SEPARATED BY EVIL

CHRONICLES OF THE SUPERNATURAL
BOOK FOUR

J M HART

COPYRIGHT

PROLOGUE

C asey, Sophia, and Tim watched as the portal Kevin had created closed. The sparkling light of the portal drew together until it faded like a dying star. The next few days were going to be strange without Shaun and Rachel and Kevin and Jade. It was the first time they had been separated since they returned the Emerald Tablet to the Tomb of Thoth. Shaun's father had stolen the tablet, opening the gate to the underworld and releasing evil, setting off a chain of events that would lead to the destruction of humanity and the earthly realm.

How much of the world population remained, Casey didn't know. Only a few people had driven past the estate where they had taken refuge since the whiteout, when the veil between the realms dissolved, releasing the imprisoned angels, demons and monsters, from around and within the parallel ethereal realms in the atmosphere of the earth.

Each week during the whiteout, they heard the sounds of increasing numbers of creatures. Casey remembered the Bible stories of the giants, and how God banished their spirits to the ethereal realms, preventing them from ever entering heaven. But the atmosphere around the earth had rumbled and moved in strange ways that made him believe the demons and monsters were making themselves at home in the earthly realm once again, and it was only a matter of time before they crossed paths. He thanked God every day for Sophia and the invisible protective dome she had placed around the estate.

Casey didn't know how Kevin and Jade would find Jade's father in the realm of lost souls, or how Shaun and Rachel would find Rachel's mother in the ruins of Israel. He prayed they would hurry and return safely with their families. As they had cleaned the surrounding towns of the dead, Casey noticed the malice of some of the lingering spirits, and he didn't think the future was going to be rainbows and lollipops.

1

HUGH: LONDON

The cold snap seeped into his bones. Half awake, he tried to maintain a distance between himself and the frost that had settled in the bedroom. The chair pressed into his back. His neck, tilted to one side, would be sore when he moved. He hadn't meant to fall asleep. For three days he had stayed alert, vigilant, but once in the warmth of slumber, he didn't want to leave. However, the icy room made it impossible to stay. Leaving the warmth meant something was wrong; something was in the room with Gwen and Bo. Something evil, something he wasn't prepared to accept.

Gwen and her daughter Bo were fast asleep, snuggled in the single bed. He could hear them breathing, and sometimes Bo gave a tiny snore. Shivering, Hugh tugged on the blanket at his knees. It resisted, caught under the leg of the chair. Opening one eye, he bent down to free the blanket. A pink clock covered with pictures of fairies sat on Bo's bedside table. It blinked, illuminating the time in red. The innocence of the fairies disappeared. 3:15 am. The two dots between the numbers blinked on and off.

In the dim light, a shadow raced across the room. Hugh listened to the faint shuffling and scratching coming from the foot of the bed. Bo had been asleep for three days, and Gwen and Hugh were worried. Gwen talked to the sleeping child, read her books, fussed over any change in her breathing and willed her to wake up.

Stealthily Hugh reached down for the yellow torch next to the chair. The sudden light drove the shadow away from the foot of the bed. Frozen under the beam of the torch was a filthy old doll. It sat on the floor with its head turned towards him, staring. A shadow raced across the ceiling. Hugh sprang to his feet, the blanket falling to the floor. He pivoted, chasing the shadow with the light. The dark mass raced down the wall and out of the window. Hugh crossed the room and looked out on the old prison on Newgate Street, searching for movement in the night.

Gwen stirred. She turned her daughter to face the wall, shielding her from the probing light, as Hugh searched every corner of the room for the doll.

"What is it?"

Hugh checked the window. Locked. "Nothing." He concentrated the light into the corner at the foot of the bed again – empty. The room was tidy. There was no sign of the doll. "Everything's okay, I'm just imagining things. Go back to sleep, it's early."

Holding the torch out like a gun, he left the bedroom and switched on all the lights in the apartment to check everything was as it should be. The dirty plates were in the sink, his book was on the coffee table, and their shoes sat in a neat row by the door. Nothing was out of place.

He checked the deadlocks and the latches. The chain rattled against the wooden door as he peered into the darkness of the hallway. He seemed to be the only one in the building awake. He waved his hand in the hall, and the sensors picked up his movement. The hall light turned on. The musty scent of earth filled his nostrils. It trailed down his nose to the back of his throat – he could taste it. The potent scent of earth masked the pleasant fragrance he associated with the apartments. He cleared his throat, resisting the urge to spit and wipe his eyes. It was as if someone had shoveled dirt onto his face – he shook his head. He stepped back into the apartment and bolted the door. As he walked towards Bo's bedroom the lights in the lounge room flickered off. He fumbled for the light switch and flipped it up and down. Nothing. "Damn it." The doorknob of Bo's bedroom was icy cold in his grip. Fear heightened his senses. Cautiously, he entered the room, shining the torch to the ceiling and away from Gwen and Bo. With a gentle touch, he pushed the door closed behind him. Holding his breath, he stifled a scream of pain as he stepped blindly into a minefield of scattered Lego. Gwen and Bo stirred. Shit! What the …?

He pointed the torch at his feet and stepped through the blocks, wondering how they had got there. He settled back into his chair by the window. The hair on the back of his neck stood on end. He picked up his blanket, pulled it up to his shoulders, and turned off the torch. As his eyes adjusted to the darkness, he listened. The smell of earth entered the room. A strip of light illuminated the bottom of the door to the lounge room. God damn it! The lights in the lounge room must have come back on – maybe it was just a faulty wire, or rats in the wall cavity. Hugh stared at the glow of yellow light, afraid to close his eyes. As Bo's digital clock flipped over to 4:00 a.m. he realized he couldn't sit another night in that chair reliving the last six months. He needed to take action. Bo needed medicine and a better place to live, somewhere away from the tavern, and out of London.

The number of people taking refuge in the tavern over the last six months had dwindled. Kraig and Patricia and their three children, Seth, Billie and Ernest, remained, and there were the tavern owners, Gary and Eleanor. Hugh didn't think any of them could hurt Bo, but someone – or something – was.

At first, he had thought it was her mother, Gwen, until he saw the marks appear on Bo's skin for himself. One day he had been alone with Bo, watching over her while Gwen had made lunch. Red raw gashes appeared on Bo's body, as if she was being whipped, or sliced with a knife. Within moments, her soft pale arms were covered in cuts and bruises. Her face broke out in rashes, and bruises circled her neck, as if someone had stran-gled her. It had scared him, forcing him to think about the impossible: maybe the past haunted the tavern.

When Gwen had returned with lunch and seen Bo's arms and neck, she dropped the bowl of pea and ham soup onto the carpet. She cried and hugged Bo, rocking her back and forth. Hugh tried to tell her he hadn't touched her, but Gwen paid him no attention. She cradled Bo, telling her everything would be alright.

She lifted the back of Bo's bed-shirt to show Hugh the scars that covered her back. "Help us!"

Over the past six months he had developed feelings for Gwen, though he preferred to avoid getting entangled in serious relationships – they didn't work out for him, and he didn't think things were going to change just because ninety percent of the population had died or vanished. But when Gwen asked for his help, he couldn't say no. Whether or not he wanted it, he was already entangled in Gwen and Bo's life.

Bo was just six years old. Now as he gazed at her he saw her face was gray, and defense wounds covered her arms. She looked as if she was dying. Three nights ago, she'd gone to sleep – and that's when Ernest, Kraig and Patricia's youngest son, began displaying the same symptoms: fever, night terrors, emotional explosions, cursing, loss of appetite, and mysterious cuts and bruises on his body. Ever since then Hugh had sat in Bo's room, guarding her from an unseen enemy.

ON THE EDGE OF DAWN, Hugh packed his duffel bag and headed for the door of the tavern. He thought it best to leave before anyone else woke up. He turned back to pull the door closed. Gwen stood at the top of the landing, looking down at him. She frowned and turned away, but not before he saw the disappointment in her eyes.

"I'm going to get help. They need a doctor, Gwen. There has to be a doctor somewhere who can help Bo. I'll be back in a few days, by the end of the week at most. I promise."

"But what about the jackals and God only knows what else is out there? It's too dangerous, Hugh. You're going to get yourself killed, just like the others."

"I have to try." He shut the door, knowing she might be right.

Before heading off to St Bartholomew's Hospital, Hugh walked across the road towards St. Sepulchre's. *I'll check the church one more time,* he thought. Only a few hours ago, as he'd watched Bo's clock tick over, he had heard the church bell toll.

There was something about the freshness of the morning air he had always enjoyed. Even as a boy in boarding school, he had collected the milk crates just to be part of the morning, but the city air was stale and old – lifeless.

A crow flew down Old Bailey. The courthouse and commercial buildings were empty. All but one of the windows were closed. Hanging from an upstairs window were a man in his late twenties and a redheaded woman. Hugh knew them as Jack and Lolita. They must have jumped, the rope tied to the window frame snapping their necks. The couple had left the tavern a few weeks ago. Something must have forced them back to Old Bailey. Hugh had hoped they'd escaped the haunting madness of the city. The crow landed on the woman's head, its claws sunk into her soft curls. It leaned over and pecked at her eye. He couldn't leave them hanging.

Before the apocalypse this building, on the corner of Old Bailey and Green Arbor Street, had been undergoing a facelift and the construction site was protected by cyclone fencing. At the front of the building was a fountain where, in better days, he had met his friends after work, before heading into the tavern for a round of drinks, but now the water was dirty and stagnant.

Hugh found a gap in the cyclone fencing and made his way inside the building. The renovations on the internal stairs were incomplete, making it dangerous to climb. He looked up, mapping a way in his mind, before tackling the stairwell and climbing up to the fourth floor. The floor creaked as he neared the open window. He leaned over the windowsill and shooed the crow away. It flapped its powerful wings and launched itself off Lolita's head, carrying her eyeball in its beak. The bodies were heavy and awkward to grasp as Hugh dragged the couple back in through the window and laid them side by side. Head bowed, he gave a silent prayer.

Hugh wasn't off to a good start. His spirits were already waning as he headed out into the empty street. He glanced down Old Bailey, and as he did, his breath shortened, and his eyes grew wide. Rooted to the spot, Hugh gazed at the scene before him. Reflected in every window along the street were men and women hanging by their necks. Their worn-out clothes were from the turn of the century. Some wore sacks or hats over their faces. Hugh craned his neck to see inside the nearest window – there were no physical bodies on the other side of the glass, and nothing to suggest what was casting the gruesome reflections in the dawn light. He shook himself and briskly walked away, sensing the watchful eyes of the dead.

He picked up his pace and rounded the corner, glancing one last time at the tavern. Gwen was at the window, watching, and waved. He waved back, then turned to head towards the church, leaving the tavern and Old Bailey behind.

Inside St. Sepulchre's, Hugh's footsteps echoed in the hollow space. A chill raced up his back as if all the dead were behind him. For a while someone from the tavern had checked on the church in case anyone had stumbled in looking for shelter. Nobody was there now, not a single living soul. He could feel it. This place creeped him out, and he couldn't get out fast enough. Back on the street, Hugh stopped to calm his nerves and shake off the dread, which was becoming all too familiar. Raising his face to the sky, he bathed in the sun for a moment.

As he approached, the makeshift triage tarps of St Bartholomew's Hospital flapped in the gentle breeze. Long before the whiteout someone had trashed the front of the hospital. A-frame signs with directions were turned on their sides. Feeling vulnerable, Hugh called out, "Hello – hello – anybody!" hoping to attract someone who could help them, but he feared he was going to attract the jackals and things that hide in the shadows.

The lonely sound of his voice prevented him from calling out again. No one was around. Hugh jogged away from the hospital, and did everything possible to stop himself from sprinting, in case someone was watching; he didn't want to look like a total chicken-shit, but to be honest, he felt rattled, and he knew it wasn't a good idea to be out on the streets. It reminded him of his first night at boarding school, waiting for the bigger kids to haze him. The waiting was the hard part, not knowing when they were going to attack. It was the unknown that scared him. Right now there was nothing familiar, no sense of stability around him. The city was a strange place, with screaming ghouls at night and howling beasts. Shadows from London's past were everywhere, but Hugh refused to acknowledge them.

He kept moving through the city, focusing on checking medical centers, drugstores and churches. Everyone had vanished. He needed a car, but he didn't know how to hotwire a car. He slapped his forehead. *Stupid, stupid, stupid!* Before the riots, before the city went into lockdown, he had taken his car to work to avoid the mayhem and crazies on the subway. He had forgotten all about his beaten-up red car. Hugh picked up his pace and jogged past the Amazon building, turned into Snow Hill Street, and there was his car, parked behind police vehicles. It had been spray painted with graffiti, but otherwise it was in good nick.

Two years ago, he had hidden a spare key under the car because his ex-girlfriend had a habit of locking the keys in the car. Hugh prayed the spare key was still bolted to the undercarriage. He wriggled his way under the car, and located the wingnut and bolt holding the metal tin in place. The nut was stiff, and at first it wouldn't budge. He wriggled further under, shifting his position for better leverage to loosen the nut. The key tin came away with the bolt.

It was comforting to be inside the car. He touched the steering wheel, enjoying the feel of something familiar. Bang, the sudden noise startled him, he kept still as a jackal climbed up on to the hood. It snapped at the windshield, saliva dripping off its teeth. Hugh shoved the key in the ignition, but the car wouldn't start. He tried again, and again. He was afraid he would flood the motor, when it suddenly roared into life. He slammed the car into reverse and the jackal's claws scrapped down the duco as it slid off the hood. He didn't ease up on the accelerator until he was out of the city and on the A1.

His sense of survival compelled him to keep driving north. At first, he felt like a heel, as if he was deserting those back in the tavern, in particular Gwen and Bo. But his instincts urged him on. He headed for Scotland and didn't stop. The further he travelled from the city, the more he could believe he had imagined the reflections in the windows along Old Bailey, that it had just been the morning light playing tricks on his eyes.

The country roads were empty. There was an almost perfect blue sky, and no one to enjoy it but him. After six hours of weaving through abandoned cars and empty towns he pulled off the road, wondering what the hell he was doing. Hugh wasn't a coward, so why did he feel like one? Swinging the car around in a U-turn, he glimpsed light reflecting on the pasture beyond a row of birch trees. He stopped at a gate and looked up the windy gravel road that seemed to lead to an empty field.

Glad to stretch his legs, Hugh got out of the car and climbed on to the roof for a better look. "Hello, anyone out there …?" Scratching his head, and feeling like a loser for leaving London, he sat down on the car roof frustrated, wondering what the hell he should do next. A few times he thought he saw something, a twinkle of light in the distance, but when he took off his sunglasses, whatever had caught his attention was gone. It must have been a bird or a fox. "Stuff this." He jumped off the roof of his beat-up car and got behind the steering wheel.

Hugh thought about heading straight back to London, back

to the apartments above the tavern and Gwen and Bo, but he didn't want to go back empty-handed. He couldn't watch Bo die. The tavern had been a good place to call home, but not for Bo. He couldn't ignore the mysterious marks on the little girl's body. Everything was wrong, and Ernest was now sick too. They were all susceptible to whatever was attacking the children. It could even be bacteria infecting the mind, creating madness. It was only a matter of time before everyone's physical and mental health was affected. He had to do something.

Once everyone was taken care of, he needed to restore order in his own life, and maybe he should go. Maybe his feelings towards Gwen would disappear after a while. A few weeks ago, he was ready to throw her to the jackals when he suspected her of harming Bo, but now he knew better, and was ashamed. Gwen was only ever caring and helpful to others when they were in need. He must find a property they could all settle in for the long haul, and it would be nice if Kraig's family, and Eleanor and Gary stayed with Gwen in case he decided to go his own way. After he found a suitable farmhouse, he'd head back to the tavern and convince them all to leave.

Satisfied with this plan of action, even if he couldn't find any medical support, he smiled and started the car. Sitting in the car alone, he felt a little more self-assured, believing he was doing the right thing. He looked out once more towards the pastures, before shifting the car into gear, but a strong sense of being watched gave him the creeps as he pulled out onto the road.

2

CASEY: COUNTRY ESTATE – AUTOMATISM

Casey leaned back from the notebook on his desk. A halo of light from the banker's lamp failed to illuminate the beds that remained cloaked in darkness. Behind him, Tim was dead to the world. The last thing Casey remembered was lying in bed talking to Tim about Kevin and Jade, who had left yesterday to find Jade's father. Shaun and Rachel had set off the same morning to find Rachel's family. It was so quiet without them. The best thing about the room was its size, the way the double-sized bunk beds were built into the walls. It was like a giant private cabin on a ship. At that moment, it felt like a ghost ship. He stretched his concentration towards the grate in the wall. Listening, and ignoring the fact he was sitting at his desk in semi-darkness in just a singlet and his boxers, the house was mute. Remnants of the herbs and spices Joe had used when cooking dinner lingered, but there were no echoes or voices. Those who had remained at the estate were asleep. The old house was still and settled.

He has never been interested in drawing, but now his fingertips were sore from drawing too much. Casey was reluctant to look at his new drawing, and focused on his hands, avoiding the sketchbook. *When did I get out of bed?* Charcoal covered his fingertips from smudging shadows on his drawings. He turned his head away, stretching his neck, evading the image, but trying to catch a glimpse of it at the same time. It looked like a town. He gave in to his curiosity and glanced down to see beyond the sense of horror the picture exuded. This was his third picture this week, and he didn't remember drawing any of them. He was auto-sketching in his sleep, and waking when the image was complete.

In the middle of a city, in the middle of a street, stood a jackal the size of a pony. Its coat was glossy black, its eyes the color of hot coals. Casey stared into the picture, into the jackal's eyes, and saw flames flicker deep inside the pupils. He held the paper up at an angle to get a closer look. Was the lamp shining on the glass of water on his desk causing the flickering in the picture's eyes? But he only had charcoals. Parched, he reached out for his glass of water and saw bloody fingerprints on the sides. His bowie knife was on the table next to his box of charcoals. He had found the box at an arts and crafts store on a supply run into town. The tip of his knife was bloody. Casey cleaned it with his singlet. He plucked a tissue from the box next to the lamp and wiped the tip of his index finger. Under the charcoal was a tiny cut. He had used his own blood to color the jackal's eyes. The rest of the picture was shades of black and gray.

The lamplight cast shadows over the sketch, making it appear even more sinister. There was a gin palace, straight out of history. Casey could see he had drawn people gathered at the windows, craning their necks to see out into the street. Women and girls wore bonnets. The faces of the people on the street showed fear, apprehension, horror, confusion, and shock. The details were incredible. The buildings and clothing were from the Victorian era. A lot of emotional energy – panic, fear, and excitement – radiated off the page. Little signs hung over the shop fronts: Cobbler, Baker, Banker; the signs went right down the street. Casey opened his desk drawer and took out a magnifying glass. He scanned the windows of the shops and businesses. An image of a man frozen in time, closing his curtains. Another, a man in a shop, in the middle of turning over the 'closed' sign. Down at the far end of the street he could see a man wearing a top hat, and Casey knew he was the source of the fear, but everyone in town was looking at the jackal. The details of the drawing were so clear.

The man in the hat was like the executioner, but he was much more than that. He was a gentleman you could not trust. This man hid his true self in the shadows. His clothing was like that of a ship's captain of the eighteen-hundreds, with many shiny brass buttons. The man was too far in the distance for any of the townspeople to see. Casey kept looking at the image under the magnifying glass, wondering why he was sketching these images from the past. *Is the man hiding from the townspeople or hiding from me?*

Flicking through the pages of sketches, he found the image he had drawn yesterday. It was of the same street, but a different scene. A row of men and women were being hanged on some gallows. People were throwing rotten fruit and vegetables. Casey had drawn the spoiled food frozen in mid-air. Other people smiled and cheered, or waved their fists in anger. A group of men with top hats were placing bets. It was like a sporting event rather than witnessing someone's death. Casey couldn't believe the joy radiating from the faces of the crowd as they watched someone die. The spectators looked insane, almost evil in the way they cheered. One man hanging from the gallows was thin and frail, with filthy clothes and muddy feet. Casey couldn't imagine him ever having the strength to hurt anyone. Another wore tailored clothes, and his boots shone. He had been someone people had trusted.

Casey placed his hand on the picture. The feelings of the spectators punched him in the chest. He pulled back his hand and leapt out of his chair, catching it before it fell and woke Tim. It was as if his entire body had been zapped with a buzz of painful energy. It was still tingling as he pitched forward and sat back in his chair. He shook his hands. *Okay, I can do this.* Again, he placed his hand over the image to connect to the emotional energy from the sketch, but this time at a safer distance. Coming from within the crowd around the gallows, he heard a prayer for the man with shiny shoes. The sound rose towards Casey. He leaned in closer to listen. Next to the man on the gallows with the shiny boots was a rounded woman – they had been in cahoots, partners in crime. A cheer rose from the crowd, cursing the woman.

"Baby killer! I hope you rot in hell!"

"Baby killer!" the crowd chanted.

What is this? Why can I hear them? Please don't start moving, that would be too creepy. Casey felt like a giant peeping Tom looking over the town. He moved his hand over a group of men who surrounded a man who was taking their money. He held a fob watch that was hooked to the bottom of his waistcoat pocket by a gold chain; he was timing the event. Casey guessed they were betting on how long it would take the men and women on the gallows to stop twitching and die.

"Sometimes the neck doesn't snap, and the noose strangles them instead – choking to death," the man with the fob watch said.

It was creepy. Casey pulled back in fright at the sound of the man's voice. It was like the crowd was going to leap off the page, or Casey was going to fall into the image. *Shit!* As soon as he moved his hand away, the sounds of the crowd stopped. Casey turned to look at Tim, wondering if he should wake him, or maybe he should go and wake Sophia. *You've got this, visualize golden light surrounding yourself like a cloak, keeping out all negativity.* He closed his eyes, waited until he felt calm. *Okay.*

Casey rubbed his hands together and hovered one hand above a group of women huddled together, their heads bowed, handkerchiefs held to their faces. They were grieving for their dead children; a man hanging from the gallows had killed their daughters. It pleased them to see the man's life ending, but they derived no satisfaction from it. It didn't fill the emptiness of their loss. The pain would last forever. They believed joy and happiness had gone from their lives forever. Casey's eyes watered. Without thinking, he took a tissue from the box and wiped his hand, as if that would stop the sadness entering him. He moved the magnifying glass away, and left them to their grief. Casey focused in on an image he had drawn heavy lines around: it was a man in the crowd who appeared to be looking back at Casey.

The sketch frightened him, so he turned away and latched onto the sound of Tim snoring. Casey peered into the darkness at Shaun's empty bed, which was above Casey's. Before leaving for Israel, Shaun had taken to sleeping in Rachel's room. He looked forward to their return.

Casey was stalling, focusing on his friends, reluctant to turn back to his desk and review the very first sketch he had done a week ago. He clenched his teeth and tried to view the image without connecting to the gruesome details. It was of a primitive mortuary. Against the wall were coffins, large and small. In the middle of the room were four tables with four bodies, each at a different stage of dismemberment. Organs lay beside each body. A woman's stomach was an empty cavity, her brain exposed, and her face peeled back. A well-dressed man, wearing suspenders and polished knee-high black boots had his back to Casey as he leaned over the dead woman's body, his hands deep in her chest. Her heart lay on a metal table beside her intestines. Casey moved the magnifying glass over to an open wooden door. A shadow was pushing a wheelbarrow of corpses through it. Casey looked back at the coffins, frustrated at not understanding the meaning of what he had drawn. He slammed the sketchbook closed.

"Go to bed, or there will be no levitating for you tomorrow," Tim said sleepily.

Startled, Casey turned in his chair. Tim's voice in the room was a hundred times louder than the voices coming from deep within the pictures.

Casey turned off the lamp, slid the notebook off the desk and stuffed it under his mattress. Moonlight spilled into the room. A feeling of something impending filled his senses. It was an odd feeling of excitement and dread, which made him think whatever was coming wasn't good. It felt as dark as his charcoal drawings. He lay in bed and looked out the circular window at the moon.

As he tried to sleep, he thought about all the people Sophia had said would come one day. He thought about Joe, creating the hydroponic gardens, over the last six months, to feed the people who were going to come. The livestock Shaun, Kevin, and Tim had collected. The barn had been converted to accommodate at least twenty people, and still no one had come except one guy in a beat-up red car who couldn't see the estate or anyone in it, and had left.

Casey let his eyes close, but feared the man with the hat was watching. He wondered if the man among the crowd of ghoulish spectators was the same man hiding at the end of the street. He turned away from the window as if that would ease his feeling of dread. Whatever was coming, Casey believed it involved the man in the hat.

His eyes were heavy. Casey lay in a state of semi-consciousness staring into the darkness until his eyes closed, and he drifted in and out of sleep as he resisted the incoming tide of dreams. He listened to the silence and wished Tim would start snoring again. Behind his eyelids he saw a flash of light. Something was in his peripheral vision. He lay still, pretending to be asleep, waiting to see what would emerge. Another flash of light. *Maybe it was the desk lamp?* He flipped both eyes open. The room was dark. There was no light. Only haunting shades of gray and black. Clouds had covered the moon.

He closed his eyes again, falling into a dreamscape he didn't care for.

The sound of hooves on cobblestones faded as the horse moved down the street. Buckets of human waste sat in corners of the jail cells. Prisoners banged on the doors or screamed in pain. Men and women hung from gallows. A stagnant fountain. The street changed. The fountain disappeared as time went backward to the eighteenth century; Casey didn't know where he was. Light streamed out of a window: the gin palace. A well-dressed man with the poise of a gentleman exited the bar and entered the night with a drunk woman by his side. He showed her to his waiting carriage. The sound of the hooves faded into the night. Images changed like a carousel. Casey now saw inside the well-appointed house of a gentleman or aristocrat. The gentleman poured the woman a drink from a crystal decanter. She collapsed, poisoned. The man dragged her by the heels down to his laboratory, her head banging against each step as he descended. Casey was helpless inside his dream, now inside a coffin. He pushed his hands against the coffin lid. *Wake up!* His hands went straight through the lid. He bolted upright and glanced down at his chest; it was an open cavity. His heart gone – stolen. The woman from the bar lay dressed on the table, while the gentleman washed his hands. Casey sat upright in the coffin, lined up against the wall next to four other coffins. Fear prevented Casey from moving as the spirit within each box rose.

* * *

THE SUN WAS UP, and Casey was in bed drenched in perspiration. He sort of expected to be at his desk with a piece of charcoal drawing as if he had a fever. Tim's bed was empty. Casey was alone. He was tired, and wanted to go back to sleep, but he could hear the morning sounds of the house and the wonderful smell of home cooking. He couldn't resist.

In the bathroom, he splashed cold water over his face. He closed his eyes, enjoying the rush of cold water. It made him feel alive and fresh. Even during the winter months he doused himself in cold water. He picked his clothes off the back of his chair and dressed, running his fingers through his curls before heading into the kitchen. Joe was cooking; he never seemed to give anyone else a chance in the kitchen.

During the past six months, the best thing for Casey had been practicing using his gift with Sophia. His favorite ability was turning electrical or motorized devices on and off with his mind, as well as levitating the others, and lifting things that weighed over a ton with just his mind. It was incredible and getting stronger, but the nightly drawings were troubling. Casey assumed they were from nightmares he didn't recall. He felt tired and knew he looked it too.

3

SOPHIA: COUNTRY ESTATE - ASTRAL PLANE

Most nights Sophia guarded the estate from the astral plane. Since the guy had driven up, stood on the roof of his car and cried out, Casey had been acting strange, distracted and tired. Sophia gave up her sleep to watch over him. She no longer took the same joy in her sleep, no longer had exciting adventures in her dreams. Her dreams had just stopped. No premonitions. No communications from those on the other side. It scared her. Sophia had read her Bible and kept an eye on Casey for three nights. She sensed something unnerving inside him, but he wasn't talking about it, and she didn't want to push him.

On Monday, the first night, there was an attempt to breach the psychic dome. An energy reverberated through the house and into her skull, as if a significant force had collided with the psychic field. Her stomach had turned upside down, shocking her awake with an urge to vomit.

Tuesday night she had stayed awake meditating. She arranged the comfy cushions against the bedroom wall and straightened her legs so as to not cross the flow of energy. She touched her thumbs and index fingers together and placed them on her thighs. When, later, she would pull her fingers apart, she would return to her body feeling comfortable and energized. Sophia left her body and entered the astral plane. She preferred to be out of her body than in it. Floating around the house was easier than walking or running. She hovered in the peaceful cosmic energy, watching over the house, waiting to glimpse the entity that had tried to get through her psychic shield.

Over the past six months a lot of energies had tried to penetrate the dome, or sneak in by hitchhiking in someone's aura when they had returned from a supply run or a search for survivors. But an entity had very little chance of attaching itself to her or Casey. It would have to be very cunning and very powerful to outwit them.

Sophia slipped back into her body and into sleep, resting her head against the wall.

With a jolt she woke up, pulling herself away from the wall and looking around in the darkness. It was surprising and concerning that she had fallen asleep. Her train of thought had put her off guard; she had lost herself in the stream of consciousness, something which hadn't happened for a very long time. It was 3:15. Sophia quickly rearranged the cushions under her backside and coached herself back into a meditation and out into the astral plane.

She floated through the dark house, checking everyone. She floated through the ceiling into Casey's room, which was like a grand dorm room he shared with the other guys – after growing up in a nunnery, everything seemed lavish to her. Tim was sleeping, Casey's ethereal body, the first layer of his aura, flexed outward, expanding. His spiritual body left the room like a shooting star rising through the ceiling. He slammed into the edge of the psychic dome – electrical shock waves flashing through the barrier wall on impact, like a magnetic lightning storm. He tried again and failed, generating more energy that rippled through the entire house. After his third spectacular attempt, unaware that she was watching him, he went back to bed. He was the source of energy. Nothing was trying to get in – well at least she didn't think so – it was Casey trying to get out.

At breakfast he wasn't so talkative. Zoned out, he stared into space.

"How did you sleep?"

"Hmm?"

"How did you sleep? You look a little tired."

"Oh, fine. It's a little odd with just you, me, Tim and Joe in the house. It'll be good when the others get back."

He gave no inclination that he was aware he had left his body during the night, and she would not tell him. Not yet anyway. She didn't want him to think she was spying on him.

The next night, Wednesday, she waited again, and the same thing happened. Sophia, curious, created a doorway to allow him to get through the psychic dome, with a lock that only the signature of his spirit could open. She watched him go. Like a snowflake, he floated over the towns. He did a lot of hovering, which was interesting, because he wouldn't levitate when awake because he feared heights. He was hiding his feelings, but he should know by now it was pointless. Sophia left Casey to his astral roaming and went back to the estate and waited for his return. Casey was more than her best friend, and she didn't want to spy on him anymore.

It was four o'clock in the morning. She hadn't seen, felt or heard Casey return from his astral roaming. Her abilities were waning. She could no longer trust her gifts. Alarmed, she hurried into the astral plane and peeped into his room. He was back in bed and sleeping. She checked the perimeter of the psychic dome to see if he had brought back any hitchhikers. A shadow of energy was receding from the outer wall. She thought it was peculiar, but nothing to worry about. Within the protective psychic dome, no harm could come to Casey or to anyone else at the estate. Sophia floated down the hall, through the door, merged into her body on the cushions, and hesitated before separating her fingers; disconnecting from the astral plane. Anchored back in her body, even though she was a lightweight, she dragged herself into bed as if she weighed a ton. She listened for Jade's breathing and remembered she wasn't there. Jade had left yesterday to find her father, after Shaun and Rachel had gone through the portal to find Rachel's family. Sophia already missed them. There was only Joe, Tim, Casey and her left at the estate.

Sophia slipped into a colorless dream for the first time since the guy with the red graffiti car had shown up five days ago. All the color in her dream disappeared, everything was shades of gray. They were a strong sense of foreboding, with misty shadows and demons just out of her sight. She didn't understand the messages of the few dreams she had. In the end she woke in a panic, paralyzed with fear. She couldn't move her body, and she didn't know if it was her fear, or the fear of the stranger with the red car, but she knew with certainty that someone was in danger.

Dear God, help me see again. All I feel is death unfolding in the universe, and I don't know how to stop it. Before, with your gift of prophecy, I could see the future, but now it is gone. Did I displease you? How can I change things? It scares me not to know what is coming. Give me the courage to stand before whatever demon comes before me and the strength to cleanse the earth. I won't fail again. Hear my prayer. Amen.

4

HUGH: COUNTRY TOWN

Hugh had scouted the country and seaside towns looking for a suitable home for Gwen, Bo, and anyone else at the tavern who wanted out of London. He ended back at the country town near where he had first pulled over. All the houses in this area had marks spray-painted on their doors. Almost every front door had a cross with a circle drawn around it. Hugh had to pick one. There was a stone farmhouse that looked like a great place for everyone at the tavern, in particular for Gwen and Bo. It had two dwellings and a big main farmhouse. It would be a great place for them all to build a new life together out of the city. Hugh climbed from his car and checked the grounds for survivors. The chances of finding anyone were slim, but he still had to check. There weren't any voices coming from the stables or the barn, and no one was attending to the cows by the dam in the back field. Someone had boarded up the downstairs windows of the farmhouse, limiting what he could see inside. At the front door, he listened for several minutes before knocking. "Anyone home?"

Hugh tested the door handle, his palms sweaty with nerves. He turned the knob. The door squeaked – the hinges need oiling. Hugh eased the door open and stuck his head inside the house. As he opened the door wide he called out into the dark hallway. "Hello?"

First chance he got, he'd pop the boards off the windows. A few jackets hung on a coat rack by the front door. Taped to the bottom of the wall, hiding a brown stain, was a child's picture. The picture flapped as he opened the door wider. The picture placed low on the wall screamed out to him. Hugh bent down for a closer look and sensed someone standing in the doorway off to his right. He snapped his head around to catch who was there – no one. A gentle breeze entered the house and flapped the child's drawing of a house, barn, cows, horses, and chickens. A boy, holding the hands of his mother and father, while two other children rode horses. Above them was a bright yellow sun with a big smiley face. The paper flapped again. Hugh peeled back the sticky tape. It covered a brown mass and a hole in the wall the size of a tennis ball. He suspected it was most likely from a gunshot at close range. He put the picture back in place. If he was going to convince Gwen and Bo to stay here, he would have to repair and paint the wall.

"Hello?" He called again as he walked down the hallway towards the back of the house. Enough light penetrated the hall to give him a glimpse into the darkness of each room. There was a lounge with a fireplace, a dining room, a sunroom or maybe a home schoolroom. It had that smell of pencils and paints. Towards the back of the house were more rooms. Hugh unlocked the back door and let in the afternoon light. A rush of air filled the hallway, flowing through the downstairs of the house. He ran his finger along the large kitchen bench, walked into a sitting area that led to a bathroom, laundry, and mudroom. Hugh headed back to the front door and checked the bedrooms he couldn't see into before. That's when he noticed the brown splatter on the wall in the hall was also on the floor of the bedrooms. It was going to need a good scrub. *Who stuck the drawing over the hole and removed the bodies?*

The kitchen was clean. It had two ovens, and they were spotless. The entire house was clean, just dusty. He went upstairs and found two bathrooms, four bedrooms plus a master bedroom with its own bathroom. This place would have cost a fortune. He felt a little guilty claiming such a beautiful home for himself. Fixing the wall and floor, and removing the boards off the windows, was all the place needed. It wouldn't take long to have it ready, maybe a few days. The owners were most likely not coming home.

He went outside and got a crowbar from his car and began popping the boards off the windows to let the light in. It made a big difference. He went through every room and opened every window. He rolled up his sleeves, reenergized by the idea of a positive future. *This is going to be the fresh start we all need. Gwen and Bo will like this house.* There were trucks and cars, pictures of a galactic battleship on the walls of both upstairs bedrooms. Bo won't mind, she can pick a room and make it hers.

His stomach rumbled, reminding him he hadn't eaten since last night. The kitchen cupboards were empty. Before he went into town for supplies, he opened the refrigerator to let it air. He'd wipe it down when he got back. There must be some cans or packets of food left in the town.

He tossed the crowbar on the passenger seat and headed for the small town. He tapped the wheel, singing. It was the best he had felt since the plague and the whiteout. It was a glorious day.

* * *

Parked in front of the town's local supermarket, he stared at the store window, thinking, *I've never picked a lock.* Being at the tavern had spoiled him. They'd had enough supplies to last a year, although some stuff would go off, but Kraig had always had a herb garden out back for his restaurant.

The crowbar, raised like a baseball bat, was light in his hands. He swung, preparing to smash the store's front window when he noticed the door to the staff entrance around the side was ajar. Careful not to alert anyone to his presence, he pulled the door towards him slowly, then stepped into the store and listened. Trying not to make any noise, he moved under the convex corner mirror at the back of the store and between the aisles. The shelves were almost bare, but there were a few items here and there. He found a basket and collected the cans. It was as if someone had placed the leftover food in bundles after raiding everything else. Out of the corner of his eye, Hugh saw a child ducking out of sight. "Hey wait!" He looked into the mirror at the back of the store, expecting to glimpse the kid turning into the next isle. A ghostly light flashed in the mirror.

"What the hell? Hey, don't run!"

Hugh put the basket down and circled the store searching for the boy. "Where are you? Come out? I won't hurt you."

Certain that he was alone, Hugh went back to his basket. *God, I'm losing my mind. I survive the virus of madness and end up losing my mind, anyway.* He laughed out loud and considered his basket, filled with cans of chicken soup, mixed beans, a can of ham and a few cans of sardines. It wasn't much; but it would get him through the next couple of days. Hugh bagged the items and left the store.

He leaned in the passenger window and plonked the bag on the passenger seat and dropped the crowbar on the floor. As he climbed into the car, the bag dropped and toppled to the floor.

At first, he stared at the bag then looked around before picking it up and placing it back on the seat. It toppled over again, as if something had pushed it. Frozen, he studied the bag and the seat. The cans had spilled from the bag and rolled, clanging against the crowbar. With a slight turn of his body, he looked between the two front seats and checked the backseat. Empty. He faced forward and swept his eyes over the outside mirrors. A glint of light faded. A young boy stood in the middle of the street. Hugh leaned out the window.

"Hey, what's your name?"

He'd tried not to spook the kid, but the boy was off and running down a laneway. Swinging the car door open, Hugh hurried after the boy. The kid had vanished down a side street.

"I won't hurt you," Hugh called into the laneway. "Come out!"

Clouds appeared and passed the sun without notice until a blazing light reflected off the window of the shop he had just exited. Hugh covered his eyes as it intensified, blinding him. The light died down as clouds filled the gaps in the sky. The boy was nowhere.

Hugh ran back to the car in case the boy was a decoy for a much larger group. His car was still there. The cans were on the floor and the keys in the ignition. Pushing into drive, Hugh buckled up and cruised the car through town, searching for the boy before heading back to the farmhouse.

An eerie sensation made him jumpy. It felt like someone was in the car with him. He kept looking in the rear-view mirror, expecting to see someone. Three times he checked the backseat with his hand. A shiver raced up his spine. The sun would set within the next hour. He hit the steering wheel with his palm. "Shit, I should've searched for candles or a gas burner. Why didn't I try the lights? Fool!"

The kid had spooked him. Feeling a little light-headed, he wiped his hand across his face, trying to shake the sensation of being watched. *Too much open space is all it is.*

* * *

He slammed the kitchen drawers open and closed, searching for a can-opener. It was hiding in a drawer, under the spoons, alongside a box of matches and candles. He put them on the kitchen countertop and opened a can of soup. He tested the gas cooktop – he could smell gas. *That's good.* He put the soup in a pot on the stove. As he waited for his soup to warm, he rummaged through the rest of the kitchen cupboards. The pantry was a walk-in, and behind the door was a jar of sweet gherkins, two bottles of water and a rifle. He ignored the gun and picked up a green glass bottle and popped off the lid. It could be vinegar, or worse, turpentine, he sniffed. It was odorless. It tasted like spring water, which meant the property might have its own water tanks or well.

He walked past the living room, noting the fireplace. *After my soup I'll start a fire just for the comfort. It's the easiest way to know if something is blocking the chimney.*

The day was on the edge of twilight as Hugh sat on the porch facing the main road and eating chicken soup. Tomorrow he'd check the stables, cabins, and sheds on the property. From a distance, the cows seemed healthy. It might be a different story up close.

He thought about the others back at the tavern. He worried about the Yorkshire family and Gary and Eleanor, not just Gwen and Bo. Kraig and Patricia might want to take their children home to Yorkshire. It would be best if they stayed together until someone in authority could tell them what was going on.

He hadn't seen so much as a wild dog since leaving London. The air even tasted alive in the country. There were plenty of vacant rural properties to choose from. They wouldn't have to live together if they didn't want to, but there was something very wrong in London. The country would be better for them all.

Not in his wildest dreams did Hugh imagine living on a property like the farmhouse, and he would not let it go to waste. It was a good idea. Good ideas energized him. Taking positive action gave him purpose. He wanted to rush back to the tavern and tell everyone, but his instincts told him to wait. With his spoon halfway to his mouth, about to scoff the last mouthful of soup, he stopped and put the spoon back in the pot. He lowered the pot onto the porch and glanced over his shoulder ...

"Hello, who's there?"

Hugh stood on the doorstep and looked down the long hallway to the open door at the back of the house. Someone's shadow passed the back door and rushed around the side of the house.

Hugh jumped off the porch and ran to intercept whoever it was. No-one was there. He hurried around the house. There were two sheds and the stables. Both were too far away for someone to have run to without him spotting them first. Hugh ran from the house to the barn and peered inside.

"Hello!"

Tractors and trailers sat dormant. He was panting.

"Hello!"

He ducked under the hoes and hooks hanging from the rafters and searched the barn. He got on his knees and gawked under the tractor, trying to see anyone's boots. He climbed up to the hayloft and looked out across the property from the open loft doors. A door slammed in the next shed. He slid down the hayloft rope and ran. The side door was ajar; it could be the source of the bang.

He entered the shed and found cars, trikes, storage boxes, and a loft converted into an office, but nobody was camping out in the loft office. There wasn't anyone anywhere. His mind went back to the brown stains on the wall and floor inside the main farmhouse. He found the septic tank and two large water tanks. There were solar panels on the roofs of the main house and the other two dwellings. In the distance, past the paddocks, was the dam where the cows were hanging out. He walked into the stables and pushed open every door. He couldn't find anyone. It had been a while since he'd been out in the open. *I'm chasing shadows.*

Using the last sliver of daylight, he found the solar-power storage batteries, a generator, and a stockpile of wood. The property was an excellent choice. He collected a wheelbarrow of wood and went back to the farmhouse.

During the next few days, Hugh scrubbed the house from sunrise to sunset and slept like a log at night. He tested all the equipment, making sure everything was in good working order. The cows were healthy. They would have milk and cheese for the next few years. He painted over the circle and cross and the brown bloodstain on the wall in the hallway. He scrubbed the carpet, but the stain was still visible. It was pure luck that he found a rug in the storage shed and used it to cover the stain. The rug would do fine for now. He made the property homely.

Hugh removed some boys' toys from the largest of the bedrooms, closest to the master bedroom, leaving the ones he thought Bo might like. As he arranged figurines of horses and farm animals on top of a floating shelf, and stacked a few board games and books on other shelves, he whistled, pleased with his efforts. Tomorrow morning, bright and early, he'd return to the tavern.

A book fell off-the-shelf, breaking his reverie. Hugh picked it up and put it back, then closed the window for the night. Again, the book thudded onto the carpet behind him. In the window's reflection, he caught a spark of light behind him as each figurine tumbled to the floor. Hugh swiveled around.

"What the hell?"

The shelf was bare, and the room was empty, but a shadow moved across the floor. "Who's there?" He collected the animals off the floor and placed them on the shelf again. Hugh closed the door.

Dismissing what had happened in the bedroom, he focused on tomorrow and made his way to the shed where the cars were and selected one big enough to carry as many of them as possible.

Tomorrow I'll head back to London and get Gwen and Bo and anyone else willing to leave the city for the country. This is a good place. Fantastic place.

He parked his car in the shed and took out the Ford Galaxy MPV that seated seven and parked it in front of the house, ready to leave at first light. He could be back in the city by lunchtime and have everyone packed up and ready to go within the hour. They could be back at the farmhouse before sundown.

He sat on the porch eating and searching the horizon for signs of smoke. Twice, after dark, he thought he had smelled smoke other than his own fire; it gave off a distinct smell he couldn't quite identify. He convinced himself a rat or a bird's nest must have got stuck in the chimney and the smell was coming from his fireplace after all. Believing he had established the smell was coming from his own chimney, gave him a sense of comfort.

An electrifying north wind blew in. The air was alive, thin, and his throat tingled with each breath. In the city, the air was so stale and empty of life – he didn't understand it. Hugh scratched his head and rubbed the back of his neck. He needed to stop thinking so much. As a kid, he'd overthought everything – it had made him anxious. That's why he enjoyed his job as a computer programmer. It was fun creating logarithms and sequences, because it was systematic and predictable. It kept his mind busy and gave him something to focus on when his external environment was in chaos. It was also why he preferred not to get tangled up in serious relationships. But now, hell, his external environment ruled everything.

The colors of the setting sun were spectacular. He sat on the porch watching the day end as he finished his dinner. For a split second, it was almost normal. *One more minute, then it's time to go inside and sit by the fire.* Hugh picked up his empty pot and went to stand when he noticed that, despite the air being a little chilly, his knee felt warm. It was as if a hand rested upon his knee. At first he thought it was because he had placed the pot of soup on his leg, but he hadn't. He'd held the pot in his other hand, so it was unlikely he would rest the pot on the opposite knee. Even if he had, his knee would be cold by now, but a consistent warmth radiated through his leg. Unsure and nervous, not knowing what to expect, he touched his knee – despite the warmth, a chill rushed up his hand and down his spine. Someone was sitting next to him, leaning on his leg, pressing against his thigh. "Nonsense!" Hugh said as he sprang to his feet.

He turned off the outside lights. His mind played horrible scenarios of all the bad things that could be in the brush across the road. The marked doors, the patches of burned grass on almost every other property were clear evidence that somebody had been moving through the towns. *What the hell have I been thinking? It's not safe anywhere. Calm down, I'm getting ahead of myself. What about the town, and the way the food in the grocery store had been left in bundles? Someone must've done it.* His mind was a trickster. *It's just been such a long time since I was on my own. Enough!*

Freaked out and frustrated, he ignored his intuition and closed the front door. He flicked on the hall lights and in the space between the light and dark he saw the poltergeist. It vanished as quickly as it appeared. The hallway was icy cold. Something walked in his shadow.

He cursed under his breath. "Serious, dude, you've got to get a grip. This is stupid. I'm a grown man seeing things. There's nothing here."

A good night's sleep would chase the shadows away. He stoked the fire and made himself comfortable on the couch. The country would heal Bo and Ernest. By the light of the fire, thinking about Gwen, he dozed. He woke up and kicked his boots off and reached down for the blanket. A child shrouded in light was watching him.

"What do you want? Who are you?"

Hugh got up and turned on the lights, but as he did the boy vanished.

"Come back, tell me what you want. Did you knock the toys off the shelf?"

He went and checked every room in the house but he didn't find the boy. Feeling foolish, he forced himself into a cold shower to smarten himself up. It was something his aunt and uncle had made him do when he got agitated or was overthinking. For five years he hadn't had a problem. He needed to stop at a drugstore and pick up a herbal remedy.

He toweled his hair dry. Feeling fresh, he headed back downstairs, clearing his throat as he went, to alert anyone to his presence.

The wood crackled in the fireplace. Hugh found his blanket and lay on the couch. Something was different in the atmosphere of the room, and he sensed he was alone. He had closed his eyes and relaxed when he heard the door open between the lounge room and dining room. A brilliant white light pulsated, and in front of the light was the silhouette of a child. Hugh wanted to react, but he didn't have the strength to jolt himself wide awake. His exhausted body took over, pinning him to the sofa. He fell into a deep sleep and watched a little boy and a young man playing jacks on the carpet in a strange house with marbles and different shaped gemstones.

The boy picked up the marbles and glanced in Hugh's direction, and said. "My name's Alex. This is my friend Shaun. You need to find Shaun and Kevin. Kevin's my brother. His friends can help Bo."

Hugh saw himself sitting on the edge of a couch and Alex, the little boy, stood up and walked towards him. "I didn't mean to scare you," Alex said.

"Are you haunting me?" Hugh asked, rubbing his eyes in his dream to see if the boy would vanish.

"No, and yes," Alex said.

"Did you live in this house?" Hugh asked.

"No. My family is behind the psychic cloak of energy, which keeps out the good ghosts and the terrible ghosts. They don't want anyone to know they're there," Alex said.

"Who doesn't want the ghosts to know they are there – your family?" Hugh said, leaning his back into the couch – but he could feel the warmth of the fire back at the farmhouse. The boy touched Hugh's knee and warmth radiated through his leg. "That was you on the porch?" Hugh asked.

"Yes," Alex said.

"How do I find your brother and his friends if they are hiding behind a cloak of psychic energy? Are they here on the property?"

"No. Go back to the spot where you stopped and sat on the roof of your car."

"How do you know about that? And how do you know about Bo?"

"I've been watching you. Bo's my friend. I don't want to be in the spirit world. I found Bo, and she was nice to me. Then they took her away – the mean fat lady. Then she came back. She keeps coming and going, coming and going, in and out of the spirit world. She told me she's not dead. The mean lady is an evil spirit that forces her way into Bo's body, which drives Bo out into the spirit world, but she doesn't mind too much, being in the spirit realm, because it hurts if she stays in her body."

Hugh sat forward. "Why does it hurt her to be in her body?"

"The man with the hat whips her. Sometimes he chokes her until she can't breathe, and then she leaves her body. Her mommy cries when she sees the cuts and bruises on her body. She doesn't like it when her mommy cries. She wants the evil lady to go away, and the man with the whip, but she's afraid they will hurt her mommy like they're hurting Ernest."

Dumfounded, Hugh asked, "Is the lady Patricia or Eleanor?" Although neither of them was obese.

"I have to go. I can feel the evil spirits watching you. Find my brother and his friends before …"

Alex vanished. The light disappeared. A soft whisper filled his dream. "Go back to where you first stopped."

Hugh sat bolt upright in a panic. He was at the farmhouse. The fire had died out and there was no Alex. It was just a dream. "Oh, dear God, what is wrong with me?" Hugh looked at his wristwatch: six o'clock. He'd slept for seven hours. He put on his boots and left the house.

The lights on the car's dash glowed orange as he turned the ignition on and drove south towards London. The crazy dream weighed on his mind, and he needed a distraction. Searching the glove compartment he found a couple of kids' nursery rhymes and music CDs from the nineties – Bob Seger. Thinking that had to be better than the nursery rhymes, Hugh put on the CD and tried to lose himself in the songs. An hour passed before the memory of the dream surged back into his mind. He glanced at the backseat in the rear-vision mirror, expecting to see Alex with his arms crossed over his chest, angry at him for not following his instructions. *No, that's just silly.* It was nothing more than a dream because of his concern for Bo and Ernest. As much as he tried, Hugh couldn't ignore his gut feeling to turn around. He slammed his foot down on the brakes, spun the car around, and headed back to the spot where he had climbed onto the roof of the car. Maybe there was someone there?

He looked into the mirror and said, "Okay, Alex, I'll bite, but then you have to leave me alone. For all I know, you could be the one hurting Bo." Hugh pushed down on the accelerator.

Something warm passed between the two front seats, as if someone had climbed over to sit in the front passenger seat.

5

CASEY: COUNTRY ESTATE – OUTSIDER

C asey opened the fridge and took out two hardboiled eggs. He grabbed a piece of toast that was lying on a plate and poured a glass of milk.

"Where's Sophia, is she up?" he asked Joe.

"She's outside." Joe said, moving quickly to turn off the stove.

"What's the rush?" Casey asked, buttering another slice of toast.

"She's walking up to the front gate," Joe said.

"And …?" Casey wiped his mouth and looked at Joe, who was taking off his apron in a hurry. "Why is she walking to the front gate?"

Joe reached for his overcoat, hung on the backdoor and placed his apron on the hook. "Because that man with the beat-up red car is back, with a bigger and better car, and he's just called out Kevin's name."

"What, Kevin? He knows Kevin?"

"And Shaun, he called out Shaun's name too."

Casey grabbed his jacket off the kitchen chair. "You heard him?"

As he followed Joe outside Casey shrugged on the jacket and zipped it up, wishing it was warmer. Even though it was the first month of spring in the UK, he thought it would've been a tad warmer. He squinted to see the road beyond the birch trees. The guy was back and leaning against a dark blue MPV.

"Kevin! Shaun!" the stranger called.

He said it as if he didn't expect an answer. As if he was calling to someone down the road rather than at the house.

Sophia was heading straight for the gate.

"What's the wee hen going to do now?" Joe said.

Casey jogged towards her and stopped. "Sophia, wait!" Terry's motorcycle was a few feet away, and Casey jumped on it and headed up the driveway.

Sophia turned to look at him. "What are you doing?"

With her arms outstretched, she gazed up at the sky and turned towards the road as if she was twirling in gratitude for the sunshine. She brought her arms together, projecting her energy outward and beyond the perimeter of the estate. Like heat weaves, the energy shimmered, surrounding the man and his vehicle. The guy swatted the air. Agitated, he rubbed the back of his head and neck as the swarm irritated him like wasps. A gray mass behind him floated away. An unwavering soft glow was by his side. There was something familiar about the light. She had removed the negative energies, cleansing the guy's aura with her psychic powers, and now Sophia was going to remove the psychic protection over the estate. She lowered her hands and continued towards the gate to let him in.

"No, Sophia!"

But it was too late. The guy stared in awe at the estate. Using his psychokinesis, Casey slammed the guy back up against the hood of the car.

"What the hell!" The guy was looking straight at Sophia and Casey. He rubbed his ears and held his nose, trying to clear his ears as if the air pressure on the road had changed when the cloak had disappeared and the sounds from the estate filtered out onto the road.

It was the first time Sophia had removed their psychic protection. She had maintained its integrity daily for the last six months, preventing the few passers-by from seeing them unless they wanted to be seen. Why was she letting this guy in? The man glanced around as if looking for answers. He wandered a short distance away from the property before returning. He rubbed his chin before opening his mouth to speak, but nothing came out. The guy just stood there with an expression of wonderment mixed with confusion. They were vulnerable. Sophia had put everyone in jeopardy by revealing the estate to this one guy. Casey kept a close watch as the man moved closer to the gate and Sophia. It would take only a single thought to knock this guy off his feet or slam him up against the car again. Casey pushed anyway, but just a little nudge. The guy slid backwards from the gate. He looked down at his feet, surprised, then up at Sophia as if she had all the answers.

"What …? How …?" the guy said.

Moving closer, Sophia said, "Take it easy. You're in shock."

"What is this? Are you a witch?" The guy reached out his hands as if trying to feel an invisible wall. "The boy told me you were hiding behind some invisible cloak," he said.

Sophia unlatched the gate. "Casey, stop pushing him," she said.

"Wait, Sophia." With a slight head shake, Casey blew out his cheeks, then released a breath. It was pointless arguing. It was already done.

Her selflessness was going to get her into trouble one day, and Casey hoped today was not that day. His pulse quickened and his grip tightened on the handlebars. He didn't want her to let this guy in, and it pissed him off that she hadn't talked to him, or the others, first. Sophia was letting him in and there wasn't much anyone could do about it. She was disregarding everyone's opinion, and that infuriated him, but he trusted her. He wouldn't want to go head-to-head with Sophia, not that she would ever harm him. The first time this guy showed up, days ago, Jade had wanted to let him in. What was it that Sophia and Jade knew that he couldn't see? Or was it something he saw that they hadn't? *What do I see? The gray shadow, I smell death. But the real problem is what I can't see.*

Sophia opened the gate wide. Casey couldn't make out what Sophia was saying over the sound of the motorcycle. The guy climbed into his car and drove through the gate. Casey stood his ground and pushed the car back towards the gate with his mind. The wheels spun, Casey turned off the car's engine. Sophia calmly secured the latch on the gate and walked through the clouds of dirt. Passing the driver's door, she held up a finger as if to say, one second.

Hands on hips, she stood in front of Casey, cutting his connection with the car.

"Give it a rest, Casey. It'll be okay."

Sophia climbed onto the back of the motorcycle and wrapped her arms around his waist. His fear melted with her touch. Casey released the clutch and turned the motorcycle back towards the house. Joe and Tim stood in front of the house beside the wreckage of the plane, watching. Casey let the guy with his flashy new MPV follow him halfway along the driveway, then he cut the car's engine and smiled at Tim.

Casey pulled up next to the plane and parked the motorcycle on the grass. Sophia climbed off.

Sophia gave Casey a nudge. "What's gotten into you? Why are you acting like a jerk? It's beneath you."

Casey glanced over his shoulder and smiled at the car stalled halfway up the drive.

"Stop messing with the guy's car," Sophia said and touched his shoulder.

Casey felt her emotions seep into his body. Her fear, apprehension, and confusion coursed through his body. His brow furrowed as he tried to read her aura and understand what had put her off guard. Her self-assurance, and her superpower, was waning.

"What's going on, Sophia?"

"Not now!"

With a slight tilt of his head, he restarted the car, and watched the guy lean forward gawking over the steering wheel, taking in all the details of the estate as he made his way up to the house.

The guy got out of the car, slammed the door shut and looked back to the road. "But how?" he said to Sophia. "How are you doing this?"

Sophia opened her arms and closed her eyes to reconstruct the psychic shield protecting the estate from the outside world.

"She won't be a minute," Joe said, holding out his hand. "I'm Joe."

"Hugh," the guy said, leaning forward and taking Joe's hand.

Hugh held his hand out to Casey. "I knew you guys were

here, the first time I passed by. I knew it, but I just couldn't see you. How does she do it? She's not a witch, is she?"

"No," said Joe, "don't be ridiculous. She's God's wee hen."

Casey kept his mouth closed and his eyes fixed on Hugh. Hugh pulled his hand back, realizing Casey wouldn't shake it.

"Tim." Tim offered his hand to Hugh. "I can understand why you think she is a witch – she's spiritual and gifted, but if she was a witch, she would be the good kind."

"Cheers, Tim. Been here long? I knew you guys were here."

Intending to intimidate Hugh, Casey kept staring at him, making sure he felt even more uncomfortable.

"We got here at the end of the psycho plague, and before the whiteout," Tim said.

Hugh glanced over at the plane wreckage. "How did you get into the country? They grounded all flights."

"It's a long story. I see you've guessed I'm not from around here. Joe and Sophia, they're from Scotland, my friend Kevin and I are from Australia. Jade and Casey are from the United States. How did you know we were here?" Tim looked at Hugh.

Casey watched Hugh glance around at each of them, and the property.

"What's your problem, man?" Hugh said to Casey, who was continuing to stare him down. Casey might have been ten years younger than Hugh, but he was a fraction taller.

"He's been hanging around Shaun too much," Tim said, trying to lighten the mood.

Joe, a little uneasy, stepped back from Hugh. *It's not just me,* Casey thought.

This guy was hiding something, and Casey didn't like it. He was ready to throw the guy and his car off the property.

"What's the matter, Casey?" Sophia whispered as she came out of her meditative state.

"I think … he smells of death," Casey said.

Hugh eyed Casey. "I've seen a lot of death, and a sweet girl I know is very sick and going to die if I don't find help."

Casey softened a little but still didn't trust him. "Where are you from? And how did you know we were here?"

Tim stepped forward, "Kevin and Shaun aren't here. Maybe you should just get back in your car and keep going. We don't want any trouble."

"Alex told me you were here," Hugh said.

Casey didn't know what to say. Did he mean Kevin's dead brother Alex?

"Maybe we should go inside," Sophia said.

"Right you are, hen. I'll put the kettle on and slice some boiled date cake. Take Hugh into the parlor," Joe said.

Casey sensed danger. He kept a close watch on Hugh, like he was circling prey. There wasn't anything about Hugh that bothered him per se – he didn't know the guy, but he had a terrible feeling gnawing at him. He couldn't see any signs of concern coming from Sophia, but she had butterflies. Sophia wouldn't put anybody in harm's way.

Joe backed away from the uncomfortable silence. At the front door he took a step back onto the porch, holding the door open. "Hugh, you coming?"

Hugh walked towards Joe, followed by Sophia. Casey and Tim hung back.

Tim stepped forward and whispered, "Casey, what are you sensing? Why are you so concerned about this guy? How could he know about Alex? If he saw Alex, wouldn't that mean you saved his soul, and the she-devil didn't consume it? If Alex brought Hugh to us, we have to help."

Casey thought about the drawings. Hugh didn't look like anyone in any of his drawings.

"Casey!" Tim said. "What's wrong?"

"I'm not seeing much of his aura, and that's the problem. I should be able to see and feel so much more than I am. Something is blocking me. I'm afraid something terrible is following this guy." Casey wondered if the fear growing in the pit of his stomach was his or Hugh's – he decided it was both. His mind flashed to the top hat and the shadow of the man hiding in one of his pictures. The one where the man was peering around the corner of a building, watching. Casey didn't think it was possible, but for the past few days it had felt as if something was watching him from the shadows.

"Casey, snap out of it," Tim said. "What is it with you clairsentients? Kevin is the same, always drifting off somewhere in his mind."

"You're right, Tim, we need to find out how we can help. Maybe it's as simple as giving the guy some of our medical supplies and then he'll leave. Let's go inside."

Casey tried to calm himself, reminding himself the drawings were just drawings. There was no reason to fear them or Hugh.

"Are you two coming?" Sophia said, sticking her head out of the parlor window and looking at Casey as if trying to read his face.

"Yeah, sure ..." Casey trailed off.

She disappeared back inside, then came out the front door. "You look a little pale," she said, walking towards him. "Are you sure you're okay, Casey?"

"Yeah, yeah, all good. I'm just a little wired, I've had a few weird nights the past week," Casey said.

"What do you mean?" Tim asked.

"Tim, give us a minute, will you? Go keep Hugh company?"

"Yeah, why not?" Tim said, and ran up the steps.

Sophia waited until Tim was out of earshot. "What is it? Talk to me, Casey."

"I don't like this, Sophia. I don't know why, but I don't like this one bit. We should tell him to come back when everyone's here. What if he's been watching us, waiting for the others to leave to ...?"

"To do what, Casey?"

"I don't know, but something is making me restless, very nervous."

"Hugh is waiting inside the house to tell us how he knows Alex. You of all people know it's possible he can see Alex. Our destinies may entwine with Hugh's. It could be why you're apprehensive. You're most likely sensing it too."

"Death follows Hugh, he's brought death to the estate," Casey said.

"I don't want things to change, but we need to find out how Hugh affects our future. The vague, though positive, future timeline," Sophia mused. "Hugh could be the eraser changing our lives."

"All the more reason to get rid of him." Casey focused on the front door and pulled it open with his mind.

"No, Casey. We need to talk to him." Sophia reached out and took his hand.

6

SOPHIA: COUNTRY ESTATE – EXPOSED

Hugh was perched on the edge of the sofa as Joe poured a cup of tea and offered him a slice of date cake. You were special if Joe gave you date cake, and Sophia knew he made it 'specially for her.

"You don't have to do that," Hugh said, watching Joe.

"Can't help it son, I owned a cafe for over twenty years. I enjoy keeping myself useful."

Hugh's eyes swept the room with concern. Tim sat opposite him in the comfy armchair on the other side of the room, next to the old bookshelf. He ate Joe's cake as if it were a slice of heaven.

Sophia waited for Joe to leave the room before addressing Hugh. She could see his apprehension and confusion. He had the jitters and studied the room as if expecting to see someone.

Sophia stood in the grand doorway and whispered to Casey, "Are you seeing any apparitions in the room? I'm not seeing or sensing anything other than Hugh. He's acting as if he expects something to happen."

"He is local," Casey said.

"Are you two just going to talk amongst yourselves?" Tim said in a soft, amused voice.

Sophia realized what they were doing. "Sorry, Hugh, if we're making you uncomfortable."

"Hugh, what do you see?" Casey blurted.

"Nothing. I thought Alex would be here. This is the room I saw," Hugh said.

"What do you mean?" Sophia asked.

"In my dream. This is the room where I saw Alex playing marbles with Shaun. Just over there," Hugh said, pointing across the room to the rug, in between the two comfy chairs where Tim was sitting.

Sophia, Casey, and Tim glanced at each other. They knew that was where Alex and Shaun had played marbles the night Casey and Sophia battled the She-Devil for Alex's soul. Alex had died before they could banish her from this realm, and Sophia had thought the She-Devil had taken Alex's soul with her, but if what Hugh was saying was true, Alex's soul was free.

"Okay, you've got our attention," Tim said.

Sophia sat down next to Hugh and asked as gently as possible, "How do you know Alex? Can you see him now?"

"No. Look, he told me to find Kevin and his friend Shaun. Are they here? If not, just ask them to come to the tavern on Newgate across from Old Bailey. I need to get back to London." Hugh grabbed the armrest and readied himself to leave.

Casey sat down on the edge of the coffee table in front of Hugh. Sophia wished he would back off. He was trying to be intimidating, and it was so out of character; now he was reading Hugh's aura. Trying to look calm and collected, Casey took a piece of cake and put it on his plate, but Sophia could see how his body tensed as he pushed down the cuticles on his left hand. Casey was ready to snap. It was so unlike him. Sophia followed the energy from Casey, that drifted through the air like vapors to Hugh as Casey connected to Hugh's super consciousness. Whatever Hugh was about to say, she didn't think Casey would like it.

Hugh challenged Casey's stare. Casey was unwavering in his examination of Hugh. She didn't agree with what he was doing, but fear drove people to do things they wouldn't do ordinarily, and right now, Casey was acting from a place of fear. Hugh had him rattled.

Hugh pulled his attention away from Casey and turned to her. "Not for a second did I want to come back. I didn't even plan to stop the first time a few days ago. I was searching London for a doctor and ended up here."

"You're a long way from London," Casey said.

Hugh rubbed the back of his neck and glanced at Casey. "Before the whiteout, I took refuge in a tavern with a few mates I worked with, two families, half a dozen backpackers and the owners. We lived in moderate comfort in the apartments until the whiteout cleared. Some people became ill. At first I thought they were just going stir-crazy being confined indoors for such a long time – one guy, a German backpacker, we think he slit his own throat."

"What do you mean, think?" Tim asked, sitting up in his seat. "If he didn't kill himself, then who or what did kill him? Did you have an infected among you?"

"We don't know; we can't be sure," Hugh said.

"Since we returned the Emerald Tablet and the whiteout, we have seen no swarms in the sky or any infected. Go on," Sophia said.

"As soon as the fog lifted, people fled, including my work mates. I should've gone with them, but there's a woman, Gwen and her little girl, Bo."

"There's always a woman," Tim said.

"Bo, the little girl, became sick, and when it looked like she was getting better, she had a turn for the worse. Blisters covered her body. It must be so painful for her. We thought maybe it was a skin disease, but I'm no doctor. I watched over Bo one afternoon and saw the marks appear out of the blue, and her friend Ernest is now sick with the same symptoms. My intention is to find help for the children, nothing more.' Hugh looked at Casey. 'I can see the way he's looking at me, but I mean no harm. I hadn't meant to venture beyond the city, but I had an urge to keep driving, to keep going. Alex told me last night in a dream it was him. He had urged me on, guiding me towards this place."

"We saw you the first time you came. We were watching you," Tim said.

"But how did you meet Alex? Why did Alex appear to you?" Sophia said.

Hugh fixed on Sophia's face. "The night before I left ..."

"Answer the question," Casey interrupted.

Hugh ignored him and went on with his story. "Alex showed himself to me in a dream. At first, I thought there was a poltergeist in the house haunting me. Toys and a book fell off a shelf while I was making a room nice for Bo. I saw shadows in doorways, always the same size of shadow, small, the size of a child. I thought I saw a kid in town the first day I arrived."

"So you thought your imagination was running wild?" Sophia said.

"There was a terrible stain on the wall and the floor that looked like blood. Then, the last night, I freaked out believing something had touched my leg. I thought I was imagining everything. I had finished preparing a property close to here for the others back at the tavern. Today I was heading back to

London to get them – I think the country air will be good for us all."

"Did you clean a bloodstain in the front entrance of the house? Was there a picture over a hole in the wall?" Tim asked.

"Yes, you know the place?"

"After the whiteout we went into town and searched every property in the district. We marked them with a cross, so we knew which ones we needed to return to. When we finished gathering the dead from those properties, we added the bodies to the pyre, and then we returned to put a circle around the cross to signify it was clean," Tim said.

Sophia saw Casey shiver as he recalled the scene at the farmhouse.

"I was so tired after getting the house ready, I fell into a deep sleep and I dreamed of Alex and Shaun in this room. That's just crazy." Hugh rubbed his hands, agitated, scanning the room in disbelief. "How can that be, how can I dream of a place I've never seen?"

"You're asking the right person," Tim said, looking at Sophia.

"I sat right here on this sofa. You're making this happen. You're witches. Is Alex your familiar? Isn't that what you witches call them?" Hugh stood up.

"A familiar is an animal," Tim said.

"I have to get back to help Bo and Gwen. It was a mistake coming here." Hugh headed for the door.

Casey was on his feet, blocking Hugh from leaving. "She's not a witch, and neither am I."

Hugh pushed Casey out of the way.

"Stop, Casey, before you do something you'll regret," Sophia said.

Casey reached out and, without touching Hugh's body, picked him up by the throat and raised him to the ceiling.

"You're not making a good case to disprove his belief that you're a witch." Tim stood next to Casey, looking up at Hugh.

Hugh grabbed at his throat as if an actual hand was around his neck, choking him. It was so unlike Casey to harm someone, Sophia thought. "Put him down!" she yelled.

Casey dropped Hugh onto the couch.

"What the hell? You're crazy!" Hugh said.

Tim stood in front of Hugh. "Before you go, listen to me. I have no special ability, so I'm most like you, but these two are instruments of God. They're of light and goodness. If Alex guided you to us for help, then we can help you. His mom is a doctor, but there's a good chance you don't need a doctor, you need Kevin, Jade, Shaun, and Rachel, but they're not here. There's only us. Sophia and Casey can help you, and you need to let them." Tim stood aside for Hugh to pass. "Remember, you're in our home and we've spoken to no-one outside this estate for months. Casey is right to be wary."

"I can't prove Alex sent me here, and I can't make the kid appear. He spoke to me in a dream, for God's sake; he didn't have to attack me. Sometimes I see things out of the corner of my eye," Hugh said.

"Maybe you're more like them than you know." Tim smiled and raised his eyebrows at Casey and Sophia.

Hugh's breathing slowed and the color in his cheeks settled.

"And Kevin," Tim continued, "could touch your chest and feel your heart and know if it was his brother in your dream, because you don't know Alex, you wouldn't know if it was him or a demon in disguise trying to get in here, trying to get to them. Did you think of that?"

Casey frowned at Tim. "Let's say for now that you're telling us the truth. Sophia let you in for a reason. I trust her. She's always been more intuitive than me. It's in her blood. She's always sensed more than she can explain ... or tells." Casey looked at Sophia sideways. "Tim's right, Kevin's mom is a doctor. You can go back to the farmhouse, and we'll come for you when everyone gets back in a couple of days. Then we'll head off to London, or you can go back and take them to the farmhouse and we'll meet you all there."

Tim broke off a piece of cake and was about to pop it in his mouth. "Or – we could go with you now and convince your friends to leave London, if Sophia and Casey can't help them." Tim finished the slice of cake to avoid Sophia's and Casey's glares.

Hugh contemplated Tim's proposal. "Okay, let's go."

7

CASEY: ON THE ROAD

"I'll wait in the car," Hugh said.

"I'll meet you out the front. I'll just grab my jacket," Sophia replied.

"Are you coming, Tim?" Casey asked before Tim vanished into the kitchen.

"You can bet on it! I've never been to London. Kevin and I were going to backpack around the world before starting university ..."

Casey watched Sophia climb the old staircase and admired her long hair. It was always silky, and the light through the windows made it shimmer. Not like his own scruffy curls, which were so hard to tame. She was going up to the room she had shared with Father McDonald when they first arrived, which she now shared with Jade. A moment later she was back downstairs wearing her jacket, and stuffing Father McDonald's old KJV Bible into an inside pocket.

"Let's go," she said.

"I'll meet you out the front," Casey said, and ran upstairs. He stuffed his sketchbook and charcoals into his backpack.

Joe was still in the kitchen. Casey expected him to at least protest about them going to London, but he didn't, which meant Sophia hadn't told him. Joe was very protective of Sophia, he cared for her as if she was his own daughter. Distracted, Sophia had headed off without telling him. Over the past few weeks Sophia had detached herself from Joe, even though she loved and adored him. Having lost everyone she'd ever loved, she kept her distance from others out of fear. Sometimes she would let Joe in, and sometimes she would pull away. Joe admired Sophia's gifts and called her God's angel. He'd respect what she said, but he'd still protest at her leaving.

"I want to ride shotgun," Tim said, opening the front passenger door.

"Fine with me," Casey said. He opened the back door for Sophia, then ran around to the other side and jumped in. It was a nice car with plenty of space to bring back Hugh's friend Gwen and her daughter. Casey had always preferred the vintage cars from the sixties and seventies; he enjoyed the rumble of a V8 motor. He was reluctant to go to London, but what else could he do? He hoped they could help get Hugh's friends out of London quick-smart. It would be better if Kevin was around. He could open a portal and transport them all to London and heal the children within minutes, by passing them through the membrane of the portal.

The car started. "Maybe we should change cars," Hugh said. "This one seems to have an intermittent fault. It might be because I put old fuel in the tank."

"That was Casey," Tim said.

Hugh's lips were a straight line, and he squinted back at Casey in the rear-vision mirror before turning the car around.

Joe came rushing out of the back door towards them. Sophia rolled down her window, and Joe stuck his head in. "Where are you off to, hen?" he said.

"Sorry, Joe, I should've told you. We're heading to London to help Hugh bring back his friends ..." Sophia touched Joe's arm, leaning against the window. "We may not be back tonight, maybe late tomorrow. Don't worry about us." Sophia squeezed his hand.

"I can't help worrying about you hen, but I know you're in God's hands. You take care of her," Joe said, looking at Casey and Tim, then stepped away from the car. He walked over to the front door and turned to watch them go.

"Why does he walk like that?" Hugh asked.

"He's got a peg leg," Tim said, putting on his seat belt.

"What's a peg leg?" Hugh put the car into drive.

"He has an artificial leg," Sophia said.

Hugh stopped at the front gate. Tim jumped out to open it, and as he did Hugh got out of the car and looked back towards the estate.

"Where has it gone?" He peered back at Sophia. "Has it disappeared?"

"No," she said. "It's there, you just can't see it. It's a psychic mirror, it reflects what's around it, so the property is behind a protective dome of energy. A psychic cloak."

"Stealth mode," Tim said.

"Well, I never. How many more are there like you?" Hugh said.

"I don't know. I grew up in a nunnery, so I never met someone like me until I meet Casey." Sophia smiled.

"For a while I thought she might've been a figment of my imagination or a ghost," Casey said.

"I know what that feels like. So, you have telekinetic abilities, and you see the dead," Hugh said. "But how?"

"It's a long story," Casey replied, rolling down the window and disengaging from the conversation.

"And there're others," Tim said. "My friends Kevin and Jade, they've gone to the United States to find Jade's dad and to bring him back. Shaun and Rachel left just before them, to go to Israel. They're searching for her family. They're all due back soon."

"How did they get to the United States and Israel?" Hugh asked. "Do they have planes?"

"No, Kevin is a portal master; he can open doorways to anywhere in the world. He can even open them into parallel universes," Sophia explained.

"I wouldn't call him a master, he's just getting the hang of it. He doesn't quite understand opening up portals into parallel universes yet," Tim broke in. "Jade helped him work out how he does it. He accesses a memory charged with an emotion of his own, or someone else's, which enables him to create a doorway to travel to the physical location, but not in the same time frame as the memory, only in the present."

"So, if Kevin was here, he could access my memory of the tavern in London and we could all teleport there?" Hugh said.

"More or less," Tim agreed.

"How long has Kevin been able to open portals?" Hugh asked, as they drove through a coastal town.

"For a while Kevin was unaware he was even opening portals. It wasn't until Jade came along that he worked how he did it. He saw Casey die," Tim said. "That's when he first met Casey."

"You died?" Hugh said, looking in the rear-view mirror.

"Like I said, it's a long story." Casey kept staring out the window.

"What about Alex, Shaun and Rachel?"

Casey clenched his teeth in frustration. The more he listened to Tim yap away, the more he wanted to scream. "Maybe you should let Kevin, Jade, Shaun, and Rachel tell their stories, Tim? I think you've said enough."

Casey tried to disengage and focus on the ocean. He'd never liked sitting in the back of a car, it made him feel sick. The backpack on the seat next to him, with his charcoals and drawings, was beckoning him. It felt like a formidable presence sitting next to him. He didn't like Tim telling Hugh about all of them. What if he was someone who planned to do them harm? He had to stop thinking these thoughts. Casey didn't like the energy around Hugh. It made him so irritated.

"Is Alex here?" Tim asked.

"I don't feel him," Hugh said.

"What about you, Casey? Sophia? Any of you guys see Alex?" Tim said, looking over his shoulder.

"No," Casey said.

"Me neither," Sophia said.

Casey rolled his window down further and stuck his head out, taking in the fresh sea air as they drove away from the ocean and headed inland.

They had passed through these towns months ago and cleansed them of wayward spirits. It was pleasing to see the towns were still clean, empty of people and lingering spirits, Casey thought. It had been tough moving the bodies, and even tougher convincing their spirits to move on into the light. But even though the towns were clean, he was still on edge, worried about what Hugh was getting them into.

* * *

"TELL me about the people in London. How many are there?" Tim said.

Tim couldn't keep his excitement in check. Casey couldn't blame him. It would usually be natural for Casey to ask questions and engage with enthusiasm, but something was eating at his soul that left an empty feeling. He moved his bag away from the middle of the seat and away from Sophia. He kept his hand on the bag, and all at once had the overwhelming urge to take out the sketchbook and draw. Without hesitation, he unzipped the bag. With the book on his lap and the charcoals between him and Sophia, he listened to Tim and sketched.

"There's a family of five from Yorkshire," Hugh said. "They might want to return home."

"We could help them get home," Tim said, sitting up in his seat.

"I think it's best we stick together for now," Hugh said. "There's Gary and Eleanor, the owners of the tavern, the Yorkshire family: Kraig, Patricia, Seth, Billie and Ernest, and then there's Gwen and Bo. There's only ten of us left."

"How many were there in the beginning?" Tim asked.

"Twenty-five, maybe thirty people. Most were there before I got there."

"Can we just drive in silence for a while?" Sophia asked.

Casey surfaced from his trance at the sound of Sophia's voice. As if hypnotized, he faced her, then blinked as the smell of her soap filled his senses.

Tim put his seat back, hitting Casey's knees. Then he put his feet up on the dashboard.

"Are you for real?" Casey snapped. "How would you like it if some douchebag jumped in your car and put his feet all over it? Show some respect."

"Somebody's got his knickers in a knot," Tim said.

"What's wrong?" Sophia said, looking at Casey's hands and the sketchbook in his lap. He followed her gaze. Charcoal covered his fingers from drawing a bedroom with a sick boy lying in bed; demons looking down on him from the ceiling. The boy's mother sat unaware and helpless by his side, weeping. Alarmed, he closed the book.

"Stop asking me what's wrong!" He stuffed the book and charcoals into his backpack, and quickly cleaned his hands on his jeans, avoiding Sophia's questioning gaze. But she didn't push him for an explanation.

He closed his eyes to collect his thoughts. It was the first time he had yelled at Sophia. It was the first time he had opened the sketchbook to draw while he was awake, but he was unaware of when he started or finished drawing. Casey had heard everything Tim and Hugh had said but had been unaware of the automatous movements of his hands. He chewed the inside of his cheek. What if Hugh and his people had known Casey and the others were at the estate? Maybe someone saw the smoke from the pyres and followed them back to the estate. Worrying thoughts circled in his mind. What if there was a group of soldiers with guns waiting to experiment on them? Silence filled his mind, enveloping him like a wash of cool water. Sophia touched his hand. He opened his eyes and welcomed the sight and smell of the green pastures; it was peaceful, calming. He felt the softness of Sophia's warm skin, relaxed and dropped into a deep sleep.

The car went over a bump and Casey jolted awake. Alert. He opened his eyes and met Tim's in the side mirror. Tim was smiling at him.

"Where are we? This is fantastic. Look at all the survivors, it's like the psycho virus or the never-ending whiteout ever happened. Who are all these people in the streets?" Casey wiped his face and stopped slouching against the door. He leaned between the front seats. "It's so good to see other people acting normal and going about their lives, doing the grocery shopping, kids running off from their parents, teenagers trying to look cool vaping. Where are we?"

Tim turned in his seat. "Dude, the street's empty."

"What? No way, just look. Sophia?" Casey leaned back from the front seats, feeling embarrassed and confused.

"We can't see anything," Tim said.

In the rear-view mirror Hugh gave Casey a pained half-smile.

Casey turned away, ashamed, unable to look anymore.

The people of the town behaved as if nothing had changed. He wondered if they had lost their lives all at once, frozen in time, stuck between two realities. It weighed on his mind and heart, as he searched for a plausible answer.

Sophia sat a little closer. "In time we'll help them all."

Casey squinted at Sophia, knowing she could enter his mind and rummage around – he wondered if she was doing that now. Creating a mental brick wall, he blocked his thoughts from her. He didn't want her to hear his worried thoughts, to feel his shame and fear, or to see his nightmares, the darkness he sensed. But she seldom jumped into someone's head these days, out of respect. Mindful of her ability, Sophia gave people their privacy. Sometimes he wished she wouldn't be so respectful, because it was hard for him to tell her how he felt about her.

"Can we pull over for a while so I can stretch my legs?" Sophia asked, breaking the silence.

"You can sit crossed legged in a meditative state for hours, why do you need to stretch your legs?" Tim asked.

"I'm going to stop in the next town. Maybe we can grab something to eat?" Hugh said.

"You'll get no argument from me," Tim said. "I'm famished."

"Something tells me you're always hungry," Hugh said.

"I like food, what can I say? I tried vaping, but food, it's so much better, and Joe's an amazing cook," Tim said.

"You don't pack it on," Sophia said.

"Thanks," Tim said and smiled at Sophia over his shoulder.

"Oh, please ..." Casey said.

Hugh made several turns until the frozen-in-time town was behind them. The next town they entered rocked Casey's senses.

"Stop the car, you're going to hit them!" Casey screamed.

"What, why, who? What now?" Hugh said, his face paling.

Casey sat up and held on to the back of Tim's seat. Dozens of ghost-like corpses staggered along the street, drunk on the fumes from their decaying bodies. Casey tried not to gag. An angry mob had ransacked the town and broken the windows along the street. Abandoned burned-out cars lined the road. Creatures, once human, appeared dark gray; they didn't encapsulate any joy or color like the people in the last town. The energy vapors were vengeful – some evil entity was trapped inside the rotting corpses that lay abandoned in the town. Casey felt concerned for the souls that once lived in these bodies, bodies that had most likely been taken over before they died. The town needed cleansing. First the ghosts would have to be dealt with, then the bodies would need to be gathered, blessed and burned. Casey couldn't see how they could go door to door, finding all the dead in every house in every town. It seemed like an impossible task. It would take the hand of God to clean every town. The very physical-looking ghouls started moving like a herd towards the car.

"We mustn't let them get in the car. Can't you see them?"

"No, what?" Tim said.

"But you sense them, don't you, Hugh?" Casey said, "Shut the vents. Close your windows."

"My body is vibrating; it's like a low hum. I feel them," Sophia said. "For God's sake, Tim, wind up your window and close the vents."

Tim's curiosity was going to get them all killed or worse, possessed. Casey slapped Tim on the back of the head. "Wake up Tim and shut your damn window."

"Don't hit me! Why can't I see, hear or feel anything?" Tim said.

"Don't go down this street, take the next left, head southeast," Casey commanded.

Hugh leaned over the steering wheel, searching ahead for a glimpse of what Casey could see before he sped into the next street and pulled up in front of a general store.

The decomposing body of a woman was exiting the store pushing a ghoul in a pram. "Bloody hell!" Casey said.

"What, what is it?" Tim said, searching through the window.

"I'm going to run in to the store," Hugh said, opening his door.

Sophia leaned forward and put her hand on his shoulder and said, "Don't go out. Casey can see things we can't. If he says don't go out, listen. You don't want a demon, or an evil entity, attaching itself to your soul. Your mental state, your physical and spiritual bodies will become depleted until you are sick and die."

"How can a ghost make me sick?" Hugh asked, holding onto the door, one foot dangling out of the car.

"By possession. The consumption of your soul," Sophia said.

"We can stop in the next town. Now's not the time to argue," Tim said, panicked.

The ghoul in the pram flipped up out of the pram and

smashed onto the hood of the car with a thud. It pressed up against the window then jumped off and threw itself under the idling car.

"Did you feel that?" Tim said, making sure he had locked his door.

"What the hell was that?" Hugh pulled his leg back as if something had touched it. He slammed the door shut and took off.

No one spoke for a few minutes. Casey could see the beads of sweat on Hugh's face.

"You all felt the thud on the hood, right?" Casey said, breaking the silence.

"Yeah, I felt something. What was it?" Tim said.

"A ghoul," Sophia said.

"Did you see it?" Casey said.

"Sort of. I saw its essences, gray-green vapors. It's trapped inside a baby. When the baby died, it got stuck."

Tim turned to face Sophia, his eyes wide. "Maybe it wasn't a baby at all. It could have been a changeling."

"Okay," Hugh said. "I'm heading straight for London."

Casey sat back, relieved to be moving further away from the town of ghouls trapped inside human corpses. They would have to come back and gather up the bodies and burn them. He let out a sigh of relief. "Thanks for listening," he said.

He didn't know how to deal with a ghoul, or changelings, he'd only ever helped the spirits of humans. Sophia was often the guiding light and together they had helped the human spirits pass over, but never a ghoul. *But Sophia is off her game, big time,* Casey reflected. *The world is overrun by evil.*

"No worries. I thought there might be a supernatural element at work ever since the whiteout. We heard some pretty far-fetched animal cries," Hugh said.

"We did too. What happened to you guys?" Tim said.

"We took refuge in the apartments above the tavern with dozens of people, which wasn't so bad. Until one day we all went to sleep and woke a week later. I was so confused, my head was heavy, and everyone felt the same. We all staggered around searching for Eleanor and Gary, the owners, for answers. Gwen and Bo found them in the basement, locked in a cell. They were face-down in the dirt. That was the first strange thing that happened, then it just kept getting worse. So, I will listen to you, Casey. I'm just not sure how much I can accept. I think I might go insane with all the possibilities."

"How had Eleanor and Gary ended up in the cell?" Tim said. "Who locked them in?"

"We don't know. We thought they were dead. I found a pair of bolt cutters and snapped off the chain. Gwen was the restaurant manager at the tavern. Before the apocalypse, Gwen and Bo lived in an apartment above the tavern. Bo and Eleanor were close, and as soon as I unlocked the door, despite her mother's protests, Bo raced into the cell and kneeled by Eleanor. Bo shook her, kissed her on the cheek, crying for her to wake up. She cuddled her. Gwen pulled her off and got her out of the cell. No one had the faintest idea what was going on, but we were all relieved when Gary and Eleanor woke up. They were in a daze like everyone else."

"The reset? When we returned the Emerald Tablet?" Tim looked at Sophia for confirmation, but she didn't answer.

"How do you know how long you were asleep for?" Casey asked.

"My facial hair had grown." Hugh went on, "Gwen and I opened the shutters and peered out of the front windows while others checked the courtyard. Fog surrounded the building. Visibility was nil on all fronts. I opened the main door to the tavern. The fog smelled of ammonia, and I couldn't see the street beyond the door. Gary shut the door, locking us all inside the tavern again. He told me not to open the door until he returned. Then he ran down to the basement and brought back ropes. Three of us volunteered to go outside. They tied the ropes to our waists, we took every precaution, we even said a few prayers, before we entered the whiteout. The fog was so thick I couldn't see my hand. The smell of ammonia was overwhelming. My chest was tight, it was difficult to breathe. I pulled my sweater up over my nose and mouth. My ears felt as if I had my hands clasped over them. Growling and muffled screams filled the fog. I couldn't pinpoint how close the sounds were, or what was attacking, or who was being attacked. I strained to hear, turned in all directions until I was confused which way would lead me back to the tavern. That's when I panicked. The rope around my waist tightened, and they pulled me back inside."

"What about the others?" Casey asked, not sure if he wanted to know the answer.

"As they untied me, I saw the other ropes go slack. Kraig pulled his rope in as fast as he could. When it neared the end, he slowed. He picked up the gnawed end of the rope and examined it. Twenty-five people or more watched on – the rope was bloody with pieces of flesh stuck to it."

"What happened?" Tim asked, leaning against his window to face Hugh.

"We don't know, but since then we've seen jackals or hell hounds."

"Jackals," Sophia said.

"During the fog, the whiteout, we heard people wailing and crying, foxes screaming, animals fighting, howling, baying, hissing and barking. It's been survival of the fittest beyond the tavern walls. For two months nobody dared to go outside.

During the third month the fog lifted, and as it did, we heard less and less horrifying sounds. It was hard for some of us to stay cooped up indoors with a bunch of strangers. The more superstitious people were, the more agitated and paranoid they became. They had to leave. Some just couldn't cope. I took comfort in little daily rituals: making my bed, exercising every morning, meditating, shaving. I watched out for Gwen and Bo, helped Eleanor and Gary to keep the place clean, and fixed anything that broke. It wasn't so bad. The fog had almost gone by this stage.

"A group of backpackers who had been annoying since day one, having late nights and drinking, making a lot of noise, scaring the young ones, and refusing to help unless they wanted something, started going stir-crazy, lashing out at each other and belittling anyone. They told scary stories and made noises during the night to scare the small children, Bo and Ernest. They had a mock ouija board and had a séance, scaring each other silly. One backpacker, who often tried to get the others to quieten down, was found dead in the basement with his throat slit. It looked like suicide, but his friends believed it was a demon that haunted the tavern. They took off within the hour. Seth, the eldest of Kraig's sons, was the one who found the body, a guy named Colin. A few days later, when he was in the basement getting supplies with me, Seth broke down and wept. I didn't know Seth and Colin had developed a close friendship. I felt so sorry for him.

"We should have rejoiced the day the whiteout cleared, but Patricia, Kraig's wife, was the first to rise that morning, and she screamed, waking me up. I ran downstairs and found her. She was trembling and screaming as she pointed out of the window. She babbled about jackals growling at her. By the time I looked, the creatures had gone, but she was certain they had been there, and was convinced it was an omen, a warning. Kraig and the children tried to comfort her. Ernest clung to her dressing gown, and Billie tried to calm her by rubbing her back. Seth and Kraig went onto the street. Patricia held her breath. No one spoke. We were worried that savage dogs were about to tear Seth and Kraig apart. I remembered the sounds of men screaming in the fog as they were being mauled. I wished Seth and Kraig would hurry back inside, but we'd all have to leave the tavern some-time. Someone had to be the first. Breaking the silence, Kraig's youngest, Ernest, called out for his daddy to come back inside. I could see Seth walk the perimeter of the intersection and stand by the fountain looking back at Newgate Street. Kraig stood in front of the courthouse on Old Bailey. They both relaxed and walked back across the road to us, unharmed. I went for a bowl of oats, and the superstitious ones didn't wait a minute longer. They packed up and left the tavern. Who could blame them? I sometimes wondered if I should've packed up and headed out too."

"Why didn't you tell us this back at the house? It explains why I sense so much death around you," Casey said.

Hugh just shrugged. "Why do you think you can see the dead?"

"Maybe it's because he died twice," Tim said.

"No way! You died not once but twice? For how long?" Hugh asked.

"Can you just let me focus? Pull over up here. The physical and spiritual space of the area is clean. We should take a break and use the bathroom. If we're lucky, we might find some food," Casey said.

They all got out of the car and found a house empty of ghosts and corpses. Whoever had lived here had fled their home; nobody had died here. Casey entered first, and gave the okay for the others to follow. There was an emptiness in the house, but it felt there was still a living presence that belonged to it, and that one day the owner would return. Casey walked around the house remembering he had sensed the same energy when he returned from school one day and his mom had gone out; she was almost always home. An unusual 'knowing' had washed over him as soon as he'd stepped into his house. The house had been telling him it was waiting for her return. To give it life and purpose. That must've been how she felt after his dad died. He had always wondered why they'd moved house after he passed away. The house might have his father's energy embedded in the walls, and be forever waiting for him to return. That would've broken her heart. He was only young when his dad passed, and didn't sense the changes in the atmosphere when somebody came and went until he was older. It was the same feeling in this house.

Tim and Hugh went outside to a tree, while Sophia used the bathroom. Casey looked in the pantry and found it packed with food. He thought about joining the guys outside, but waited for Sophia to finish instead. Tim and Hugh came back inside and joined him, searching the pantry. The toilet flushed. Sophia jumped up to sit on the countertop, opened a nearby drawer and took out a can-opener. He took the opportunity to use the bathroom.

After washing his hands, he took the can of beans Sophia had opened for him. Enjoying the clean atmosphere, Casey walked outside to the garden, with his beans, and sat in a garden chair.

Hugh came out and sat in the seat next to him, offering him a can of ham. He had a whole can of ham and was eating it with a spoon. "It's good to have meat," Hugh said. "What's it like seeing ghosts?"

"You never see the ones you want to, and the ones I see are troubled. It's not nice."

"I can't image it's fun," Hugh said, and continued to eat the processed meat in silence. He looked grateful for the protein.

"When your friends are healed," Casey said, "if everything goes okay, we'll need to go back to the town of ghouls and clean it. You saw Alex, so I think you can see the ghosts too, but you're suppressing it. I know I do, but I'll teach you how to see what others can't."

"I don't want to see," said Hugh.

"What don't you want to see, and why wouldn't it go okay?" Tim said, coming out to join them. "What aren't you saying, Casey?"

"Stop being so melodramatic, Tim," Casey said, dismissing his words but knowing full well he was hiding a terrible feeling in the pit of his stomach.

"I can't believe we're going to see other people," Tim said. "I'm just so excited. It's been a long time."

"You'll like Seth, he's about seventeen, Ernest is seven, he's Bo's friend, and then there's Billie, his sister, she's about fifteen," Hugh said scrapping the bottom of the can and getting up.

"Awesome! It's so good to know that more people have survived," Tim said as they cleaned up and left the property as they'd found it.

"Do you ever wonder where everybody went?" Tim asked Hugh.

"I do," Sophia said.

"Me too," Hugh said. "It's so eerie to see the city empty of people."

"They're all dead," Casey said.

"You don't know that," Sophia replied.

8

HUGH: HIGHGATE CEMETERY

Hugh's legs were stiff from driving, but he was almost back at the tavern. Another fifteen minutes, tops. He didn't know who Casey, Sophia and Tim were, but he prayed they could help Bo and Ernest. He opened his mouth to stretch his jaw muscles and release the tension, then held his nose and blew out his ears to unblock them. His temperature was rising, his body overheating the closer he got to London. Dark clouds obscured the sun. Thunder rolled as lightning split the sky in half. Haunting sounds filtered into the car. Hugh felt a puff of air on the back of his neck. He looked at the rear-view mirror. Sophia and Casey had put on headphones. The wind picked up a notch. A faint sniffle and cry made the hairs on the back of his arms stand up.

"Did you hear that?" Hugh said, glancing at Tim.

"No. What did you hear?" Tim said, searching the road ahead.

"Someone's crying and people are speaking in whispers. There. Listen. Did you hear it?"

"Are you alright? You look like you're burning up." Casey asked, not taking off the headphones.

Tim indicated they should take off their headphones.

"Yeah, I'm hot." Hugh stayed vigilant, listening for the mourners. "Are you sure you can't hear them?" he asked Tim.

"I hear them," Casey said. "We're passing Highgate Cemetery, not a good place to stop. It might be why you're burning up." He went on, "I don't always see the dead. I know spiritual guides or angels draw close to protect us at times like these. When there are people or entities close by that need healing, the angels and guardians will shower us with healing light, especially if those people or entities are malicious and intend to cause us harm."

"How do you know?" Hugh asked.

"It's what I feel when Metatron is close, I burn up with his healing light, and I've had time to read a book or two during the whiteout."

Hugh looked into the rear-view mirror again, watching Casey adjust his headphones back over his ears, and move away from the window. He couldn't help watching Casey. He seemed normal, but in the pit of his stomach Hugh sensed Casey's torment. It would be horrendous to see visions of the dead, but amazing to see an archangel. He could tell by the passion in his words that Casey believed in what he saw, and that he believed Hugh had the ability to see beyond this world into the spirit realm. But Hugh just wasn't sure if he was ready to believe in the supernatural. Regardless, he knew the Highgate Cemetery stories and would drive past as fast as he could for Casey's sake. *How difficult it must be for them, not knowing if something is going to jump out and scare the shit out of them.* He could empathize but preferred not to imagine it.

A web of emotional entanglements was growing around him,

he could sense it, and preferred not to be caught in it. As soon as he had helped everyone at the tavern move out of London, and made sure Gwen and Bo were all set up on the farm, he'd leave. Gwen would have everyone from the tavern, and Casey and his people close by. They didn't need him. He would find solitude. Helping others out occasionally was okay, but it had been too long this time and was affecting his decision-making. It was crazy that he was even heading back into London. He had tried long-term relationships, and they didn't work; short and sweet was best.

How would Casey react if they drove down Old Bailey? They were thirteen minutes away and Hugh was getting edgy. He shivered, his sweat making him cold. What would a ghoul look like? He tried to get the gruesome picture out of his head. Gory horror films weren't his thing, they always gave him night terrors. He shivered again and glanced over at the hedges surrounding the cemetery. Birds fluttered around the shrubbery, unafraid of the brewing storm. A black cat lay low, watching the birds. The wind picked up, making it difficult for the tiny birds. Hugh tried to shake off the sensation they were being followed as a rat ran from under the hedges. Hugh sniffed the air. "Can you smell that? A woman's perfume?"

Tim sniffed and shook his head. "Sorry. Nothing. I wish I could."

Hugh remembered when he first went to boarding school over fifteen years ago, and how in the dorm boys liked to tell spooky stories to the newbies. Hugh had joined in and always kept a level head, but he didn't feel so level-headed now. His heart was racing, and his mind filled with old ghost stories. Hours of driving had made his body stiff. He straightened his back, then hunched forward over the steering wheel again.

Sophia was fidgeting in the back, digging into her coat

pocket. He looked from the road to Sophia in the mirror. She opened a Bible and mumbled as she read. Casey's eyes were closed. *They're just a bunch of religious nutters.*

Tim sat upright in his seat. "What is it?" he peered out the window. "I thought I saw something up ahead."

The afternoon sky had turned black, as if night was falling. Hugh's skin crawled. The steering wheel was slick under his sweaty hands. He slammed on the brakes, stopping inches away from an emaciated woman who had walked onto the road. Casey opened his eyes and Sophia read her Bible more loudly. Hugh held his hands over his ears as a shrill voice filled the car. The woman's high pitch wailing could've shattered the car windows and his eardrums.

"Go! Go! Go!" Casey yelled.

Hugh floored the accelerator and headed straight for the woman. He braced himself for impact, but she dissolved into a green mist that covered the car as if she was made of smoke. The tires screeched as he flung the car around the next few corners at breakneck speed, trying to put distance between them and the dead wailing woman.

Shaken, he eventually pulled over and waited for the ringing in his ears to stop, and his heart to stop pumping so much blood into his throbbing head. His ears hurt and felt warm. He touched them and blood came away on the tips of his fingers. Hugh opened and closed his mouth. Tim's ears were bleeding too.

Hugh's hands were shaking, he was rattled. "What the hell was that? If you knew it was going to happen, why the hell didn't you warn us?"

Casey removed his headphones. "I didn't know that was going to happen. Your ears are bleeding."

"You knew it was going to happen. You both did. That's why

you both put headphones on." He saw Casey frown as if he was in pain.

Sophia raised her eyebrows and shook her head. "I didn't know." Not knowing bothered her more. She was used to knowing everything.

Hugh felt a little embarrassed – they were as frightened and mystified as he was. He could see Casey panting as if exhausted. Sophia was out of breath too.

"I saw whispers of energy floating through the air, from the graves," she explained. "I heard the pleas of the dead as they tried to leave their graves and move beyond the earthly plane. Something has trapped them here. I put the headphones on to block out their pain. The sounds are dreadful, their pleas gut-wrenching, and I'm helpless. It's agonizing not being able to help them. I don't know what's happening, and I didn't know that woman was going to attack."

"You did know something!" Hugh said, challenging Sophia.

"I felt the evil, the pain and suffering, the feelings of abandonment and heartache, so I started reading from the Bible to open a passageway for them to return to heaven, but like Casey said, something is holding them back."

"Can we keep moving?" Tim said, finding tissues in the glove compartment and stuffing them in his ears. "Let's just get to the tavern."

Hugh narrowed his eyes, focusing in on Sophia. She looked calm. *This is real to her, she believes she can create a passageway to heaven. Who are these people?* He faced forward and turned to Tim, the only sane one in the trio. "I'm with you, let's get out of here."

"Did you see the woman, Tim?" Sophia asked.

"I think we all saw it," Tim said. "Come on, get us out of here."

"We're less than five minutes away, and we're about to enter Old Bailey. Brace yourselves." Hugh put the car into gear. The church bell chimed twelve times.

"Who would ring the bell? One of your people?" Tim said, checking the tissue to see if his ears had stopped bleeding before glancing up at Hugh. "Could it be someone from the tavern?"

"Nobody's at the church. I checked it before I left," Hugh said, more to himself. "It's possible, but we don't like to leave unless it's for essentials. We have everything food-wise at the tavern. Sometimes Kraig and Seth go out to search for survivors, and Billie has tagged along a few times, but they're never gone for very long, and we've never rung the bell."

The traffic light in the middle of the intersection swung from the wires, threatening to come crashing down on the car as it stalled, and the light turned red. Dust swirled faster and faster at the crossroads.

Tim yelled over the noise. "Stop it, Casey. It's not funny."

"It's not me," Casey said.

The bell stopped ringing, and everything went still for a few seconds while Hugh tried to restart the car. The wind returned with a vengeance. Gale-force winds rocked the car, and the gathering dust became a twister. A dust storm was moving towards them.

"Get us out of here," Tim shrieked.

Hugh made sure the car was in park and punched the ignition. "It's not working." He looked at Casey for help.

Casey focused on the dashboard for only a second, and the car revved into life.

The edge of the twister spun the car three hundred and sixty degrees. Hugh regained control and made a sharp turn onto Old Bailey.

"What's that?" Tim said, pointing out of the front window.

"What? What did you see?" Sophia asked as she and Casey leaned forward, peering between the front seats.

"An enormous black dog ran across the road, and I mean huge," Tim said.

Hugh stopped the car. "What do you mean? Like a retriever?"

"No, it was like a massive Rottweiler with pointy ears."

Everything went silent. The twister disappeared up into the sky.

"Sophia, Casey, what can you see? What's happening?" Tim asked.

Sophia closed her eyes and calmed her breathing.

"What's she doing?" Hugh asked.

"I'm going to surround the car with white light to protect us."

Casey put his hand on the window and said, "We're being attacked by a mob from the eighteen-hundreds." He pulled his hand off the window, leaving a steamy imprint.

The mob materialized in front of Hugh. They were solid, waving farming tools and fiery torches, some wielding canes, all as if they were out for blood. The clothes were from centuries ago. Some men wore waistcoats with fob watches and long winter coats. The angry mob banged their weapons against the car. Tim leaned away from the window. Hugh couldn't deny what he saw, but it was impossible.

He stole a glance of Casey in the mirror. "Why are they attacking us?"

Casey pushed both hands out towards the window. The glass in the windows rippled. Hugh felt the energy reverberate through his jaw and the metal of the car, then the angry men and women disappeared.

The light in the car brightened; Sophia radiated light like an angel. She opened her eyes.

"Where have they gone?" Tim asked, looking out at the ground, as if expecting someone or something to lunge up and attack.

The tavern was at the far end of the street. Hugh clutched the steering wheel. But before he could put the car into drive, he heard Casey draw in a deep breath.

"What the hell!" Casey said.

"What now?" Hugh asked.

"Where the hell are we? There's nothing but death here," Casey said.

Hugh didn't need Casey to tell him what he could see. Hugh saw the bodies hanging from the closed windows, just as when he exited the city. He had hoped they had disappeared, or better still, that they had been a figment of his imagination.

"Get out of my head," Casey yelled at Sophia. He smacked his forehead as if knocking away a bug. Hugh felt nervous laughter brewing in the pit of his stomach.

"What, Casey?" Hugh said over his shoulder.

"Dead men, men and women hanging from the windows," Casey said.

"And you?" Hugh said to Tim. "What do you see?"

"Nothing," Tim said, straining forward.

"I can feel the energy," Sophia said. "And I have an image in my head of a dirty muddy street with horse poo and puddles, women wearing bonnets and long dresses that trail through the dirty street. Men hanging from the gallows as a crowd of women cheer." Sophia rubbed her brow as if to erase the images. "And I'm not in your head, Casey!"

Maybe he should jump from the car and make a run for the

tavern, leaving the bizarre trio behind. It was getting crazy. *Best to avoid getting entangled in other people's crazy lives.*

"Can you see them?" Casey asked Hugh.

"The ghosts? No." Hugh lied. He had had enough of this ghost and poltergeist shit.

"They're not ghosts," Casey said in a matter-of-fact tone, regaining his composure. "They're not restless spirits. They're memories, residual energy from events that occurred over a century ago. If you were to stick your head out of any one of those windows, you'd be short of breath, your throat would feel constricted and you'd feel as if you were dying. There is a lot of medieval madness lingering here too."

"London is a beautiful place, and I wouldn't live anywhere else," Hugh said, "but it has a dark history."

"Don't we all have a dark history, one way or another?" Casey said.

"The sooner we get out of here, the better. This place gives me the creeps," Sophia said.

Hugh aimed the car down Old Bailey. The storm gathered above them. *If the storm doesn't blow over, we might not be heading back tonight,* Hugh thought.

Sophia and Casey spoke softly to each other. He caught a few words, "ghosts" and something about being trapped in this realm. What did they mean by "realm"? He just wanted to get this over and done with.

* * *

HUGH PARKED across the road from the tavern and shut off the engine. Battling the wind, he raced across the road, expecting the tavern door to be open, but it was locked. He banged on the door and rammed it with his shoulder, before stepping back into the wind. He shielded his eyes, trying to see into the apartment windows above. A shadow appeared to move across Bo's bedroom window. He yelled over the storm, "It's me, Hugh, open up!" He peered in through the downstairs windows and could see the bar area. Most of the time everyone gathered in the main bar area before dinner. "Gary! Eleanor! Open up."

He stopped shouting. Ernest had climbed onto a barstool. He was not allowed to sit at the bar. He was facing away from Hugh, watching through the mirror. A hideous demonic reflection glared back through the mirror. It wasn't the face of the child he knew. Its skin was so tight it was almost as if it had been burned in the fires of hell. It covered Ernest's face. The boy poured a shot of vodka from a glass skull. Hugh couldn't see the sweet face of the innocent boy he knew. He could only see the face of death. Ernest slid off the stool and walked over to the front door. Hugh heard the locks disengage.

Ernest looked like his old self again. Hugh couldn't take his eyes off the boy's face; the demon had gone, and Ernest didn't even look sick, but his eyes were piercing and cold, and he didn't smile or blink. It made Hugh uncomfortable. The boy appeared agitated, twitching. He didn't recognize Hugh standing there on the threshold.

The others emerged from the car and crowded around him, trying to get out of the storm.

"Ernest, where is everyone?" Hugh said.

Ernest kept his hand on the door, blocking them from entering. He spoke as if in a trance. "Around, somewhere."

"What do you mean, *somewhere*? Ernest, let me in," Hugh said.

"They're upstairs in their apartments." Ernest sighed as if tired of answering Hugh's questions.

"You look like you're feeling well," Hugh said.

"Who are your friends? Have they come to play with me too?" Ernest tilted his head to the side as if listening to someone behind him – he giggled. "We've been waiting for you."

Sophia spoke up. "You're a handsome young man. You must eat all your vegetables to be so strong and unlock all of those latches. When I was your age, I would've required a chair to stand on to unlock the one at the top. May we come inside?"

Ernest stepped forward and parted the group to take her hand. "They've been expecting you." Ernest led her inside. Tim followed.

What's he talking about? Does he know why I've brought her here? Hugh wondered. A tight feeling was growing in his stomach and he felt a little light-headed. He was reluctant to step over the threshold and go inside, afraid he may never leave. Casey was beside him. They were both hesitating, and together glanced down at the piece of polished wood separating the outside world from the inside of the tavern as if it was a border they weren't willing to cross. What had changed to make the tavern so uninviting?

"There's no way out of this, is there?" Casey said, raising an eyebrow.

"I'm afraid not," Hugh said, looking up at the windows. "I hope for your sake that everything you see will disappear if you ignore it." He smacked Casey on the shoulder.

"Here's hoping. I've practiced over the past few months how to block energy. When I touch someone or an object I feel left-over energy, good and bad, from the living and the dead. I see their strong emotional images and experience their pain or joy, it doesn't matter which. *Most* of the time I can handle someone's residual emotional energy, like yours now, but not always."

"Is that why you touched the window in the car?" Hugh

asked, stalling, turning up the collar on his overcoat. He shoved his hands into his pockets.

"No, I avoid the experience as much as possible. I was pushing the entities away." Casey ran his fingers through his hair, exasperated. "I'd prefer not to see what's inside the tavern, but there's no avoiding it. Every gruesome moment in history haunts this city. Emotional energy surrounds us, and there are creatures I don't even know – I don't know what they are, or what realm they're from. The further I venture away from the estate, the more mayhem I see that's not of this world. It's like hell opened up and vomited out all the evil."

Hugh yelled over the sound of clapping thunder. "Well then, this is another great opportunity for you to practice." He shook himself. "I don't know why I'm so jumpy. Let's get inside, before lightning strikes."

As they stepped over the threshold, the storm outside ceased, and the flying debris dropped to the sidewalk.

9

HUGH: TROUBLE AT THE TAVERN

"I'm going to check upstairs," Hugh said.

"Let me show you around," Ernest grinned at Sophia and Tim.

Hugh watched Ernest guide them past the bar. Hugh paused before going upstairs, hoping to catch Ernest's reflection. He saw nothing more than a little boy who had a captive audience.

"Come with me," Hugh said, waving Casey over.

Just as Hugh was about to touch the banister. Casey shouted, "No, don't. Don't touch it."

But it was too late. His hand was already in motion and he grabbed the banister as it turned into a snake. It hissed. In one motion Hugh let go and jumped back as the serpent dissolved into a pungent black gas. As if poison had been secreted into his hands, Hugh rubbed them on his hips. Crows cawed outside, laughing, *Ahhh, ha, ha.*

"What the hell …?" Hugh shook his hand, it burned as if he'd touched hot coals. The banister had transformed back into wood. "Did you foresee that?" he asked Casey.

"No. I saw dark gray energy covering the handrail. I didn't know it was going to turn into a snake. The dark energy is coming from down there," Casey pointed to the basement door.

"That's the basement and the old jail cells," Hugh said, climbing the stairs.

"Jail cells, are you serious?"

Hugh nodded, aware Casey was watching his back.

"Oh, great!" Casey said. "Well, just so you know, I'm not going down there. Let's get your friends and get out of here. Is that creepy kid downstairs acting normal?" Casey said.

"No, he's not. I'm surprised he's walking around. He was sick as an old dog when I left. They must've found some medicine, or got someone to help." Hugh stepped onto the landing.

"Maybe that's who was ringing the church bell?" Casey said.

"Maybe."

"Did you go into the church basement?"

"No. No, I didn't." Hugh started down the hall and stopped. Everything was so quiet. He wanted to hear Gwen talking to Bo, or reading her a book, anything but the silence and the floor squeaking under their feet. Kraig's family was rowdy. It would be normal to hear Seth and Billie arguing. They were often trying to get one up on each other. It was all quiet, except for the soft hum of a sewing machine drifting into the hallway.

"That's Patricia," Hugh explained. "Soon after the jackals took the two men, we found the backpacker Colin dead, and Patricia retreated into herself. She said she could hear the sounds of a wailing woman, and cackling. We all thought she was going insane, but now after our experience outside High-gate Cemetery, I'm inclined to believe there are elements of truth in her story. One night she woke up everyone in the house, screaming in her sleep. Kraig said she believed a gray alien watched them all sleeping. That's just a little too crazy for me. Kraig had bought her the sewing machine for her birthday. She began making clothes. Patricia loved it, and it distracted her from the madness, but in the last few weeks that's all she's been doing. It's become an obsession. She never sleeps anymore."

He knocked on the door of Patricia's apartment. He tapped again and pushed the door inward. The stink of stale urine filled the room. It was like a sewer pipe had burst. Patricia sat in her nightie at the sewing machine, humming a nursery rhyme, pushing material along under the needle. It looked like she was making a white party dress with a red ribbon around the bottom. It was identical to others that hung off the cupboard door. She was gazing out of the window as her finger travelled with the material under the needle. The needle stabbed her finger multiple times, and the crimson of her blood seeped into the white fabric of the dress. Without urgency, she lifted her foot off the pedal under the table, cutting the power. She took hold of the machine's wheel and retracted the needle, pulling it out of her finger. Droplets of blood continued to spoil the pretty white party dress.

"God Patricia, I'm so sorry, have I startled you?" Hugh said.

She put the finger in her mouth and sucked the blood. "Oh, it's alright," Patricia said, holding up her hand. All her fingers had puncture marks, and there were bruises under her nails.

"Maybe you should stop sewing for a while," Hugh suggested.

Placing her hands on the edge of the sewing table, Patricia pushed herself up as if her body weighed a ton. She rose from her chair and walked slowly, as if in a trance, over to Casey. "Who is your friend?"

The cushion she'd been sitting on was wet, the back of her nightgown soiled. *How long had she been sitting there?*

Casey stepped backwards out of the room. "Nice to meet you," he said with a shaky voice.

Avoiding eye contact with Patricia, Casey turned side on and folded his arms across his solar plexus. "Hugh, I'm going to find Sophia and Tim. Get your friends packed up ready to go."

With his hand over his mouth, Hugh opened the window. "Patricia, maybe you should have a shower and get dressed. Where is everyone?"

"Having a nap," Patricia said.

"Shouldn't you guys be getting dinner ready?"

Patricia didn't answer.

Hugh left and went into Seth's room. It was cold and dark, the air musty. In the darkness, he could hear Seth snoring. Hugh turned on the light. "Seth, wake up!" Hugh opened the window for fresh air. "Why are you sleeping? Are you sick?"

Seth blinked, puzzled. He focused on Hugh as if trying to remember who he was. "Hugh, right? Weren't you going to find medicine for Ernest and Bo? Gwen said you'd already left."

"I'm back, it's been five days," Hugh said. "Are you alright?"

Throwing his legs over the side of the bed, Seth sat up. "You're pulling my leg. Stop kidding around. Is the heating working? It's freezing in here." Seth hugged himself.

"It's Friday evening. I left on Monday morning," Hugh said. "Have you been sleeping since Sunday night? Find your dad. Your mother needs a shower, and check on Billie. Ernest is wandering around downstairs. Then I want you to pack. I'm going to go check on Bo and Gwen."

Hugh ran out and listened at the door to Gwen and Bo's apartment, staring at the room number for a few moments before he rapped on the door. Fifty-eight triggered a sense of dread because it conjured up a passage from the Bible, Peter 5:8 which he hadn't thought about in a decade. The seniors used to recite it to the freshmen: *Be sober, be vigilant; because your adversary the devil, as a roaring lion, walketh about, seeking whom he may devour.* Dread crept up his spine as he barged into Gwen's apartment.

The smell was the first thing to penetrate the gloom. It was the stale sour smell of spoiled food. The curtains in the lounge were closed, making it as dark as Seth's room. Hugh opened the curtains. The window looked out at the intersection, and jackals were prowling out the front. He shivered and backed away from the window, bumping into the dining room table. Leftover food from their last meal together had maggots wriggling around the carcass of the roast chicken. The dishes were still in the sink. *What the hell is going on around here?* He took hold of the brass doorknob of Gwen's door, and tapped with his knuckles before entering.

"Gwen? Are you in there?" It smelled like a septic tank inside her room. A pipe that ran through the apartments must have burst. Heading towards the window, he stumbled over a pile of discarded clothes. Careful not to startle Gwen, Hugh only opened the blinds a sliver to raise the window for fresh air. The jackals were still out there, waiting. Gwen was curled up on her side, facing away from him.

"Gwen, honey, where's Bo? Are you awake, Gwen? Gwyneth!"

She stirred, stretched, and turned towards him, rubbing her eyes. "Hugh," she tried to smile. "I have the worst headache. Shut the blinds. It's too bright."

The gap between the curtains was minimal. There was no piercing light; heavy dark clouds hung over the city.

"Hugh, did you open the window? It's freezing in here, and I can smell the horse manure from the street." She pushed herself up and dropped back. "Can you get some aspirin? It's in the cabinet."

Hugh turned to leave, but she took hold of his wrist. "Can you empty the bucket out the window first please, it's in the corner," Gwen said.

There was no bucket, but there was a plastic gray wastepaper bin next to the chest of drawers. There was a roll of toilet paper sitting next to her hairbrush. He walked towards the bin and found the source of the odor in the room. The basket was heavy with excrement. He covered his mouth and took the basket to the bathroom. He held his breath and poured the contents down the toilet and flushed. The water turned black, thick as tar, as it rose to the top of the bowl, threatening to spill over. It settled back down, to his relief. The painkillers were at the back of the vanity cabinet wedged between mouthwash and sanitary products. With the packet of aspirin in hand, he shut the vanity door and returned to Gwen. He handed her the glass of water that was on her bedside table and put the tablets in her hand. "I'm just going to check on Bo."

Hugh opened Bo's bedroom door and was super surprised to see Bo sitting on the floor, in the middle of the room, playing with her dolls. She had them lying down in boxes lined up like they were in beds in a dorm room.

Bo jumped up off the floor and hugged Hugh around the legs. He didn't have time to step back or react. He looked at the dolls. She had made some out of wool. There was a scruffy doll with a dirty dress and singed hair. You could see the holes in the scalp where the hair had been. It was the same doll he had seen the night before he left. The doll had one evil-looking eye open, and one half-open. It watched Bo play. On the doll's lap was one of the woolen handmade dolls, with pins and needles sticking out of its hands.

"That's my new friend, Miss Amelia," Bo said, stepping back from Hugh and following his gaze.

"How are you feeling, Bo?"

"Much better, thank you," Bo said.

"Where did she come from?"

"I found her when we first came here. I heard her calling out from under the floor. She said I'm her savior. What's a savior?"

"Hero," Hugh said. "Maybe you should take her downstairs and put her in the laundry for Mommy to wash?"

The doll blinked. Hugh held his breath. *No.*

Bo's body stiffened as she walked back to the dolls. Bending down to the old Victorian doll, she tilted her head as if listening to it whisper in her ear. She looked back over her shoulder at Hugh and giggled.

"Why don't you keep playing with your dolls while I go talk to your mommy," Hugh said.

Bo leaned into the doll, listening, then she stood straight and said, "We missed you. Thanks for coming back. We don't like the new house."

Hugh did a quick double-take as he stood at the door and looked back at Bo and the doll.

"We want you to stay with us, Hugh. We don't want you to go away again. Stay with us. Mommy loves you," Bo said. "Miss Amelia said you can't leave us like my real daddy did. Promise you'll stay, or dolly will get mad."

He crouched down beside her. "How do you know about the house, Bo?" He was feeling nauseous and wanted to leave the room. For just a second he thought he saw Bo's eyes turn black. When he blinked, they were normal, beautiful and blue. Her breath reeked as if she hadn't brushed her teeth for months, but there was another odor coming from behind her. He stood and scanned the room. In the far corner, almost hidden by the open closet door, was a plastic wastepaper bin. Why was everyone using wastepaper bins as toilets? This wasn't the Middle Ages.

Bo looked embarrassed.

"Bo, how do you know about the house?" Hugh asked again.

"You're mad at me, aren't you?" Bo started crying.

"No, Bo, I'm just curious."

"Alex told me, before dolly made him leave. She said it's an awful house and we should stay here!"

"When did you see Alex?"

"I don't know – before the man in the hat came back and took him away because dolly told him to. He takes all Miss Amelia's naughty children."

"What man in the hat?" Hugh asked.

"I can't talk to you anymore." Bo wiped her tears.

"Where's the man in the hat, now?"

"Inside me."

10

CASEY: TRAPPED IN HISTORY

Hugh's friend Patricia was peculiar. Casey protected himself by standing side on, so her energy couldn't connect with his solar plexus. The smell in her apartment was disgusting, and she looked like she hadn't showered in days. Casey doubted that was normal for her, just as the boy he met downstairs wasn't himself either. There was something sinister about the tavern; he felt dark spirits rising. Casey saw apparitions all over London, but the tavern was dense with entities. Something was hiding just out of sight. Moving along the hallway towards the stairs, there was a blur of paranormal activity behind every apartment door. He tried to ignore the painful emotions emanating from the rooms. He even tiptoed for a moment or two along the paisley-patterned carpet. Casey didn't want to know what was behind those doors.

Apartment 1800 was numbered out of sequence – there couldn't be more than twenty apartments in both wings. The cries of a distressed child filled the hallway. He stopped and placed his hand upon the door of apartment 1800. Images flashed through his mind: a raging fire, a child cowering in a corner, crying and coughing. The images faded as he pulled his hand away. Black smoke drifted under the door into the hall. A piercing scream filled his head. He touched his fingertips to the door. It was hot. There was a fire inside the apartment. Casey pulled his sleeve down over his hand, grabbed the door handle and forced his way into the apartment. The room was ablaze, the heat and flames were unbearable. He stepped back and covered his face with his forearm, trying to see. A woman watched her daughter screaming for help. A girl crouched in a corner and hugged her doll. She coughed and cried to the woman to save her. The girl dropped her doll and the doll's hair went up in flames and burned to the roots. The girl braved the flames and picked up her doll by the feet. She rolled it on the ends of the curtain. The curtain caught fire and roared up to the roof. The girl cried into her smoldering doll. Casey searched for a way through the flames. He pulled his jacket over his head and ran into the flames towards the girl. In one fell swoop he picked up the girl and the doll. He protected them with his jacket as he ran through the flames and out of the door. He yanked the door shut. As gently as possible, Casey put the girl down and knelt beside her to check she was okay. Her face and clothes were black from the smoke, and she smelled like the doll's burning hair. They were even wearing the same outfit: a white dress with a red silk ribbon around the bottom. He took the girl's hand.

"You're okay now. Was that your mommy in there with you? Where are your parents?" he asked.

Traumatized, the girl didn't speak.

"Wait here." Casey ran back to the stairs where he had bumped his elbow on a fire extinguisher. He pulled it off the hook, released the pin and ran back to the room. He kicked open the door and sprayed foam over the curtains, but there was no fire and no smoke. The room was in perfect condition. He turned back to the girl. She had vanished. Casey lowered the fire extinguisher and shut the door to the apartment. He found the pin on the carpet and returned the extinguisher to its hook at the top of the stairs. As he looked down the silent hall once more, he half-expected Hugh to come out to see what all the commotion was about. Casey went back to apartment 1800 and checked each room. The apartment was empty.

In the past Casey had seen and felt how people had died, but this time it was stronger. It felt real somehow. It was like the past and the present had become one. He wasn't just having visions, something else was going on. He had to find Sophia and tell her about his dreams, the drawings, and what he had just experienced. He had to tell her everything.

Casey ran down the stairs and tripped.

CLIP-CLOP, clip-clop. A horse neighed out on the street. Casey opened his eyes. Smoke from too many cigars mingled with the smell of alcohol polluting the air in the bar. A roar of excitement filled the packed room, along with the sound of glasses clinking together. People dressed in old-fashioned clothing crowded around the tables and booths. The bartender rolled his sleeves up and moved up and down the bar pouring drinks.

"Get up lad, if you can't hold your liquor, be off with you," he said, flicking a dirty rag he'd using to clean glasses at Casey.

The tavern's front door was wide open. Horses pulled carriages along the muddy street, and a boy wearing knicker-bockers and a golfer's cap was moving a large hoop along with a stick, trying to keep the hoop upright. Crows cawed from the top of the buildings. Casey stepped outside into the path of a horse and cart. He tilted his body back and out of the way.

Time shifted. A woman leaned out the widow crying; "Gardyloo!" then emptied a bucket of water out of a second-story window. Casey quickly stepped out of the way, and out of the Middle Ages.

Time shifted. Women wearing bonnets and long dresses that dragged through the mud rushed past him. They were like the ones in his drawing. A woman held her skirt up and rushed to catch up with the others, as if worried she'd miss some important event. *Maybe it was a church day,* Casey thought. Other people were rushing, too. Men wearing top hats and smoking cigars walked the streets with fashionable canes. *How was this happening, how was time changing?* He didn't know – he wasn't even certain which era he was in, or if he was seeing a vision.

The tavern disappeared, and Casey stood facing a riveted iron door. Above the arch of the door were the words Newgate Prison. Two guards dressed as though they had stepped out of the eighteen-hundreds opened the heavy metal door. Rows of shiny buttons stood out on their black uniforms.

Two more prison officers pushed a procession of prisoners wearing hoods over their faces into the street. Shackles around their wrists and ankles clanged together. Some wore shoes, but most were barefoot. Their dirty feet slapped down on the mud as they shuffled forward. Excited women in long dresses rushed past Casey, discussing how to secure a suitable position to watch the hanging. It was as if they were going to a spectacular outdoor entertainment. Casey craned his neck in the direction the women were headed. At the far end of the prison's walls gallows had been erected.

Casey froze. In the middle of the filthy, unpaved road lay the hat from his dream. He turned and found himself on the opposite side of the street. He dodged the horses and cart, and headed to where the tavern should have been. Halfway across the street, a man on a horse blocked his way. Casey took a few steps to the side to go around the horse, but the rider flicked a whip in his path, stopping him from moving.

"Pick up my hat!" The man yelled down at him. The horse reared up, its hooves inches from Casey's face.

Casey could see the hat over his right shoulder. He didn't want to touch it.

"Pick it up!" The man yelled.

As Casey was about to put his hand on the hat, a constable said, "Everything alright here, warden?"

"This scoundrel here is trying to steal my hat."

"No, that's not true. He asked me to pick it up," Casey said.

"Where are your knickerbockers? What are you wearing, boy? Where did you steal those fine threads from?" The constable, slapping his baton in his hand.

Casey pulled the sleeve of his jacket down over his hand, to block as much energy as possible from transmitting from the hat into his being, as he picked up the hat. He held it up for the warden to take. Casey bowed his head to avoid eye contact with the warden and the constable. He didn't want to see into the warden's face; he could feel the man's eyes boring into his soul. The rider had curled the whip at his side. He flicked it out, hitting Casey in the face.

"Look at me, boy. Do I know you? Answer the constable." The warden's voice was getting deeper and slower. Suspicious, he titled his head to get a closer look.

As the constable reached for Casey, the warden's whip connected with his back. Casey turned to protect himself – the horse reared up. Casey ducked under the hooves and ran across the street into the entranceway of the building where the tavern should have been. He stood in the doorway and braced himself, ready for the hand of the constable to fall upon his shoulders. With his head lowered, he waited. When the blow didn't come, he glanced back towards the street – the constable and warden had vanished. Casey touched his cheek. He was bleeding. It reminded him of the day his mother died, when he was crossing the rope bridge, and the rope snapped, flicking up and cutting him on the face while the raging river dragged him to his death. He ran his fingers along the scar.

The scene changed in front of his eyes to a vacant block of land, as time shifted again. He watched mesmerized as laborers built a Post Office. They erected it within seconds. Night and day came and went, the city of London moved on, changing from century to century. Then, like a merry-go-round, the city came to a stop. After a long day of manual labor, men with dirty clothes entered the post office, which was now a drinking den. Casey's head was spinning. He closed his eyes. Time stood still. Excited murmurs filled his ears. He opened his eyes and saw thousands of people crammed into the street around a tall gallows, different from the first one. Time was slipping backwards and forwards through history. The constant switching from one era to another was making him sick.

Peasants were at the back of the crowd while wealthy women in hooped dresses had front row seats as if they were at the opera. He visualized Sophia wearing a bonnet, looking beautiful as she adjusted her white gloves and held up the circular skirt of her long handmade dress, like the other women of society, trying to avoid getting mud on it. Her voice filled his mind. He worried she was in the crowd. Casey felt himself melding into this new time frame. He had to get out, back to his own time. *How was this even happening?* A lot of people were waving their fists, angry and yelling for justice. Impatient, they mingled, waiting for the hanging to begin.

Male and female prisoners looked awkward walking in shackles, heading up the steps of the gallows. The hangman came forward and placed a noose over each prisoner's head. Just as the hanging was about to reach its high point, the gallows collapsed, killing the prisoners and crushing the spectators. Casey rushed to help, and skidded to a stop when he saw the man with the hat laughing at him – he too seemed to jump through time. "Get out of my head!" Casey ran back to where the tavern should've been, or would be in the next decade.

Sophia whispered, her voice calm, seeking him. "Where are you, Casey?"

He thought he could feel the softness of her hands enclosing his face, and warmth filled his heart. She was in his mind – she was in his head and his heart. He welcomed her. The street disappeared.

Casey opened his eyes. He was in the tavern, lying at the bottom of the stairs; alone.

CASEY PUSHED himself up onto his knees and sat back on his heels. His heart raced. His cheek was bleeding. The sting of the whip against his face was a fading memory, like waking after a night of dreams. He must have hit his head when he fell down the stairs. He stood and looked back up the stairs to see what he had tripped on. The steps were narrow and the rise a little higher than usual. He could have misjudged the step. He hadn't noticed how narrow they were. His feet were big, but they weren't that big ... He struggled to come up with a plausible explanation. It had felt like someone had grabbed him around the ankle, causing him to fall.

Remembering his concussed hallucinations, Casey was quick to check the tavern, making sure he was in the right century. The door to the tavern was closed, and it was the same as when he had entered with Sophia, Tim and Hugh. There was no bartender. That was an excellent start. Hugh's car was visible through the window. Casey did a three-sixty, looking for Sophia, certain she had woken him, but she was not around. Light glowed under the basement door.

Casey covered his hand with his coat sleeve and opened the basement door. He stood, listening, and looked down the stairs. Voices. Soft, whispering sounds floated up. As he placed his feet firmly on each stair, it squeaked under his weight as he descended.

At the bottom of the stairs was an old iron shelf, and on it sat an oil lantern casting a faint glow but not bright enough to have radiated up the staircase. Shadows concealed the walls and corners of the basement. It was as if he had stepped into a medieval dungeon. He wanted to get out. Smothering his fear, he headed back up the basement stairs, and halfway up the door at the top slammed shut. He ran up the last few steps and yanked on the door handle. Images burst into his mind as a carousel of people from the past who had touched the doorknob raced into his head as he pushed on the door. It wouldn't budge. He let go of the handle, and the intruding parade disappeared.

Casey went into the basement for the lantern and held it close to the door, scanning the edges to see why it had jammed. When he pulled the lantern away, light penetrated the cracks. There was no obvious blockage. There was no key in the square lock. He turned the handle again, pushed and pulled. Still the door wouldn't budge. Indistinct whispering came from deeper in the basement.

Casey wanted to dismiss the sensation of paranormal activity, but he knew it wouldn't be long before apparitions materialized. Holding the lantern high, he made sure he could see the way forward as he moved down the stairs once again.

"Sophia? Tim?" he called. His voice lacked strength and confidence. He coughed as he moved forward; a nasty odor made him gag. It was the same as the apartment upstairs. He shivered from the cold. The iron bars of the cells looked nearly new – as if the cells were in use. The doors were closed and, he assumed, locked. Through the bars, he could see men lying on filthy cots, curled up without blankets, shivering from the cold or jail fever. Keeping himself at a distance, Casey tried not to touch the metal bars, but he couldn't stop the entities from touching his aura.

"Sophia!" He yelled, but the only sound he heard was the echo of his own voice. The basement felt more and more like a medieval dungeon. He walked a little further into the damp space and reached out with his mind, searching for Sophia, or at least a powerful essence of her being, but there was only the faintest hint that she had been down here. She meant everything to him. He would give his life to save her.

Certain she wasn't in the basement, he didn't need to look any further and couldn't get out quick enough. As he turned to leave he stepped on a rat, which gave a sharp squeal. As he jumped back, feeling the rat's body under his boot, Casey fell against the bars of one of the cells and the perils of the past burst into his mind.

Men, women and children were crying, screaming, and pleading. Clanging chains and the jumbled noise of captive people filled his ears. Sounds of madness surrounded him. The horrific smell of faeces, sickness, and decay was everywhere. An invisible presence pressed up against him and pinned him to the bars of the cell. It was as if he was having a night terror: he couldn't move. He closed his eyes, and projected his telekinetic energy outward, repelling the entities until the pressure ceased and he could peel himself off the bars. He didn't want to know what had pressed against him and ran through the basement, looking for another way out. The screaming of a dozen or more babies filled the air. The sounds of the dead surrounded him. Casey gulped, trying to catch his breath, experiencing what the babies had felt during their last moments before death. There was nothing he could do for them. He needed Sophia so that together they could at least help them into the light of God.

A set of stairs loomed in front of him. He kept running. Trying to ignore the heartbreaking sounds of the babies, Casey made a beeline towards the stairs. A spirit materialized in front of him, blocking his way. He didn't want to connect to it by going through it. It was the figure of a large round woman in a long filthy dress, her hair pinned so tightly to her head it stretched the skin of her face, giving her an unnatural look. Her bodice pushed her bosoms way too high, and she stood with her hands on her hips. There was nothing meek and frail about her.

In a booming voice, she screamed at him, "Go shut them babies up!"

Casey looked over his shoulder, and a darkened room appeared behind him containing rows of small boxes. He stepped into the room. In each box was a baby, some wrapped in cloth, some naked and stiff. Shocked, tears pooled in his eyes. He held back the vomit. He could hear the babies crying. It reminded him of his dream and his sketches. He wanted to kill the woman; she was a monster, but she was already dead. The heavyset woman pushed him. Casey stumbled backward, trying to think. *How can she push me? She's a poltergeist.* So was the warden, the man with the hat. He thought he had stepped into an emotional memory loop, but it wasn't that. *The woman is a poltergeist, it must be the residual energy of one of the babies.* It was hard to think, his head hurt.

"Shut them up now, or I will shut them up," she said, pushing him to the ground. "You're worthless. I don't know why I bother keeping you alive. Look at your soiled apron. Take this." She shoved a potato sack at him and kicked him aside to enter the room, and as she did, the room changed into a nursery. Casey reached out and took the sack.

"Come on, girl, what are you gawking at? Hold the sack open."

The woman took four dead babies and dropped them in the sack. She stopped to count. "One more, Doc wants five." The woman looked over at the crying babies, and picked the one with the weakest cry and put her hand over its mouth and nose. Casey put the bag down and attacked the woman, trying to pull her hand off the baby's mouth. With no effort, she slapped him across the room. He banged hard against the wall, which freed him from the emotional memory loop. A girl of about twelve stood with her back to him. It was her memory. The woman took the potato sack and added the suffocated baby, which fueled the girl with rage.

"Get that look off your face, or I'll give you to the Doc to experiment on. Off with you and make sure he pays you two pounds for the lot."

Casey watched the girl. He vowed to free the girl and the babies and send the woman to hell.

"Yes, Miss," the girl replied.

"Yes, Miss what!" the woman said, stepping forward and slapping her hard across the face.

"Yes, Miss Amelia." The girl turned and climbed the stairs with the heavy load.

Casey ran out into the night after her. It was dark, and he was facing a church. They had come out from a side entrance which faced Gilchrist Street. The girl placed the sack into a wooden wheelbarrow and pushed it non-stop down the unpaved street. Keeping a safe distance, Casey followed. She entered an alleyway and knocked on a door. A man with his sleeves rolled-up checked the street before acknowledging the girl.

"Who are you? What do you want?" The man said.

The girl curtsied. "Delivery from Miss Amelia, sir."

Prior to taking the sack from the girl's wheelbarrow, he stepped outside and checked the street again. He wore high-waisted pants with suspenders, and an unbuttoned waistcoat with a watch attached to a chain. He checked the time and tucked the watch back into the waistcoat pocket.

"You're late!" the man said.

As he stepped forward and reached for the sack, moonlight reflected off his shoe. Casey recognized the shoes as the ones worn by one of the men man hanging from the gallows. The woman who had been beside him on the gallows must have been Miss Amelia. It gave Casey a smidgen of satisfaction to know that they had been hanged for their crimes. The man Casey assumed was the Doc put his fingers into his pocket and brought out a few coins. The girl took the coins and began pushing the wooden wheelbarrow back to the building she had come from.

Casey didn't follow her; instead, he walked to the intersection to get his bearings. He turned a corner and saw the prison. He looked up at the corner building and the tavern was a gin palace. *Close enough*, Casey thought. A man with a cane was smoking a pipe in the shadows, watching a woman in front of the prison across the road.

Casey shivered. *No more, God please take me back.* He pulled his collar up and kept his head down as he passed the man with the pipe, and hurried into the building. A hat floated in the air and as he followed it, he saw his body lying at the foot of the stairs. A tall skinny monster was standing over his body. It had pale wet skin like a salamander and was throwing something in his face. He could no longer see.

Inside his body at the foot of the stairs, it was dark. He smelled freshly dug earth. It was difficult to move his arms as the salamander tossed grains of dirt into his eyes and over his body.

11

SOPHIA: THE HAND OF THE DEVIL

Desperate to let go of the boy's hand, Sophia had to stop herself shaking off his grip. She had to trust her instincts. He was very gray, his skin the color of a corpse, his eyes sunk above prominent cheekbones. Everything about him was haunting. Ernest's fingernails felt long and sharp in her hand, even though his hands looked small and fragile. His arms were super skinny. Sophia peeked inside his mind, searching for a remnant of the life energy of the real Ernest. Deep within his subconscious, he was struggling to talk to her, calling out for Sophia to help him. She was cautious as she strengthened the connection, careful not to alert the demon possessing Ernest. It dug its finger-like claws into her hand. There was more than one entity clogging his aura, fighting for his soul – there were many.

It was like evil was free to roam the world, something she had tried to prevent by returning the Emerald Tablet, which now seemed futile. She feared the earth belonged to the army of the devil: demons and monsters that would do anything to gain physical bodies in the mortal realm. She got the sense that some of the entities inside Ernest were wandering human spirits seeking redemption, thinking he was the light or their saviour. But it was the legion that possessed Ernest, and she worried that he and Bo were offerings to the devil for his physical manifestation. She found the real Ernest embedded deep inside his subconscious, deliberately hidden by his own super-consciousness.

"Ernest, I'm your friend. I come from the light of God, guided to you by Hugh. I will come for you and return you to your family soon," Sophia reassured the little boy. "I will return when it is safe for you to rise back into your consciousness and take back your body forever, the vehicle given to you by God to travel upon this earth. Hide, Ernest. Hide within your favorite memory until I can return." Sophia spoke with her mind into Ernest's mind. A vision of Blackpool, a festive night, with colored lights bringing joy, surrounded Ernest. His memory was of a holiday to the Pleasure Beach amusement park, holding his sister Billie's hand as they rushed towards the rides on a glorious warm summer night.

Sophia disengaged from Ernest's mind, leaving him in his memory with his sister. Sophia pretended to drop something on the floor near the bar. She reached down to pick it up, allowing her to let go of the boy's clammy hand and severing the demon's physical connection. She could feel it trying to penetrate her aura. It was too dangerous for them to stay at the tavern. Sophia used all her mental power to keep her pulse rate low, and the legion of entities out.

Like an angry parent, Ernest held out his stiff hand for her to take. His eyes transformed to yellow and blinked like a reptile's. He glared down at her.

Sophia moved her gaze away from his eyes. "I think I lost a

contact lens," she said, pretending not to have noticed his transformation.

"Can you help me find it, Tim?" Sophia said.

She watched Tim drop the boy's other hand and his vagueness receded as if he had snapped out of a micro-sleep. Tim blinked several times to focus. He crouched down, keeping his eyes on Sophia. She could feel the butterflies in his stomach, and see the rise and fall of his chest as his breathing became more rapid. He searched the ground for the contact lens that didn't exist.

"What game are you playing?" The boy's voice was deep and grave. He coughed like a smoker.

Sophia didn't wear contact lenses, but Tim was quick to play along.

"You okay?" she asked Tim without speaking.

Sophia locked her eyes with Tim's, praying he wouldn't speak out loud. She could see him struggling to understand how he could hear her inside his mind. He looked like he was about to speak out loud, and she could hear in his mind what he wanted to say.

"What's going on? I feel like I've been sleepwalking."

"Don't let on we're talking. Keep it together, Tim," she said inside his mind.

"This kid is so damn creepy. What just happened?"

"I feel so many entities around; it's hard to know which one is doing what. Stay close to me, and go along with whatever I do, unless you think I'm not me."

"What do you mean, if you're not you?"

"I don't know how strong some of these demons and entities are, and they could try to take possession of our bodies."

"Us?"

"Keep cool and go along with me." Sophia kept stroking the

carpet. *"We need to keep everyone alive and get out of here."*

Sophia pretended to put a contact lens in her eye. She stood up and took Ernest's hand. "Where is your family, Ernest? It would be nice to meet your brother and sister. Is your mother making dinner?"

"Sleeping," Ernest said.

A glass flew off the bar, missing Tim's head. "What the …? Did you do that?" Tim asked Ernest.

Ernest put his hand to his mouth and giggled.

Glass after glass flew across the bar, hitting Tim in the back.

"That's enough," Sophia said. "If you don't stop this nonsense, we will not play with you anymore."

"It's not me," Ernest said. "It's them from over there." He pointed towards the street.

Tim kneeled on the cushion in the booth to get a good look out the window. He turned back to Sophia. "No-one is out there."

Sophia listened to the rise and fall of Ernest's voice as distinct entities and spirits came through. "I'll show you one more place that's spooky, then I'll take you to meet my mommy and daddy."

Sophia and Tim were reluctant, but went along with Ernest. Tim moved with caution, hesitating, as if he expected something else to come hurling towards him. Sophia decided it was worth the risk to save Ernest and get the human spirits seeking redemption into the light, when the demon was busy elsewhere. "How long have you lived here?" she asked casually.

"A long time ago, I used to live across the road. Then there was a big fire, and I got trapped between the walls, but then I found Ernest."

"You lived in the courthouse?" Tim said.

"No, the prison," the ghost said.

"If you say so." Tim shrugged.

Sophia frowned at Tim, he should leave the talking to her. "How did you get trapped between the walls? Were you alone?" Sophia was leading him towards the upstairs banister.

His head twitched, and a puff of smoke came out of his mouth. The voice changed back into a deep, croaky voice. "He doesn't like to remember."

"I need to find my friends," Sophia said, not looking into the yellow eyes of the demon.

Sophia's focus changed as she became aware that someone, or something, was behind her, close to her shoulder, and if she pushed her long hair back behind her ear, she might see an unknown face. A chill filled her body. She spoke to Tim, trying to gain composure and take back control.

"I think Casey and Hugh went this way." She disengaged from the demon inside Ernest and, holding onto the banister, started upstairs.

"No, you promised." It was the spirit that had died trapped between the burning walls. "We're not going up there, silly, we're going down there." He pointed down the hallway to a single door.

"Is that where you and Ernest like to play?" Tim said as the three of them moved towards the door.

"Ernest's not allowed to play in the basement. His big brother played in the basement, he's like you," he said, pointing a finger in Tim's face. "And his boyfriend got killed. The guard doesn't like people like you."

Sophia ducked under the low beam at the entrance. "Watch your head," Sophia said to Tim. "And stick to me like glue."

They walked down the stairs to the cold and musty basement.

"I don't like this. There are shadows everywhere," Tim

whispered.

There was a gas lamp on a shelf and a packet of matches. Ernest lit the wick and replaced the glass dome over the flame. He raised the lamp up high and switched off the overhead light.

"What are you doing?" Tim said and flicked the switch back on.

"Us down here, we don't trust the magic of electricity." The boy's voice changed again as he flicked off the lights.

Sophia wondered which entity or spirit was coming forward, taking over Ernest. The ruling demon must be busy elsewhere to allow other entities to make conversation like this.

Now was the time to get the spirits seeking redemption to pass into the light. The boy held the lantern high and in a croaky old man's voice said, "These cells were part of the tower. When I lived across the road it was my job to make haste through them tunnels. I had to collect the jugs of gin prepared for the warden, the guards, and the prisoners that could afford it."

"Were you trapped in between the walls because of the fire too?" Sophia said.

The voice stopped and the entity scrutinized her, as if seeing her for the first time, and then turned to Tim. He squinted his eyes as if trying to see better. He pushed the light into Sophia's face and then Tim's. Tim stepped back, covering his eyes.

She reached out her hand. "I don't think we've met. My name is Sophia, and this is my friend Tim. What's your name?"

"James." The old cell door screeched as James opened it. It surprised Sophia that the hinges even moved.

Sophia felt trapped, as if they were mice about to be pounced on by a cat. Before Tim entered the cell she said, "Tim, tie your shoelaces."

Sophia followed Ernest into the cell, blocking Tim from James. Tim dropped to the floor and pretended to tie up his shoelace. Sophia's atoms started taking on a life of their own, scintillating and building force. Her energy gathered into her arms and hands. In a controlled burst forward, she pushed the energy outward, throwing Ernest's body hard against the stone wall. While he struggled for air, Sophia stepped outside of the cell and slammed the heavy iron door shut with another burst of energy. Tim secured the lock through the loop of the chain on the door, sealing Ernest inside. It had been a few days since she had used her powers, and it felt good, but she feared she had now drawn the demon's attention and it wouldn't be too long until it showed itself. She saw a hideous vision of a burned man sniffing her aura. Using her power may have been foolish, but it was the only way to help the trapped spirits and Ernest.

"The lantern!" Tim said.

Ernest had become a doorway for the dead to enter this world. He had dropped the lantern on its side.

Sophia created a psychic barrier around her and Tim and went to work. "Our Father which art in heaven, Hallowed be thy Name ..."

"What are you doing?" A light gray puff of smoke escaped out of Ernest's mouth. "Open this door!" the voice of the old man cried.

"Thy Kingdom come, Thy will be done on earth, As it is in heaven. Give us this day our daily bread ..."

"STOP! STOP!"

"And forgive us our debts, as we forgive our debtors. And lead us not into temptation, But deliver us from evil. For thine is the kingdom, The power, and the glory, For ever and ever. Amen."

In one breath, a dozen voices cried out and trails of smoke left Ernest's body.

His eyes rolled back in his head, exposing the whites of his eyes. A pleading, soft female voice cried out, "Release me! Release me!"

"I can set you free, and I will ..." Sophia said, stepping closer to the bars.

"Wait," Tim said, holding her back. "It could be a trick."

"What are you doing?" It was a woman's voice now coming from within Ernest.

"Let me out of here," said a woman crying. "It's so hot, please don't let us burn. I promise not to steal again. My children are starving, waiting for my return. I must return to them."

Ernest's body hunched over like an old woman who shouldered the pain of the world. He gripped an invisible collar, as if clutching a shawl around his neck, as another desperate ghost possessed his being like he was a puppet.

"Please, I must get home to my family, don't let me burn!" said the lost and frightened woman.

"I'll help you, but you must help me first," Sophia said.

Tim grabbed her arm. "What are you doing? Let's just get out of here."

"Anything, be quick, before the demon returns," the woman said.

"I want you to round up all the good people trapped between the burning walls and bring them forward with you."

"No, I cannot."

"Yes, you can, what's your name?"

"Mary. The warden will feed me to the dogs. Please, please let me go."

Sophia walked away.

"Wait. I'll do it."

"Go. Find them all, reach out, and let them pass through you. Nurture them as you would your own children – hold them in the bosom of your heart like you would cradle your own baby.

You can do this, Mary. You're not bad, you're not evil. I see you only stole a loaf of bread to feed your children. Now help those around you to be free. It's time for you all to return home. Mary, you can do this," Sophia said.

"Do you promise you will set me free?" Mary pleaded in Ernest's trembling voice.

"Yes, I promise," Sophia said.

"I don't belong here with this madness," Mary said.

Sophia felt her body tingle with fear, something she had refused to feel. The Bible of her old parish priest, Father McDonald, pressed against her left breast, and the canister of holy water against her right. In the lower pocket of her coat was the velvet satchel of dried sage. In the past, she had chewed on pieces of sage when negative energy lingered. Now, she hadn't even thought about putting a piece in her mouth, or giving some to Tim for protection. Since Father McDonald died, Sophia had left herself vulnerable, forgetting to protect herself because there had been no need – until now.

"I promise, Mary, I will see that you are set free. I will show you to the door so you can return to your children and feel the love of God in your heart."

Tim gave Sophia a curious look as she handed him some sage. "Chew on it and don't swallow," she said.

"Now, Mary. Our Father who art in heaven, shine your light upon me to help free the spirits trapped between the realms who seek your forgiveness and light. Open the gates of heaven. Hear my prayer for the poor and desolate, they have suffered and been kept from your love, help them adhere to your healing light. Amen."

Radiant light from all directions filled the basement and was channeled into and out of Sophia and out through the bars to the west wall of the cell.

"Are you ready?" Sophia asked the woman.

"Yes."

"Understand this, you all are going home with the grace of God, it is not for me to judge; those found unworthy will be cast aside. Go now, Mary, shepherd your folk before the door closes."

Apparitions of men, women, and children of all ages crowded the cell.

The woman led the way into the light, clutching her shawl around her shoulders. Looking ahead into the light, she cried, "I see my children! God bless you." Mary merged into the light and the procession of spirits followed. A few exploded into black smoke, giving off a foul odor. Sophia reached into Ernest's mind. It was free from the clutter of spirits and the dark forces were at bay, forced back by the light, but she knew that once the doorway to heaven was closed, the legion would surge forward again.

Sophia pulled Ernest into consciousness.

With an expression of shock and horror, Tim stepped away from the cell as Ernest's features flickered and wavered. The boy's face was pale with just a tinge of pink, his eyes sunken and drawn.

"My eyes behold the light!" Tim said. "But I can't see anything beyond it."

Sophia baulked at closing the doorway, but it had to be done. She closed her eyes and let out a sigh as it shut.

Sophia stopped channeling the energy into and through her solar plexus. The lantern's glow was minuscule compared to the receding light. It was a slight comfort in the basement's darkness.

Ernest collapsed to the ground as the last spirit passed through him into the light. Tim moved to Sophia's side.

"Tim! Help me. The key, get the key," Sophia said.

Tim hesitated. He closed his eyes, as if afraid. "Where are the keys?"

"There's a row of hooks at the bottom of the stairs with a ring of keys."

"What? I didn't notice," Tim said.

"I have a thing for old keys," Sophia said.

Tim ran back to the bottom of the stairs, found the row of hooks and took the big loop of keys.

Sophia reached between the bars for the lantern. Tim handed her the keys, and she studied them.

"Just pick one!" Tim said.

Their eyes met. "Here goes."

The anticipated click seemed to take longer than the millisecond it actually took. Sophia picked up the lantern and held it in Ernest's face.

"Tim, can you pick him up?"

"Easy," Tim said.

"Hurry, Tim. Ernest is very weak, almost an empty shell. He is vulnerable to even the weakest spirits. Anything could possess him within a second." She crouched down. The lantern shone over Ernest's face as she reached into the inside pocket of her coat, producing a silver canister. She unscrewed the lid and put her finger against the opening, tipping a small amount of blessed water onto her finger. She made the sign of the cross on Ernest's temple.

The boy stirred, then let out a tremendous wail as if he'd been holding his breath for a long time. He cried for his mother; he recognized Sophia and pulled his knees up under his chin and hugged himself tight, sobbing.

"Hey, you're okay," Tim said, picking him up. "Let's go find your mommy."

Tim cradled Ernest and carried him up the basement stairs. "He's gone all limp. Is he dead?"

Sophia checked the boy. "He's breathing."

"He's so light, is he okay? I'm worried about this kid," Tim said.

"I think so, let's get him upstairs and find his family."

* * *

"WHERE THE HELL IS EVERYONE?" Tim was carrying Ernest along the upstairs hallway.

"Casey!" Sophia called out. "Casey, where are you? Casey! Hugh! Where are you guys?" She glanced back towards the stairs. It felt as though Casey was coming up behind her. His spiritual energy was slight, but he was around, she could feel a faint pulse of his life force stretching out, moving further and further away. Hugh poked his head out of an apartment halfway along the hall.

Hugh saw Tim and opened the door wide. Sophia went ahead into the apartment. The smell was disgusting. Humming an old nursery rhyme, a woman with short black hair sat at a sewing machine, oblivious to the commotion. There was another man who pushed open a door that she assumed led into a bedroom. Sophia thought he must be Ernest's elder brother, Seth.

"In here," Seth said. "What happened?"

In a sleepy state, a teenage girl walked out of an adjacent room wearing a nightie, rubbing her eyes as if waking from a deep sleep. She crossed her arms over her breasts when she saw Tim.

"Hugh, what's going on? Who are these people?" Billie asked.

The woman at the sewing machine was in a terrible state. Seth held the bedroom door open for Tim and Ernest.

"Go get dressed, Billie," Seth yelled at her. "We slept for five days."

"How is that possible?" Billie said, confused. "Mom? What's going on? Mom, answer me? What's that awful smell?"

"Go get dressed, Billie, she's not herself. Get her into the shower. Then maybe make her a pot of tea. And chuck out that chair," Seth said.

Sophia reached into her pocket and opened her pouch of sage. She handed some of it to Billie. "Put this in her tea, it might help. You should have some too."

"What is it?" Billie said.

"Sage and basil. They will help cleanse her body of the negative energy within her, and it will help to keep you free from the spirits I imagine are waiting to take over your being and shove your soul into the depths of despair. As they would like to do to all of us. Be careful."

Sophia followed Tim into the bedroom. He placed Ernest on the bed and stepped back for Seth to take over.

"Ernest! What happened? How long has he been out of bed?" Seth asked.

"We got here fifteen minutes ago, and he let us in. He was sitting at the bar when we arrived," Hugh said.

"I'll take it from here," Seth said, looking from Tim to Sophia as if dismissing them. "Hugh?"

"This is Sophia, and Tim. I brought them here to help us," Hugh said.

"Where's Casey, Hugh?" Sophia said, checking the dark cold bedroom. She pulled the curtains open to let in some light.

"He went to find you," Hugh said.

Ernest opened his eyes. "I feel sick," he said, screwing up his face and holding his stomach.

Seth turned him on his side just as Ernest vomited over the edge of the bed. He hurried out and came back with a bucket, a towel and a wet facecloth. Seth was careful as he rubbed Ernest's face clean.

"You'll be okay, buddy, just take it easy," Seth said and began scrubbing the carpet.

"Let me help." Hugh crouched down, cleaning the carpet with the face cloth.

"Seth!" Ernest said in a voice much older than his own. "Seth, look at me," the new voice said.

"It's happening again. We have to get out of here before it happens to us," Tim said to Sophia. "How many more ghosts are there?"

Unhappy ghosts would fill the city, but this was new to Sophia. She could sense a lighter energy that seemed almost to still be alive, as if it had died not long ago.

Seth stood and turned his back to Ernest. He looked hard into Sophia's eyes. "What sort of trick is this?"

"Seth," Hugh said, taking a step back and tapping Seth's arm. "You, we, know that voice. It's Colin. I can see a ghostly haze of his body covering Ernest. Turn around and look. This is impossible!"

Seth peeled his eyes away from Sophia. She saw the recognition on his face. It hurt him to hear the voice, but still he would not look. He seemed torn, his rational thinking unable to process what was happening.

"Look at me, for Ernest's sake, Seth!" the voice pleaded. "I have little time."

"Why are you doing this, Hugh?" Seth's face was red with anger. "I trusted you."

Hugh whispered, "Talk to him."

Seth turned around and looked at Ernest, and his anger dissolved as he saw the apparition of a man in his early twenties or late teens covering Ernest's body.

"I didn't kill myself. This place, it's filled with evil spirits surging out from hell. This place is no longer the world of God, it belongs to the devil. I am trapped here and can't move on to heaven. Ernest and Bo are the closest thing to heaven and the light. The devil's legion wants Ernest and Bo's inner light, and they want yours, too. They are seeking to claim every living soul before God's light warriors can take us home. After the blood drained from my body, I asked why I was killed. I was told God wouldn't want me because I loved you, that I belong with them in hell. It's not true. The devil's legion tells nothing but lies. Ernest is strong. I'll protect him as long as I can. You must expel the demons, and then you'll save us both."

"I didn't believe you killed yourself," Seth said, standing close to the side of the bed.

"Let her help you ..." the apparition of Colin flickered, turning into white noise. "I have to go, it's not safe. The evil is returning. I can feel it creeping back in." The voice faded away to silence and the ghostly vapors disappeared.

Seth hugged Ernest's limp body and spoke in a soft voice. "We're coming for you, Ernest. Don't be frightened. Colin will keep you safe. I trust him. We'll get you back. These two will help us." He placed Ernest's head on the pillow and stepped away from the bed. A tear escaped Ernest's closed eye.

"Can you help him?" Seth asked Sophia.

"I'll do whatever I can." Sophia didn't know if she could help. In theory, she knew what she had to do.

Ernest murmured and struggled as if in a bad dream. His head thrashed from side to side. *God help him,* Sophia thought as another entity came forward to take over his body. A fire rushed around in the pit of her stomach, alerting her to the dangerous nature of the entity. Ernest pushed himself up off the bed, his eyes rolled back in his head. A scream poured from his mouth, and he launched himself off the bed at Sophia. She stepped to the side, and he latched onto Seth, grabbing him around the throat.

"Let go, Ernest, you're hurting me," Seth said. Ernest squeezed tighter and grinned at Sophia. The whites of his eyes turned yellow, and he blinked like a reptile as he smiled.

"Did you see that?" Tim shouted, pointing at Ernest.

"Get him off me," Seth shouted.

Hugh and Tim wrestled to peel Ernest's hands away from Seth's neck and pry his legs from around Seth's waist.

"That's not Ernest, and it's not Colin either. It's a demon," Sophia said. "Tim, Hugh, get his arms. Tie him to the bed so he doesn't hurt himself, or anyone else. You heard what Colin said, they forced him to kill himself."

Ernest thrashed on the bed under the weight of Hugh and Tim as they tried to restrain him.

"What? No! We can't tie him to the bed," Hugh said.

"With what?" Tim said.

Seth rubbed his sore neck. "There are belts hanging on the back of my bedroom door." His voice sounded as if he was still choking. He left the room and came back with a bundle of belts and dropped them at Ernest's feet at the end of the bed.

Ernest's thrashed as Hugh and Tim held him still.

"Hurry, Seth," Hugh said.

"I'm trying. Keep him still." Seth wrapped a belt around Ernest's ankles, holding them together. He looped another belt around the bottom of the bed and fastened Ernest's legs to it. Without hesitation, he attached the other belts to the bed and Ernest's out-stretched arms.

"Get your filthy hands off me!" said Ernest in a hoarse female voice, which turned into cackling laughter that made Sophia's blood run cold.

"We need holy crosses. Lots of them, and place them in the children's rooms," Sophia said. "I'll bless the children."

The entity screamed and laughed. "You're all in hell. You're all going to die."

Sophia took out her flask of holy water and splashed it over Ernest's body. The holy water cut him like a knife, but the wounds didn't bleed. They sizzled like water on coal and steam rose from his body. Sophia squashed her fear and moved closer. She made the mark of the cross on his forehead with the holy water and a beast cried out in pain. The thrashing stopped, Ernest wet his pants.

"Clean him up, Seth," Sophia said. "Is there a cross or any religious symbols in the building?"

"There's a church across the road," Billie said, wiping away tears as she stood at the door dressed in jeans and a woolen sweater.

Sophia didn't know how long Billie had been watching, but before anyone could stop her, Billie ran off.

"Here, take my crucifix," Tim said, and removed his necklace. The chain was long, and he put it over Ernest's head.

"When Billie gets back with the crosses, nail one to the wall above his bed," Sophia said. *But where the hell is Casey?*

A cold mist was coming out of Ernest's gaping mouth. His body was still and relaxed as a chilling frost filled the room.

"He should sleep for a while. It's best you clean him up now, Seth." Sophia shivered.

Seth cut Ernest's boxers away with a pair of scissors and cleaned him up. With Tim's help, they untied his legs to put on clean boxers. Hugh made sure Ernest stayed still while they changed him. Sophia continued to read her Bible. Tim helped Seth change the sheets. They had to make half the bed at a time and push the sheet under Ernest's body.

Sophia hugged herself and checked the radiator.

"Get everyone together, Hugh, and let's meet downstairs at the bar. Can you look at the heating? It's freezing in here. I'll go find Casey," Sophia said in a soft voice.

"Okay. I still need to check on Bo and see if Gwen can come downstairs. Bo is acting weird, but she doesn't appear to be as sick as she was when I left. It's bizarre, she's up and playing."

We need a priest. I need Father McDonald. Sophia put her hand to her chest, pressing on Father McDonald's Bible as if pressing it into her heart. "Our Father, which art in heaven, Hallowed be thy Name. Thy kingdom come, Thy will be done on earth, As it is in heaven. Give us this day our daily bread. And forgive us our debts, As we forgive our debtors. And lead us not into temptation, But deliver us from evil. For thine is the kingdom, The power, and the glory, forever and ever. Amen."

"What the … who is that?" Tim said as they were about to leave the room.

A young girl in a white dress with a red satin ribbon tied into a bow around her waist stood in the doorway. Next to her was a black jackal that looked like a hungry Doberman. Sophia took a step back. The girl's hand rested on the beast's back, stroking its smooth shiny coat. The jackal snapped and snarled at Sophia. Saliva dripped from its sharp yellow teeth, and fires danced in its eyes. The girl clutched a doll that was missing most of its hair. A woman was coming up behind her.

"Bo, honey, what are you doing out of bed?" Hugh asked, stepping forward in front of Sophia.

"I want to play with Ernest, and I want those people to leave."

"They're here to help us," Hugh said.

Bo laughed and laughed and laughed. Her voice multiplied from one to a dozen, and the jackal barked.

"What the hell is going on? Bo, get that thing out of here!" Seth yelled.

The door slammed shut.

"Everyone just calm down," Hugh yelled over the barking and laughing coming from the other side of the door.

"Bo, take that dog outside right now!" Hugh said in an authoritative voice. "Animals don't belong in the house! Outside, now!" The laughing stopped, and the jackal went quiet.

Sophia could blast the door open with a bolt of energy, but she was giving Hugh the chance to take control. If she forced her way through using the power of the cosmic life force that surged through her body, Bo and Gwen wouldn't survive. Sophia pressed her ear against the door.

Bo started crying. "Miss Amelia said you're going to go away and leave me and mommy."

"If you do not take that animal outside right now I'll shoot it," Hugh said.

Sophia tried to hear if Bo and the jackal were leaving. All was silent. Hugh pulled the door open.

"Gwen, where are they?" Hugh said.

Gwen was shaking. "She went downstairs with that thing."

Seth pushed past. "Billie's out there, Hugh." Seth took off down the hall to the stairs.

"Go with him, Tim," Sophia said.

Before leaving the room and closing the door behind her, Sophia reached for Ernest's wrist to check his pulse and listen to his breathing. Both were still regular.

Starting with the apartment next door, Sophia searched every room for Casey. She heard him scream out in her mind.

12

HUGH: JACKAL

The jackal ran out of the tavern into the street. Hugh grabbed Bo's arm as she went to follow the beast. She collapsed at his touch, and the filthy doll in her arms fell to the ground. Hugh kicked it out into the street. The jackal entered the intersection and vanished. Hugh scooped up Bo and was about to grab the door with his other hand to close it when he saw Billie running towards the tavern, dragging a cross behind her. Around her neck dangled three or four crucifixes, and she had two brass and two wooden ones stuffed in her pockets and under her arms; she was always trying to prove herself, and didn't see just how exceptional she was.

"Quick, inside," Hugh said, holding the door open for her. She was hot, and her cheeks were rosy. Her eyes were wide with fear.

"Was ... Was that a jackal I just saw? Is everyone okay?" Billie panted.

He locked the door behind her. "Yes."

Tim and Seth came running down the stairs.

"Help your sister upstairs with the crucifixes."

"I can manage," Billie said, regaining her composure, but losing her grip on the big cross.

"Let them take the big one. You've done well, Billie," Hugh said as Gwen pushed back the loose strands of hair from Bo's face.

Tim and Seth looked awkward as they lifted the large cross onto their shoulders and headed up the stairs. Hugh followed behind them, Bo light in his arms. Gwen walked close to him.

He whispered in Bo's ear, "You'll be alright. When we're out in the countryside and you're feeling better, you can get a pony if your mom agrees."

Bo was such a sweet girl, it was heartbreaking to see her wither away. Hugh couldn't imagine how Gwen felt. He glanced over his shoulder at Gwen as they walked back to her apartment. Her salmon-colored sweater stood out against the flowery blood-red wallpaper. Gary and Eleanor should've torn it down and painted the hallway when they first arrived. What would possess them to keep something so hideous? Gwen checked Bo's breathing and touched her arm.

"Do you think she's hurting?" Gwen was a bit breathless as she tried to keep up as they moved down the hall.

"She fainted when I touched her. The jackal took off into the street." Hugh entered the apartment and sniffed the air. "Can you smell roses?"

"Yes. Where is it coming from?" said Gwen.

"You tell me. I don't know." Hugh pushed the bedroom door open with his foot.

Hugh eased Bo onto the bed and pulled up the blankets. The room was still chilly. On the other side of the room, the blinds he had opened were now closed. He opened them, letting in the light. On the child's plastic chair lay the doll, Miss Amelia. Her body was facing Bo, but its head had turned right around as if watching him.

He left the doll where it was and watched Gwen stroke Bo's head. "I'll go and help to hang the crucifix."

Out in the hall, Billie struggled with the crucifixes. "Leave them there, Billie, against the wall next to the big one Seth and Tim brought up. Go hand out a necklace to everyone. Start with Gwen and Bo. I'll be right back," Hugh said.

"Where are you going?" Seth asked, still angry at Hugh.

"Basement, you want to come?" Hugh said, stopping at the stairs.

"I'll help Billie," Seth said. "What should we do with the big cross?"

"Oh, maybe its best you put it at the end of the hallway," Hugh said, leaving them to it. He wasted no time getting a hammer and nails from the basement. *Where the hell are Gary and Eleanor?* he wondered as he headed back upstairs.

He paused outside Ernest's bedroom, listening before peeking in. Ernest was sleeping. Careful not to disturb him, Hugh leaned over Ernest's head. Hugh feared Ernest would wake up, fly off the bed and start choking him. Trying to be as quiet as possible, Hugh blinked half a dozen times and tried to calm himself as he positioned the cross on the wall. Strapped to the bed, Ernest moved in his sleep. Hugh wanted to gag him and set him free all at the same time. His insides were churning to see a small child tied up, but he was glad just the same.

Ernest was looking very pale and blue-gray. Whatever menacing creature was inside him was making him weaker by the minute. Painful-looking open sores covered his face and arms, and his breathing sounded as though his lungs were full of phlegm – he needed to sit up and cough. Hugh finished putting the cross on the wall above Ernest's head. He laid the hammer on the bedside table and checked they had turned the heater on. He ran his hand over the top and felt the warmth seeping out of it, but the room was freezing.

Squeak.

The crucifix swung back-and-forth, upside down. He was alone with Ernest. A shadow hung from the ceiling. Hugh picked up the nails and hammer, and took care adjusting the cross. This time he nailed down all sides of the cross so it couldn't move. He had one nail to go. He put it in his mouth ready while driving in the second last nail with the hammer. Hugh swallowed and coughed, choking on saliva, and almost swallowed the nail. He took it out of his mouth and cleared his throat. Composed, he tried to shake off the uneasy feeling something was playing tricks on him. Watching, and mocking him. He lined up the last nail and drove the hammer down. The nail slipped sideways, catching the web of skin between his thumb and index finger. Hugh screamed out in pain, dropping the hammer inches away from Ernest's head. He reached down for the hammer, careful not to tear his skin, cursing as the blood dripped down his wrist. The pain was excruciating. What he'd done was near impossible. Hugh turned the hammer over and pulled the nail out of the wood, tearing his skin free.

"God dammit," he said, shaking his hand.

Ernest's eyes flew open, and he laughed. Hugh jumped back and stumbled, falling to the carpet. Holding up his bloodied hand, he scrambled to stand as an adult voice spoke through Ernest.

"Ahh … You underestimate us. Ha ha."

Hugh took a couple of tissues from the box and went to apply them to his wound. There was no blood, and his skin was undamaged. "What in hell's name is going on?"

"Ahh. Your parents are here, Hughie. Would you like to talk to Mommy dearest?"

Hugh staggered backwards, away from Ernest. "What are you?"

"It's Mommy, Hugh. You shouldn't tie Mommy up like this. It's not good, Hugh."

The dressing table slid across the room, barricading the door.

"Ernest, stop this! Stop this nonsense right now!" Hugh said.

"He isn't here right now. Ahh, aren't you glad it's Mommy? It's been a long time. Be a wonderful boy and loosen the straps for Mommy, and take down that hideous cross. You're already in hell."

"You're not real. You're not my mother," Hugh said. "Who are you, what do you want?"

So much time, decades, had gone by since he had heard his mother's voice. But he had watched hours of home movies, and no matter how similar the voice was, it wasn't his mother.

"Ahh, come and give Mommy a hug. Ha, ha, ha ..."

The insane laughter became the voice of his uncle.

Hugh put his shoulder to the chest of drawers and moved it away from the door. Terrified, he turned the handle. He yanked and pulled, but the door wouldn't budge. There were no locks on the bedroom door. He shuddered from the Arctic cold.

"Ernest, you need to come back. Colin, help me."

Terrified, Hugh pounded his fists against the door. "Patricia! Patricia, open the door!" The horrifying laughter filled his ears as he pushed the window open. It slammed back down with a force that made the glass shudder in its frame. Lying on Ernest's desk was a wooden ruler on top of a drawing of black dolls with evil red eyes. He ignored the picture and quickly picked up the ruler and propped the window open with it. The ruler snapped and the window slammed shut, just missing his fingers.

"Ernest, open the door." Hugh returned to tugging on the door; the door handle and barrel came off in his hand. He fumbled with the handle until he fixed it back on the door.

Drawers flew out of the chest of drawers, striking him in the back. Simultaneously the drawers of the bedside table banged open and closed. The cross pounded against the wall as if trying to free itself from the nails. Everything was a projectile aimed at Hugh. He ducked down and protected his head. Without warning, the bed floated off the floor and plummeted back down, landing on to the carpet with a muffled thud. It rose and dropped, rose and dropped. Hugh held his breath. Then everything moving in the room stopped. Ernest cried.

"Hugh, help me," Ernest pleaded.

Hugh stood up and pushed aside the surrounding clutter.

"What's happening? Why am I tied up?" Ernest lifted his head off the pillow and looked down at the bottom of the bed. "Who are all these people in my room?" He let his head drop and pulled at his arms and legs.

Hugh wanted to go to him, but this might be his only chance to leave the room.

"I'm sorry, but it's for your own good." Hugh felt like a real jerk. He wanted to help the boy.

"Mommy! Daddy Help me! Seth! Billie! Where is everyone?" Ernest wept, pulling at his restraints.

"It's okay," Hugh said, making his way to the bedside. "Is that you, Ernest?"

"You're scaring me, Hugh." He pulled on the straps. "My arms are sore."

Hugh went to the door and opened it.

"Don't leave me, Hugh," Ernest said, in between hiccups and sobs. "Mom-my Mom-my."

Hugh ducked out of the room, defeated. He couldn't bear to

hear Ernest's cries. It clawed at his core. He wanted to untie him and reassure him everything would be alright, but he didn't know everything *would* be alright, he didn't understand what was happening at all. This was madness. He recalled the many voices coming from Ernest's body, including his mother's. He couldn't trust it wasn't one of that legion playing tricks, using Ernest and people he cared for to get him to release the straps.

Hugh couldn't hear Patricia singing at first, until Ernest stopped wailing. Patricia was sitting at the sewing machine with a different chair, washed and in fresh clothes. Her short hair was still wet, tucked behind her ears as she sang an old nursery rhyme.

"Oranges and lemons,
"Say the bells of St. Clement's.
"You owe me five farthings,
"Say the bells of St Martin's.
"When will you pay me?
"Say the bells of Old Bailey …
"Here comes a candle to light you to bed.
"And here comes a chopper to chop off your head!
"Chip chop chip chop the last man is dead."

"Patricia, stop. Get up. Come with me." He tapped her on the shoulder. "Come on, let's get you a cup of tea."

She stopped singing and the sewing machine went quiet. She looked out of the window, Hugh followed her gaze. The bell at the old church of St. Sepulchre was ringing.

"It's got to be Kraig," Hugh said.

He thought Patricia was about to speak. She was coming around. She looked him up and down and opened her mouth. "All you that in the Condemned Hold do lie prepare you, for tomorrow you will die. Watch all, and pray, the hour is drawing near, That you before the Almighty must appear. Examine well yourselves, in time repent, that you may not to Eternal flames be sent. And when St. Sepulchre's bell tomorrow tolls, the Lord have mercy on your souls ..." The bell stopped, and she turned back to her machine.

"What the ...? Patricia!"

She's gone mad. Maybe we're all mad. What if I never left? What if it's me that's gone insane? He had to stop thinking this way. If he wasn't mad already he would soon drive himself crazy. He checked in on Ernest. The room was a mess, but Ernest was asleep. As Hugh closed the door, something moved, a shadow in a corner the light didn't quite reach. He closed the door and went towards the front door of the apartment, when a loud thud came from Ernest's room. Hugh ran back into Ernest's room and saw the bed rise to the ceiling and crash to the floor again and again.

The belts came loose. Ernest floated above the bed. Hugh ran over and pulled him down. He was icy cold. Hugh pressed Ernest onto the bed, tightening the belts to Ernest's arms and legs as quickly as he could. Hugh covered him with the bedcovers. He got another blanket off the floor and placed it on top of Ernest.

Where the hell is everyone? It was like an awful dream that he couldn't wake from.

Gwen came running into the room as he was tucking the blankets under Ernest's chin.

"What's going on in here?" she said, pulling her jacket tight. "It's so cold in here, Hugh, and what's that smell?"

"He somehow got loose and floated above the bed."

Down the hallway Bo screamed. Gwen took a deep breath in fright. Her eyes widened. "God, no!" She ran as quick as she could back to her apartment. Hugh jogged behind her.

Bo was having an epileptic fit. Gwen tried to hold her daughter's thrashing body as Bo hit her mother in the face and kicked her off the bed. Bo sounded like a wild animal. Hugh helped Gwen up. Bo went limp. Gwen broke down and cried, cradling her daughter.

"What's happening to us, Hugh?" Gwen rocked Bo.

There was nothing he could say that would comfort her. Something had to be done, but what? He went into the hall and picked up another cross. The hammer was still in Ernest's room. Hugh walked down the hall to Kraig's apartment. He didn't want to go back in there, but when he poked his head around the apartment door, Patricia was still singing. He crept into Ernest's room for the hammer, but it wasn't on the nightstand. He looked at the floor and scanned the mess. In the middle of the room, sticking out from under a pile of clean clothes, was the hammer. Hugh darted into the room, snatched up the hammer and ran out, afraid the door would swing shut.

Without any reservations, Hugh marched into Bo's bedroom with the hammer and nails and nailed the wooden cross to the wall.

"I can't wake her up now. She's sleeping way too much." Gwen was frantic.

"Something is wrong with her, Gwen, you know that. You've been hiding it for a while. What happened after I left? Everyone slept while Bo had played with her dollies and Ernest roamed around the tavern. Don't you think there's a bigger problem than Bo sleeping way too much?"

13

CASEY: TICK-TOCK

Out of breath, his heart racing, Casey could feel the beads of sweat on his brow, and his clothes sticking to his body, as if he had run a marathon. He couldn't remember where he was or what had just happened. Relief washed over him as he smelled the clean soapy scent he associated with Sophia. He opened his eyes, and she was leaning over him. It surprised him to see he was on a double bed, and not at the bottom of the stairs.

"Your head's bleeding," Sophia said, concerned.

Casey wanted to answer her, but a ticking inside his head marking each second became so loud he couldn't hear anything but *tick-tock, tick-tock*. He grappled for a fragment of a memory; whatever had happened to him was important.

"Dammit, I can't remember," he said through gritted teeth. "Can you hurry and get my backpack?" he asked, holding his head.

"Where is it?" Tim asked, rushing towards the door. Casey hadn't noticed Tim was in the room.

"In the car? I left it behind the passenger front seat on the floor." He searched his mind for a glimpse, a thread of the dream to hold on to. It had seemed so real, more than a simple passing dream. As Tim opened the door, chilly air rushed in. Fear washed over him. He swallowed, searching the doorway. He shivered. Nothing was there.

Sophia spoke. "Tim won't be long."

Frosty air circled him. He allowed his eyelids to shut as he reached for the thoughts swimming in his mind.

Tim returned, panting, and dropped his backpack on his legs. With his eyes closed he pushed himself into a sitting position. Feeling a little dizzy, he opened his eyes just a fraction for a second or two. He didn't want to focus on where he was, but rather on where he had been.

Casey crossed his legs and leaned against the bedhead. He took out the art book and charcoal. His drawing was frantic as he tried to hold on to the sleepy state, and concentrated on taking relaxed even breaths to scan the darkness behind his eyes. The charcoal scratched across the paper. Tim gasped. Casey kept his eyes shut until whatever was inside him was on the paper. He licked his finger and turned the page, continuing to sketch. It was hard to hold on to fragments in his mind. It was exhausting. The charcoal between his fingers burned. He dropped it and opened his eyes. He didn't want to look at the images – he glanced at Sophia sitting next to him on the bed. Tim was standing over him.

And then he saw a girl and a guy he didn't know had crept into the room.

"Where did he come from?" The girl said.

"This is Casey, he is our friend," Tim said. "Casey, this is Seth and his sister Billie."

Behind Billie, a dark shadow blocked the corner of the room.

Casey's skin crawled. "Did you carry me up here?" he asked Sophia.

"No, I found you here. What happened to you?" Sophia asked.

Casey tilted his head down, trying to talk to Sophia without the others hearing him. "I fell down the stairs." He didn't want to say too much in front of the strangers.

"What are the pictures of?" Billie asked. "Can you show us?" She was looking at him as if he was some kind of freak.

"Maybe later," Sophia said, looking at Casey. "Why don't you just put ..."

He didn't wait for her to finish and turned his gaze to the last picture he had drawn; it surprised him to see an emaciated salamander. The four fingers on each of its hands looked almost human. Casey flicked back at the next picture; a man in shadows leaning against a wall. The man's hat sheltered the glow of his pipe that revealed part of his face. Casey had drawn this man before; he didn't appear fictitious now. Casey pinched his lip and ran his fingers through his hair. It worried him how sinister and real the man appeared.

Casey kept moving back through the pictures: a girl pushing a wheelbarrow; a woman pushing the same girl to the ground. There were images of babies lined up in boxes. Frustrated, he slammed the book closed – he didn't understand their significance, they were just pictures. Frustrated, he shoved the book and charcoal in his bag, before rubbing his hands on his pants. He got up and threw the bag onto the foot of the bed, and stumbled a little as he got his balance.

"Wait," Seth said. 'I think I've seen that man with the pipe before, and the woman. At college, I studied the history of the penal system. The barbaric conditions horrified me. I studied Newgate Prison and the Old Bailey. I got lost down a rabbit hole. The woman in your drawing was a baby farmer – hanged for murder around 1896. Her name was Anabella or Amelia something."

As Seth said the name Amelia, he heard the girl inside his head say, *Yes, Miss Amelia.* "And the man?" Casey asked, unsure if he wanted to know.

"He was a prisoner in Newgate. It used to be just across the road." Seth said.

"Prisoner?" Casey said. It didn't sit right. He felt the man was more than a prisoner. He waited for a recollection, an image, or a sound like the girl saying *Yes, Miss Amelia,* but nothing came.

Sophia turned to Billie and said, "Did you give your mom a cup of tea with the herbs I gave you?"

"No, not yet," Billie said.

"Maybe we can all use a cup of herbal tea," Sophia said.

Casey watched Sophia round up everyone and herd them into the hallway. The last to leave, he turned to close the door and saw it was room 1800, the room where he had rescued the girl from the fire. He shivered; he could do with a hot cup of tea and something to eat.

"Has the jackal gone?" Sophia asked Seth and Tim. "And where's Bo?"

"It ran off. Bo collapsed at the entrance to the tavern. Hugh carried her back to bed and said he would nail the crucifix above Ernest's bed," Tim said.

What the hell were they talking about, jackals and crosses? Casey wondered.

Sophia turned to Tim. "Why don't you and Seth help Billie? When we've all eaten, we can fill Casey in on what has been happening around here."

* * *

CASEY SHUFFLED into the booth and looked out the front window of the tavern. The road was patches of old and new bitumen and lay empty and quiet. The MUV, not a horse or a cart, was out the front where they had left it. He wondered if the water in the fountain was dirty or clean. Casey tried to ignore the surge of emotion and frustration that was swimming through him; he was missing something. There was a slight wind blowing, and a hat tumbled in from a side street. The walk sign beeped and flashed. He almost expected people to cross the road. He knew the hat wasn't real, it couldn't be. It belonged to a time long gone. He ignored the ghostly hat and looked back at the still fountain. He wondered if the bottom was slippery, and whether an albino salamander with tiny human hands lived under the water. His mind played tricks as he imagined a four-fingered hand reaching out of the fountain and holding onto the capped edge, twice as long and wide as a man's.

The smell of manure drifted into the tavern, but he was getting a little warmer and grateful the shivering had stopped. Looking through the window was like watching a black-and-white movie. It flickered like a poor signal, and he saw the warden picking up his hat.

"Casey!" Sophia said, poking him in the arm. "You're nodding off. Maybe you should have some coffee with sugar. You need to eat more, Casey. Say something, you look like a deer in the headlights. I will jump into that head of yours if you don't say something."

He felt like he had no eyelids and couldn't blink. Anxious, he tried again to blink, and sighed in relief when everything went dark. He opened his eyes again; they felt so heavy. He was so tired.

"I'm fine," Casey said. "Maybe some coffee will be good." He could smell it brewing and drew in a deep breath.

"Do you want to talk about it?" Sophia asked.

Billie carried over a tray with a pot of percolated coffee, cups, sugar and milk, careful not to spill the hot coffee, and joined them. Tim and Seth followed her with croissants, toast, scrambled eggs and tomatoes with wilted spinach. It smelled delicious. Casey's stomach rumbled. Seth put a stack of plates and cutlery on the table for them to help themselves.

"Where did you get all this food from?" Casey asked.

"We have a lot of frozen food, but Eleanor and Gary like to make everything from scratch when they can. We have plenty of supplies at the tavern, but we also have the entire city to raid," Seth said.

"But the eggs?" Casey said.

"Frozen."

Casey picked up a croissant and spread strawberry jam on both sides, then stuffed it with scrambled eggs. He was famished. "It doesn't taste fresh. Why are the croissants so soggy?"

"We microwaved them. I don't know where Eleanor and Gary are, but it doesn't look like Eleanor has been in the kitchen for a while," Seth said as he sat next to Tim.

Sophia poured him a coffee. It was hot and warmed his insides. He slowed down, noticing the energy around Tim and Seth as they talked. He could see their auras moving towards each other in soft waves of color. Their energy fields were mingling. They liked each other. Casey watched them interacting a little longer, noticing that Billie also liked Tim, before taking a slice of toast and putting a layer of spinach and a squashed-down tomato on top, and folding it over into a half sandwich. He was on his second cup of coffee before he started feeling like himself.

"You're not eating?" Casey said to Sophia. "You haven't eaten all day."

"No, just coffee for me right now," Sophia said, leaning towards Seth.

"Tell me again the last thing you remember before Hugh woke you up half an hour ago," she asked him.

"Wait a minute," Casey interrupted. "You slept for what, four, five days?"

"Yeah, and I can't tell you why. I have no recollection, just a sensation I've forgotten something important."

"That's how I feel," Casey said.

"That's weird," said Tim. "What about you, Billie?"

"Sunday dinner, and Mom wouldn't get off that stupid machine. I had to help Eleanor get meat out of the freezer. I hate that room, I'm always afraid the door will close, and I will freeze to death. I took Mom a tray and went to my room to read," Billie said. "Where are Eleanor and Gary now?"

"Has anyone checked their rooms?" Seth asked.

"I don't think so," Billie said.

"Where are their rooms?" Sophia asked. "I have just about combed through every apartment on the north wing searching for Casey."

"There on the left, not where the guests stay," Seth said cleaning his plate. "We should check." He stood up.

"No, wait, we need to be clear about what we're doing," Sophia said. "We're here to help you all leave the city , and move out to the countryside where some towns are clean and safe. But Bo and Ernest need to healed before they can leave. They're possessed ..."

"What the hell?" Casey turned towards Sophia.

She gave him a half-smile and continued. "I will try to clean them of the entities, so we can get out of here."

"You're talking about an exorcism?" Billie said, hugging herself.

"Yes." Sophia took a deep breath.

Casey could tell she was nervous. He couldn't recall seeing her this fazed before; but whatever had happened while he was unconscious had got her spooked.

"We need to find the owners and your dad," Sophia said, looking at Seth. "You will need to convince them to leave. We'll need another two cars, ready to go." Sophia took a sip of her coffee. "I think it's best we stay awake. No lying down and no sleeping. You in particular, Casey."

"Gwen has caffeine tablets. She asked my dad to get them on a supply run. He brought back an entire box of them," Billie said.

"Okay, Billie, you're in charge of dispensing the caffeine tablets. Don't give your mom any until she has had the herbal tea. Besides the little ones, she may be the only one who has been awake this entire time, and could use a few hours of sleep, but someone will have to monitor her. Seth, find Eleanor and Gary, explain to them everyone is leaving, and convince them they have to come too. Then find your father. We don't want to leave anyone behind."

"What's that noise?" Casey said. "Who's upstairs?"

14

HUGH: MISS AMELIA

B illie, Casey and Sophia barged into Gwen's apartment, startling Hugh. He didn't know how much more he could take. He was twenty-six years old and felt like fifty-six.

"What's all the banging about? What's going on?" Seth said, his face contorted in confusion.

"Ernest has a poltergeist with him, and Bo had an epileptic fit," Hugh said.

"What? How do you know it's a poltergeist?" Billie had her hand on the door, ready to bolt down to her apartment and Ernest.

"Hang on, Billie," Hugh said. "Ernest is okay for now. While I was in his room, the chest of drawers moved across the floor, barricading the door. Clothes, toys, drawers, and books were thrown across the room. Drawers, and the cupboard doors, were banging. It didn't last long, but long enough to scare the shit out of me, and turn the room upside down."

Casey and Sophia gave each other a knowing glance.

"What do you know?" Hugh said.

"Has Bo ever had an epileptic fit before?" Sophia asked Gwen.

"No. Never." Gwen looked at Sophia.

"She's fighting the demons trying to claim her body and soul, but she's too weak."

"Hugh, I'm getting Bo and leaving right now," Gwen said, panicking. "You coming?"

Hugh's eyes moved from Gwen to Sophia, trying to decide the best thing to do. His mission was to get help for Bo, but he couldn't see how Sophia and Casey could help her now. Taking her away from this place might be what she needed.

"Pack her stuff, we're leaving," he said to Gwen.

Gwen ran into her room and grabbed a pink suitcase with wheels, standing by the wall. She tossed it onto the bed and flung it open. Hugh helped her grab as many of her belongings as possible. Freaked out, her hands shaking, Gwen stuffed her suitcase.

"You can't run," Casey said.

Hugh carried the suitcase, ignoring Casey, and left it in the middle of the living room next to the couch.

"I'll check on Ernest and Mom," Billie said as she moved out of the room. "Seth, we have to find Dad," she shouted from the hallway.

"Don't go into Ernest's room, just peek inside," Seth called back.

Gwen, putting on a woolen hat, pushed open Bo's door and filled Bo's suitcase. Sophia followed her and stood in the doorway. Gwen was squashing everything she could into the bag.

"You can't leave," Sophia said.

"Here, let me help you with that," Hugh said, pushing past Sophia.

"Wherever you go, it will follow you. It's inside your daughter. Your daughter is in danger."

"I'll help you, Gwen," Hugh said, holding her hands steady.

Bo was in bed snuggled into her ugly doll, Miss Amelia. Hugh watched Gwen ease Bo off the bed along with a blanket and the ugly doll. Concerned, Hugh glanced at the plastic chair where he had last seen the doll. In her haste Gwen tripped on a piece of frayed carpet. Hugh caught her arm and steadied her.

"Alright?" Hugh said, holding her elbow.

"Yeah, I just want to get out of here," Gwen said, moving into the living room.

He picked up Bo's stuffed bag and collected Gwen's suitcase by the couch.

"Hugh, you came to us. No matter where you go, it won't leave Bo alone until she is dead, and it has her soul," Sophia said.

"You're crazy. Get out of my way," Gwen yelled in Sophia's face, knocking her with Bo's dangling feet.

"Sorry," Hugh said. "She's right; we have to leave this Godforsaken place."

"Let's go too," Tim said.

Hugh stopped. "Come with us. Let's all go, right?"

Hugh caught up to Gwen, and ran down the stairs behind her.

"She can't leave," Casey shouted at them.

"Come with us," Hugh yelled back.

Casey chased him down the stairs. "You heard Colin. It doesn't matter where you go. Hugh, you can't leave Ernest like this. Help us save them both."

Out of breath, Billie jumped down the last few steps after him. "Hugh, I don't know where my dad is, my mom has lost the plot and my brother is fighting for his life. Help us, Hugh."

He stopped and looked back at Billie. "Eleanor and Gary will help you." He put the bag down to give her a reassuring hug. She pushed him away. He felt bad, but there wasn't anything else he could do for them.

"Are you coming?" Gwen said. "If not, put the bags in the car and give me your keys."

"I'm coming," Hugh said, shaking Seth's hand.

He turned the deadlock and paused, nervous, then opened the front door and peered outside. The street was empty and there was no sign of the jackals. They could make a dash for the car. Hugh stepped into the street, and the door slammed shut behind him. He turned back and banged on the door. "Open up! Gwen!"

He could hear Gwen on the other side. "Hugh, open the door."

"I can't, it won't budge."

The handle was turning, but it wouldn't open.

"Open the door, Seth."

A soft calm child's voice beside Hugh said, "She doesn't want Bo to leave."

Who said that? Hugh stepped from the sidewalk onto the street. A flickering image of the boy from his dreams was standing by his side. "Alex?"

"Uh-huh," said Alex.

"Who won't let her go?"

"Miss Amelia."

"Can you go in there and unlock the door?" Hugh asked, feeling stupid for asking.

"No, I don't want them to find me. It's too scary in there. Too many evil ghosts. They're everywhere, but they're all being attracted to this place, it's Satan's doorway. Ask Bo to open the door. Tell her you're not leaving anymore, you made a mistake. Go on, try it." The ghost of Alex flickered.

"Bo, if you want to stay, open the door, sweetie," Hugh said. "I don't want to leave. I like it here."

Hugh banged on the door. "Open up, goddamn it! Open up!" *This is ridiculous.* Hugh rubbed the back of his neck and scratched the stubble on his face. He looked down at Alex. The boy had gone. He wondered if he had been there in the first place, and then he heard the door click open.

Gwen was on her knees, and Bo was unconscious in her arms.

"What happened?" Hugh crouched beside her as he searched everyone's faces.

Gwen looked at him with fear in her eyes. "The door slammed shut in my face. Nobody touched it. It closed on its own, Hugh. Sophia's right, something is trying to stop us from leaving."

"We tried to warn you," Casey said.

"Help me take her back upstairs, Hugh."

Hugh took Bo from Gwen, and the doll fell to the ground. He kicked the doll out of the way and started up the stairs.

Bo's eyes flew wide open. She reached out for the doll on the floor. "Don't forget Miss Amelia."

"Oh, baby," Gwen said, picking up the doll and tucking it under the blanket with Bo.

But Bo was out cold again. Hugh grabbed the bags and followed them back upstairs.

Gwen's demeanor changed as she placed her hand on Sophia's arm. "Can you help my daughter? Please."

"We will try," Sophia said. "There are a few things that we will need first." She put her arm around Gwen and helped her up the stairs.

Once Bo was back in bed, Hugh sat down on the couch in the living room. "There's something not right with that doll. We should throw it away. It's filthy, Gwen; it must have germs on it. It's not healthy for Bo."

Gwen tossed her coat on the arm of the couch and sat next to him. "I know, Hugh, but she won't part with it. I washed it."

"I've heard that name before," Casey said, "Miss Amelia." He looked tired and perplexed. "I just can't remember where."

Seth pulled out the kitchen chair. "The baby farmer. I was telling you about her before. They hanged her in 1896."

"That's horrible," Gwen said.

It surprised Hugh to see Sophia making herself comfortable at his feet. She crossed her legs, made herself comfortable, and closed her eyes. "What's she doing?"

"Searching," Casey said.

"For what?" Gwen said.

"Help. Information. Be patient," Casey said, pushing himself deeper into the armchair.

Gwen took Hugh's hand and they sat in awkward silence, but it was better than the sounds of the beds banging, or Bo having a seizure.

Hugh stiffened; he was ready to spring out of the chair. Sophia frightened him.

Sophia's breathing changed, her eyelids fluttered and as she spoke, she sounded far away. "The evil thoughts, words, and deeds of the past saturated the city. You must heal the children before they can leave. We must take them back from the evil entities. There are a great number of souls that need help, but it is not for us to do. It is not the will of God. We must concentrate on the living. There's not one demon, but an army and centuries of evil that govern the earth. Miss Amelia won't give up Bo unless she gets Doc's payment. If he pays, she will hand over Bo. He already has Ernest, and is feeding off his life force."

Sophia's eyes fluttered open. She squinted as if the light in the room was too bright for her. "I don't know how you all lived here for so long. There are hundreds of ghosts, poltergeists, demons and emotional memory imprints all over the city."

"Who's Doc?" Hugh said.

"I don't know. He is like a middleman for the devil," Sophia said.

"He was a doctor, hanged in 1892 for murdering his patients. Maybe the baby farmer sold him the babies?" Seth said.

"We don't have to help everyone, just Bo and Ernest, and get them the hell out of here," Gwen said, squeezing Hugh's hand.

"We can't put the lid back on Pandora's box," Sophia said, stretching out her legs. "They're all here, and they will not go back where they came from."

"We can help some ghosts find their way to the light, can't we?" Casey asked.

"Maybe," Sophia said.

"And how are we going to do that?" Tim asked, swatting away a fly.

"We have to protect our souls first." Sophia reached into her coat pocket and produced a plastic zip-lock bag containing dried herbs that looked like grass to Hugh. She gave out handfuls of herbs. "You chew them, smoke them. Make sure you have some with you at all times. If you have a cross or any religious symbol, wear them – this way, we all may get out of here alive."

"Sophia ..." Casey began.

"Later we can come back and clean the city, but not today," Sophia said. "Let's get ourselves far away for now. We can come back when Kevin, Jade, Shaun, and Rachel return; we can come back and clean the city together."

"Is this something you have foreseen?" Tim asked.

"No, I have not seen the future for some time," Sophia said. "I need to get supplies. Is there a herbal shop around here?"

Hugh watched Sophia rise. There was something she wasn't telling them that made him uncomfortable, but he didn't think probing her was going to reveal it.

"I know a place," Seth said. "I'll take you. Someone needs to find my father. Maybe we can look for him on the way?"

"I don't think there's time ..." Sophia said.

"I'll go," said Billie, walking into the apartment with Eleanor and Gary half asleep.

"I'll help her," Gary said. "Billie brought us up to speed. We should go before it gets dark."

Eleanor sat next to Gwen and rubbed her back. "Come help me in the kitchen," Eleanor said, trying not to make eye contact with anyone. "We should get Patricia and stay together. It might be a long night."

"Whatever you do, don't fall asleep," Casey said, standing up.

Loud banging broke the silence. It was coming from Bo's room.

"Oh no, hell no, not again," Gwen said, rushing out to her daughter.

Gwen was in the bedroom a flash, Hugh right behind her. He couldn't believe how violently Bo's body was thrashing upon the bed.

"Don't touch her!" Sophia said.

"What, why not?" Gwen ignored Sophia and tried to hold Bo, but was knocked back by Bo's flailing arms.

Sophia reached into her pocket and drew out the same canister of holy water she had used on Ernest. She splashed it over Bo's body. Bo screamed – her body jerked and squirmed as she cried in pain.

Gwen pulled at Sophia's arms. "Stop, stop, you're hurting her. You're hurting my baby girl."

"It burns! It burns!" The voice was terrifying, deep and raspy.

The room turned Arctic cold and smelled of sulfur. Hugh gagged. Gwen, on her knees, cried. Sophia handed the holy water to Casey. She took her Bible from the inner pocket of her coat, and began reading from it. Bo's body stopped shaking and stiffened. Without hesitating, Sophia drew the symbol of the cross on Bo's forehead with her thumb and continued reading the Bible. Hugh, stunned, watched with his head bowed, feeling helpless. *God, please help Bo.*

Hugh held onto Gwen's hand. Bo's breath slowed and became even. Hugh watched her tiny chest rise and fall, until it slowed into a peaceful rhythm as though she was asleep. Sophia pulled the blankets up around Bo's chin and took away the doll. "We're coming for you, Bo," she said. "Hang in there."

"Can I give her a kiss?" Gwen asked, wiping her tears.

"It's best not," Sophia said, giving Gwen the doll. "Get rid of it." Sophia tucked her Bible away in her coat and took the canister of holy water back from Casey.

"Come on, Seth, there are things I need to get before either Bo or Ernest wakes up again."

15

SOPHIA: STREETS OF LONDON

Sophia gathered Tim, Seth and Casey in the hallway. "Seth, where is this shop you mentioned? I need you to take me there."

"I'll get a jacket and meet you downstairs," Seth said.

"I'll go with him," Tim said.

"Okay. Meet us out front by the church," Sophia said.

"What about the black dogs, the jackals?" Tim said.

"We must take our chances," Seth said.

They stopped outside apartment 1800. "Casey, get your backpack," Sophia said. "We'll need it to carry the supplies. I'll wait out here while you go in."

"You're not coming in?" Casey asked.

"No. I felt drowsy in there; I don't want to fall asleep. If you're not back in three minutes, I'll come and get you."

"That makes me feel confident. I think I'll stay here with you and bring the bag to me."

Tim grabbed Seth's arm before he went into his apartment. "Wait. Watch this," Tim said.

"Watch what?" Seth said.

Casey pushed the door open with his mind until he could see through the lounge to the bedroom where Sophia had found him sleeping. She watched him will the bag to him. It rose into the air and shot straight out the door, smacking into Casey's outstretched arms.

"What the …? How? Is he a wizard? Wow! Can you teach me?" Seth asked.

"No, I'm no wizard. I don't know how to teach you, I am what I am."

"Manic, right?" Tim said to Seth.

"I don't care what you say, you are a wizard," Seth said.

"Or possessed," said Billie, walking out of Gwen's apartment with Gary.

Tim nudged Seth. "Let's get your jacket."

"I'm in control of what I do," Casey said. He turned to Seth, who was about to enter the apartment, and stopped him in mid-stride.

"Hey man, what gives?" Seth said, turning around.

"I have telekinetic ability. An ability I've had for nearly three years. It started soon after my thirteenth birthday. A gift from God, I like to think."

"I heard about a few people like you," Gary said. "They headed for Stonehenge before the whiteout."

"There are other people who can move things with their minds?" Casey stared wide-eyed at Gary.

The sooner they all get out, the better, Sophia thought. Her stomach was in knots, and she wanted to scream, but held it in. Everything *was* manic, but not in the way Tim meant. She was constantly aware of the surrounding madness that was dipping into her aura. She scratched her arms. It made her nervous.

"Yeah, and there were people having the same dream, telling

them to go to Stonehenge. There was a flyer in the window of that alternative medicine place, telling everyone who had the shared vision to go to Stonehenge," Gary said.

"Why didn't you go?" Sophia asked.

"I had people staying at the tavern; I couldn't get up and leave them. I thought they were just crazy dreams. I had to stay and look after the patrons who didn't have the dream."

Sophia ran back to Gwen's apartment. "Hugh, did you have the dream?"

"What dream?" he said, looking at Gwen.

"About Stonehenge," Sophia said with a note of frustration.

"How do you know about the dream?" Gwen sat up, surprised. "I had the dream, so did Bo. Did you have the same dream, Hugh?"

"I did, but I thought it was because I saw the flyer at the crystal shop."

"You mean the herb shop, the alternative medicine place?" Sophia asked, trying to get things straight.

"Yeah, that's the one." Hugh said. "Why, what's wrong?"

"I'm not sure, but I'm getting the feeling you're not meant to be here. Did you guys even talk about it?" Sophia asked, bewildered.

"I didn't know Hugh then. It wasn't safe on the streets with the infected killing people. I needed to keep Bo safe, and this was a wonderful job. I love it here at the tavern with Eleanor and Gary. They looked after us like family. I wasn't going anywhere because of a dream."

"Did you know Gary had had the dream?" Sophia said.

"No, he didn't mention it. Gary asked me if I had, but I said no. I didn't want to look like I was crazy, or worse, infected."

Sophia couldn't believe they hadn't told each other. It was significant. *I don't think they're supposed to be here. They weren't among the forgotten, they just didn't listen. I've had no dreams of the future, and I miss it. I wished it away, complained about what I saw and how I wanted to be free of the painful visions of death and destruction; it was so rare for me to see positive visions. It was always nasty shit, and I had had enough. Now I want them back. It's scary not knowing what will happen, because I can't prepare, or find a way out. For the first time, I'm walking in darkness. I can't hear the prayers of others – only their thoughts if I forage through their minds. Death is all around me. My sense of certainty is gone. Every other thought is of what I don't want. I don't want to feel or see bad things anymore; I don't want to see inside people's heads; it makes me feel dirty – like a peeping Tom, even though I crave to peek and know. I don't want everyone to rely on me. It was so much easier when I was sheltered by Mother Catherine and Father McDonald at the church. I don't want this alternate life. The frustration is eating me up inside. I should talk to Casey, but I don't want to burden him. He has his own issues going on. I can feel it. I have to focus on what I want and stop feeling sorry for myself.*

"Sophia? Sophia? Are you alright?" Hugh touched her shoulder. "You seem flustered; maybe you should sit down for a while."

"Thanks, but no. We will not get out of here with me sitting on my ass. Gwen? Billie said you've got a box of caffeine tablets?" Sophia said.

"I do, do you want some?" Gwen got up and opened a high cupboard in the kitchenette.

"Yes, can you also hand them around? We need to stay awake." Sophia held out her hand and took the tablets and water.

"I'm glad you're here. Were you studying for the clergy?" Eleanor said.

What an odd question, Sophia thought. She hadn't even

noticed Eleanor sitting in the armchair; she didn't see or feel her. It made her feel uncomfortable.

"No, but let's talk more about it when we're safe, at Casey's estate."

"Just as well. Did you know, in 1533 a Protestant priest was burned at the stake? And in 1555, at St. Sepulchre's, just across the road, we burned the vicar as a heretic. In 1595 a Jesuit priest was hanged, drawn and quartered not too far from here. The list goes on. You're not a heretic, are you Sophia?"

Sophia quivered and opened her mouth to speak but closed it again. It wasn't Eleanor talking. She didn't want to know who it was.

Gwen put the glass on the bench and went to Eleanor. She glanced at Hugh before fixing her eyes on Sophia and mouthing, "She's asleep!"

"Eleanor honey, let's go fix tea for everyone, Eleanor?" Gwen said, holding her hands.

Eleanor blinked several times and stretched. "I must've dozed off."

Hugh got up and fetched a glass of water and two white caffeine tablets and gave them to Eleanor. "Go, Sophia and hurry back," he said.

Sophia slowly closed the apartment door behind her.

Casey's mouth was wide open, "Come on! What was that all about?" He took the two caffeine tablets from Hugh. "Did she say we burned the vicar?" He knocked back the tablets and swallowed them without water.

Sophia didn't want to talk about it and raced towards the stairs, meeting Billie and Gary coming from the south wing. "Find your dad and make sure you're back before dark. He might be in the bell tower. Someone had to ring the bell earlier."

* * *

SUDDENLY SOPHIA FELT the weight of her coat. She stood a little closer to Casey, wanting to lose herself in his aura, wishing he would pick her up and fly them both away from all the chaos. She watched him unlock the deadlock on the tavern door, and waited nervously for him to give her the thumbs up. He checked for signs of the jackal or anything else that could harm them. She felt agitated and skittish, hypersensitive; the veil between different realms was as thin as tissue paper here, and anything could happen. She could feel the atoms in her body pulsating and separating, ready to release energy to defend herself and Casey. It was a long time since she had felt this vulnerable, not since her journey to find the Emerald Tablet had begun, when a lone gunman killed her friends at the church fete. The pain of the memory cleared her mind. It had happened eight months ago, but it was like yesterday. A fly buzzed near her head, and she zapped it with her energy, knocking it dead and shattering pieces of sandstone off the building across the street. *Poor fly*, she thought.

Casey was two feet in front of her and turned in surprise. "You're so jumpy, it's not like you. Are you okay? Do you sense something?" He stepped towards her, concerned. "You look like glitter."

Tim and Seth stopped and turned to watch them.

"I just need a minute." She went to lean against the outer wall of the tavern.

"No, not there. Lean on me." Casey took her in his arms.

The warmth and gentle embrace of his muscular arms gave her a sense of security. She sighed and leaned against him. The tingling in her body that gave her a glittery aura dissipated as warmth filled her body.

"That's better. You even feel more solid, if that's possible, and you don't look like stardust," Casey said.

She leaned against him for a few more seconds, breathing in his strength. "I'm feeling a little better now."

Casey kept his arm over her shoulder as they crossed the road towards St Sepulchre's church. He hadn't revealed what he had seen, but she knew something was happening, and he had chosen not to tell her, but she wished he would. She was feeling lethargic; it was as if her vitality was being drained, forcing her to sleep. She had expected to feel perky after taking the caffeine pills, not anxious and tired. Casey stood on the church lawn and looked along the street as if he had fallen into a psychic memory loop.

"What is it?" Sophia asked, stepping away from him.

"There are two spirits, grave robbers, digging up the lawn. As long as they don't see us, I'm fine to let them be," Casey said.

Sophia didn't see the grave robbers, but she sensed their energy. They entered the old church; it was beautiful, and Father McDonald would have loved to have seen it. She thought she could feel him in spirit but he wouldn't be lingering in between realms, he wouldn't be a ghost. Father McDonald had been a selfless man, and he would be with God. Perhaps he might be a spiritual guide or doorkeeper.

"You know there must have been a cemetery somewhere close by," Casey said.

"I don't doubt it," said Sophia. "It feels haunted, but everything is, isn't it?"

Casey stopped in the front yard. "I'm missing some memories from the last hour, and I think they're important. Ever since we got here, I feel like I've been sleepwalking."

"You were asleep when I found you. There has to be an explanation. We'll find it. If it was a gas leak, we would smell it.

What are you looking at now?" Sophia said, shaking her head in confusion. "Why can't I see?"

Casey turned sideways as if to let someone pass him by. "An old pastor is walking the grounds. Can you see him?" he asked, moving his arm from around her shoulders.

"I should be able to, but I don't. I sense death and darkness circling us; I'm also aware of the vitality of the life force that makes up everything flowing through us. I'm struggling for control over my psyche. It's eerie. Let's get this done."

"I'm with you, the sooner we can get out of the city, the better," Casey said, tightening the straps on his backpack.

"The images you drew in your sketchbook, are they all from your dreams?"

"I don't remember dreaming about them, and I don't recall drawing them, either. Today was the first time I made a conscious attempt to grasp the dream and draw. Over the past few days, I've woken up in the early hours of the morning to find myself at my desk with charcoal-covered fingers. I didn't want to worry you, or anybody else for that matter. Everyone was adapting to the new way of life. It was a breath of fresh air to see people smiling again. Everyone had gone through so much; I didn't want to burden them with my nightmares. The others think I'm super-blessed with my telekinetic and levitation abilities. I shouldn't complain."

Sophia tucked her blonde hair behind her ears. "I've got to confess, I knew something was happening. Twice I saw you leave your body – astral travelling."

"What? But how was I getting out?"

"Without bodies, we can all come and go as we please. I just had to open the shield for you."

"But why did you let me go?" Casey said with concern.

She was beginning to feel she had made a mistake, and should have stopped him. "I'm sorry, I didn't want to interfere."

"Shh, what was that?" Casey said, glancing behind them. "I thought I heard a growling." He put a protective arm around her again.

It wasn't like him to be so bold. She liked his boldness; it made her feel safe.

"I can see your energy fields, Sophia. Your aura is being depleted of the life force. It's washed out."

"You don't like me peeking inside your head, so don't peek at my energy centers," Sophia said, tapping him on the solar plexus, and giving him a zap of energy.

"You need a boost, let me ..." Casey said.

"Back at the tavern, when I found you, I sensed there was something else in the room with you – watching. I ignored it, I didn't want to give it any power. It could have followed you. Perhaps it was luring you out of your body before we even got to London."

Casey shivered at the thought. He pushed open the side entrance Billie must have used. The leaves that were scattered over the black-and-white tiled floor crunched under his foot. Sophia stayed close to him, and Casey took her hand.

She stopped in front of a glass box with a bell inside. "You know Miss Amelia, I think this bell rang for her."

Sophia let go of Casey's hand and headed for the altar in silence. She didn't want to think about all the people that the bell would have rung for, announcing their impending death. She searched for stoups of holy water or a baptistery. The last time she had been in her family church she had laid down and slept under the warm rays of the sun that shone through the old stained-glass windows back in Scotland. It seemed so long ago.

She blinked away the tears that pooled in her eyes, abandoned her daydream and checked every entrance. There was no holy water. How could there be no holy water? Behind the altar was a side door. She entered, praying it was the baptistery. It was the pastor's private room where he prepared for the services.

Twisting around at the sound of feet slapping on the tiled floor, Sophia felt her neck cramp. She massaged the pain away. It sounded as though someone had run through the main hallway and was headed in her direction. Sophia found the thurible incense burner in the pastor's private room. It was like Father McDonald's; he had waved it over coffins during funerals. She would use it to cleanse the tavern, and help those ghosts prepared to move on.

On a shelf was a glass vessel of water she hoped was holy water and not gin. She opened it and sniffed, wondering if gin had a fragrance. It smelled like water, so she took it and rushed from the room. Tim and Seth were at the altar with Casey.

"Did you see the bell?" Tim said.

"That bell would be rung the night before a prisoner was going to die," Seth said.

"That's just creepy," Tim said.

They walked back towards to the glass display box, and Seth explained how the bell was used and why. "There's supposed to be a tunnel that connects the church, the tavern, and the prison, but it's just a tale."

"What prison?" Tim asked.

"The courthouse across the road was once a prison, and they used to hang the prisoners from the gallows. Male and female," Seth said.

Half-listening, Sophia lowered the thurible by its chains into Casey's backpack. Casey yawned. "Are you okay?" she said, wanting to touch his face and hold him.

"You're not stealing that, are you?" Tim asked, breaking her thoughts.

"I'm borrowing it, but if people return to the church, I'll bring it back. There's no-one around that needs it right now as much as we do."

"I'm okay," Casey said, smiling at her.

She tucked the small glass bottle into the inside pocket of her coat next to her bag of sage.

"Isn't that coat heavy? It can't be comfortable for you to wear it all the time," Tim said. He turned to Seth. "She even has a bowie knife in there somewhere."

"How far is it to this herbal shop?" Sophia asked Seth, ignoring Tim.

"About a forty-minute walk. It's in Whitechapel," Seth replied, following Sophia out of the church. "This way," he said, taking the lead.

The way he said "Whitechapel" gave her goose bumps; she was sure he was implying something terrible had happened there. Whatever it was, she didn't want to know about it.

"How much daylight do you think we have left?" Tim asked.

Seth turned towards Tim, who matched his stride. "We've got about two-and-a-half hours." He looked towards the sky. "I want to be back way before that."

Sophia walked behind Seth, with Casey next to her. She felt they were being followed.

"I'm praying we find what we need and can get back with time to spare," she said. "As soon as we perform the two exorcisms on the children, we're leaving the city. We can't hang around in case someone else becomes possessed. We'll need at least another vehicle, and we'll leave under a cloak of protection, so we don't leave a trail of light to the estate." Sophia paused. "That's why I'm so jittery! Everyone stop."

Sophia closed her eyes and held out her hands, palms up. She connected to the light of the creator that was waiting for her to call upon it. The light travelled into her crown and through her body. It circled out towards the others and snaked around them, binding them together, concealing them from whatever was on the haunted streets. "Hold hands everyone," she said, taking Casey's and Tim's hands, and they took hold of Seth's. "Left hand up, right hand down," Sophia said.

"Tell us what you can see, Casey," Tim said.

"A golden chain of light has tethered us together; it stretches as we move apart. A sparkling cloak covers us like an umbrella."

Sophia opened her eyes. "That feels better, so, so much better. It will protect us while we travel back and forth. Stay close."

"I feel like running," Seth said. "I have so much energy. Is that the cloak or the caffeine tablets?"

"Perhaps both," Casey said.

Tim and Seth walked ahead. Tim explained to Seth what Casey and Sophia could do. Every few seconds Seth glanced over his shoulder at them.

"Bullshit." Seth stopped, causing Sophia to bang into him and give him an unintentional zap of energy.

"Was that you? Show me," Seth said.

"Show you what?" Sophia took a step back.

"That you can blow up that car over there," Seth said.

"We don't have time for games, Seth," Sophia said, feeling drained.

"We have to keep moving," Casey said.

Sophia gave a fake smile to humor Seth. "Is it this way?"

"Can you fly?" Seth asked.

"No!" they both said.

"He can. He can lift us up from the ground," Tim said.

"Can we just stay focused?" Sophia said, annoyed by Seth's questions. She wondered if his questions had triggered fear in her, and that's why she felt irritated. Sometimes she thought way too much. That reminded her of Jade. She smiled, wondering if Jade and Kevin had found Jade's father. "Can we keep moving?" she snapped at the guys.

"Down this laneway," Seth said.

It was still daylight, but the sun was behind the buildings. Sophia rubbed her arms and hugged herself.

"Watch where you're walking, Seth," Casey said.

"What, why?" Tim said, glancing over his shoulder at Casey.

"Are you sure you want to know?" Casey had a smirk on his face.

"Maybe not," Tim said.

"Let's have it," Seth said.

"There is a man hiding his face. He wears a long coat, a top hat, and walks with a cane, though he's agile. He's rushing from doorway to doorway. It's night and he's following a woman. He's heading in our direction. It's best to avoid him. His energy is sinister, gut-wrenching. Seth, if you stand in his way you will know what I mean. There are others, it's like the streets are stuck on a time loop replaying the 1800s."

Seth moved closer to Casey. "Where?"

"On your left," Casey said, pulling Seth out of the way.

"It could be Jack the Ripper," Seth said. "Can he hurt us?"

"Not while we're cloaked under Sophia's umbrella of protection. Pray it's a memory loop, but I prefer not to find out if that's okay with you. I want to get off these streets tout suite."

"How can you function, being so sensitive? Maybe you should take the lead, and I'll tell you where to go," Seth said.

Casey gave him a half-smile.

Sophia stepped out to the side and felt the energy Casey

referred to and wished she hadn't. It made her feel sick to her stomach, and pain shot through her abdomen.

"The woman is passing you now, Sophia," Casey said.

But she didn't get out of the way. She could feel the woman more than her assailant. Sophia saw a mental image of the woman holding her stomach as if afraid it would spill onto the ground.

"Let's jog." Tim grabbed Sophia's hand and pulled her forward.

"It's not far now. Straight ahead and down the next alleyway," said Seth.

Sophia and Casey turned a corner. Seth had stopped in his tracks and Casey pushed Sophia back against the wall. "Wait. Where is it? Seth?"

"Four doors down. See the green plaque with the golden writing? Hallow Curative Emporium. That's the shop," Seth whispered.

"Okay, let's go," Casey said.

Sophia stayed close to him, and could feel heat of Tim's body behind her. They were all jittery. She smiled. Tim was a gentle soul, his energy was light and playful. No matter how old he got, she hoped he never lost his childlike nature. She reached behind her, and he took her hand. Sophia filled him with energy. She could calm his racing heart and make him feel at ease, but they needed to be on edge; the fear could keep them safe.

Sophia pulled out her bowie knife, a Christmas present from Kevin. "You might need this." She handed the knife to Seth.

Seth's eyes opened wide as he looked from her to the knife. A closed smile grew on his face. "He wasn't kidding," Seth said, taking the knife. He jimmied the lock and opened the door.

16

CASEY: THE CURATIVE EMPORIUM

"This place is incredible! There is so much light and color," Casey observed.

"I can't see much," said Tim, flicking on the light switch by the front door. A bell over the door rang as Seth let it close behind him.

"It's perfect!" Sophia said.

Casey drank up the energy in the room. It was invigorating. Built into the wall behind the counter were rows and rows of drawers, labelled in old script. There were jars of alcohol with preserved plants, roots, bones, and animals. An array of colored crystals filled the glass cabinets and wooden shelves. A huge purple rock sat in a corner of the east wall, glowing with serenity and peace. If he could, Casey would have crawled inside it. His chest expanded as he breathed in the magnificent light in the store. The amethyst twinkled as he drew close. There was so much stuff for sale. Books, medicine, angel cards, baskets of unpolished crystals, pink rock salt, necklaces, bracelets, trinkets, even clothes made from hemp. What fascinated him the most was a glass cabinet with crystal wands, drums, and a rattle made from a turtle shell.

Stained-glass incense burners hung from the ceiling, and similar leadlight lamps and teapots were arranged on a tabletop. It was a wonderful place, and he could understand if customers didn't want to leave. It was clean and spiritual. He gravitated towards a glass display case of fairy and angel statues. He reached out in awe to touch the glass, to be closer to a bronze figure of archangel Metatron. Metatron's wings were open wide. In his hands, held high above his head, was the sacred geometry cube, filled with connecting circles – the flower of life, which held within it every shape imaginable in the universe, the embodiment of all physical matter. The statue bore a slight resemblance to the angel who had saved his life.

"Sophia, look at this! You've got to see this," Casey said, astounded. "I don't believe it."

Sophia and Tim came and stood by his side.

"It's the same as the etchings on the back of the Emerald Tablet and on my necklace," Sophia said. "Casey, it's Metatron, our guardian angel."

"Who is Metatron? I've never heard of an angel called Metatron," Tim said.

"When I was born in the church where Father McDonald raised me, an angel appeared to him and said I was precious to God, and he must protect me until the day he returned for me. The angel told him his name, and it was Metatron. On earth he was a man called Enoch, a very special man precious to God. They removed the Book of Enoch from the Talmud, and left it out of the Bible to became folklore."

Casey opened the cabinet and touched the statue with his fingertips. He felt the artist's passion for Metatron flowing into his being. Joy filled his mind and his heart expanded with love for the angel. He would like to learn more about Enoch, and why he was so precious to God that God would make him an angel.

"Metatron's the reason I'm alive today," Casey said. "He fished me out of a raging river, he cleansed me when I became infected with the shape-shifting virus, while trying to find the Emerald Tablet. I owe him my life, Tim."

"Tell me what you know about this shop?" Sophia said to Seth. "Who was the owner?"

"I don't know a lot. At college my friends would come here to get aromatherapy oils or herbal teas when they had the cold or the flu, or they would get a potion to rub on their wrists, because they believed it would help them during their final exams. They used the oil blend to help them recall what they had studied when they needed it the most. They stayed calm, free of anxiety during the exams.

"The woman behind the counter was warm and kind, a foreigner, exotic to us. She opened the store about three years ago. I can't remember her name. Her eyes were mesmerizing, but I couldn't tell you what color they were. She didn't say much, she was quiet but always seemed to know what somebody needed. Sometimes I would wait outside and watch through the window. People browsed and touched things, circled the inside of the store as if they never wanted to leave. So, I'd just tag along with my friends. Some guys would come in because she was sexy and mysterious. I hung out with girls more than guys, they were more serious about their studies and getting help to succeed. They looked at that woman as if she was some kind of oracle."

"This place smells so good," Casey said, turning towards the window. Light refracted off one crystal onto a flyer in the window. It might be the one Hugh and Gary had mentioned to

Sophia. Careful not to tear it, Casey peeled it off the window and read it out loud. *"The Gods have chosen you. Accept your destiny, traveller of the stars, child of God's light, it's time to travel beyond this realm, back to where you came from."*

It had a picture of Stonehenge at night, illuminated by the stars shining above it. There were other posters on the window, for private healing seasons, astrological charts, workshops and meditation circles, but none had the same vibrational energy radiating off them as the flyer.

Casey looked about the store and felt waves of healing energy touch his aura – there was no doubt it was a place of healing. He loved how clean and organized everything was. It had been such a long time since he had felt comfortable enough to touch things.

On the edge of the counter was a pile of pamphlets. The top one read, *Accept your destiny and honor the calling.* It was a more detailed version of the flyer on the window, with a map of the location, and a nutritional guide to prepare the body for transformation to the next stage of life among the stars.

Sophia walked past Casey, and he felt her aura brush his. It shocked him how flat her energy was. He thought the shop, and its emporium infused with light, would have enthralled her as much as it did him. Something was troubling her. He could feel how jittery she was, and she was trying to catch her breath. The caffeine tablets were muddling up her natural energy flow. Sophia was never jumpy, she was always calm. She moved behind the counter towards the wall of herbs. She took out her Bible. Tucked in the back of the book was a folded piece of paper. Casey wanted to reach out to her but could only watch her as she put the Bible back into her coat pocket and scanned the labels on the drawers.

Casey joined her behind the counter. He scanned all the

drawers and was just wondering how to get up to the top row when he noticed a ladder on wheels. He pulled out a drawer close to him labeled *Passiflora Incarnata*. The sweet fragrance of passion flower filled his nose and he could taste it at the back of his throat. He closed the drawer and opened another labeled *Glycyrrhiza Glabra*, which smelled like licorice. He went to open a drawer labeled *Salix Alba* but instead watched Sophia studying her list. "What do you need? Can I help?"

"I need sweet basil seeds, dried white sage leaves, white willow bark, crushed pink rock salt, sandalwood oil and root, amethyst crystal flakes, rose quartz flakes, myrrh cakes, clergy sage oil, frankincense dried leaves, zinc, magnesium, matches, and we're going to need a lot more holy water. Unless you know the botanical names of any of these herbs, I don't think you'll be much help. Thanks anyway," she said, dismissing him.

It shocked him how edgy she was, but he thought it was best to give her space. She was right; he didn't know the botanical names of plants.

Casey went into the back of the store where Seth and Tim had gone. There was a wall of old books in a back room that looked like an office. He picked up one with his mind and it hovered in front of him, so he didn't have to touch it. *Biblia Vulgata*. He assumed it was a Bible written in a foreign language. The spine was coming away. It was very delicate and old. He put it back and kept browsing all these books hidden from the public. He read some of the titles out loud: *Hands-on Healing, Spiritual Healing, Crystal Journey Light Workbook, Color Therapy,* and *A Course in Miracles*. So many old books, all of them not for sale, but what caught his eye was *The Book of Enoch*, and another called *The Sumerian Gods*. They were both in white leather binding, with gold lettering. Intrigued, he summoned the books from the shelf. They floated down, and he guided them onto a cluttered desk piled high with books. With a gesture he made room for *The Book of Enoch: keys to transformation* and *The Sumerian Gods*.

The white leather binding of *The Sumerian Gods* bore gold embossed images and ancient symbols: angels and lions with wings, and creatures that looked like humans with wings or the head of a bird. He studied the images and wondered if he dared to touch the cover. Casey focused on the energy the story the images portrayed might project into his being – images, or emotions and physical sensations he might be better off not experiencing – but he wanted to touch it and see what was inside. He wanted to peek inside both books but felt as though he was trespassing. With his mind, he opened *The Sumerian Gods*, and turned a few pages. The pages were old and stiff, resembling ancient parchment – and blank. Surprised, he closed the book, leaving it on the desk. He focused on *The Book of Enoch* and studied the letters and wings on the cover. There was a similar picture of wings on the cover of *The Sumerian Gods*. He felt they were somehow connected and was about to place his hand on the cover when Tim called out to him.

Casey withdrew his sweaty palm from the book and stepped back from the desk. He left the books and the room. Tim stood behind the counter in the storefront, next to the cash register.

"Look what we found," Tim said.

It was a chunky notebook bound in soft leather with a medieval-looking latch, and it was stuffed with papers.

"Seth and I found it under the counter. Some parts are in old script with English translations underneath. There are drawings and details of herbs, symbols, astronomy, angels, mythological creatures, and beings, and look what else we found."

Seth was holding the leather cover closed. When Tim looked at him, he opened the book to a particular page. Casey stepped back and bumped into Sophia, who was putting herbs into a brown paper bag. "Sorry." But Casey didn't take his eyes off the image. His heart raced. His skin was cold and clammy. He tried to swallow, but his mouth and throat were dry.

It was the salamander from his nightmare. The page was titled *"Homoharenae"*, and there was a paragraph above the picture.

"What does it mean?" Casey asked.

Seth pointed to the title handwritten below the images. "Latin, *Homo* means man, and *harenae* means sand: Sandman." He began to read out the paragraph:

"Beware – guard your dreams from the sinister Sandman. It is death. It will steal the life from you. Its movements are disjointed. It stalks you at night. It hides in the shadows and corners of your room. It waits for you to sleep and seals your eyes tight. It enters your dreams and turns them into nightmares. When you do wake, you forget it came for you at night. You will feel exhausted and confused. You will avoid sleep without knowing why, but when you fall asleep, it will drain you of your life force and never again shall you wake. If you ever experience sleep paralysis, it might be the Sandman stealing your life force."

"What's wrong?" Sophia stood next to Casey, and set down a copper bowl containing a mix of herbs and minerals. Waiting for him to answer, she focused on his eyes.

"That would explain why we found you asleep, and the strange feeling I had of being watched when I found you," she said.

"And maybe it's why everyone at the tavern has been falling asleep for days on end," Seth said.

Tim pinched his upper arm, scared he was already asleep. "How do we know we're not asleep now?"

Casey latched on to a sliver of awareness of Sophia touching

Tim on the shoulder, balancing out Tim's energy by pushing away the fear.

"It's possible to have shared dreams, but that is not happening now. Casey's sleep problems started before he arrived at the tavern," Sophia said.

"Did I lead it to the tavern?" Casey asked, concerned.

"You couldn't have, it has been happening to us on and off ever since the whiteout," Seth said.

"I think it might have followed Hugh. You started astral travelling the night after he first appeared."

"I just wish I could remember my dreams. All I have is the drawings."

"There are heaps of potions in here," said Seth, looking through the book. "There's got to be one to help you remember your dreams."

"Stop, go back a page," Sophia said. "*Sanctus Aquam,* perfect."

"What does that mean? Will it help Casey remember?" Tim leaned over Seth's shoulder.

"No, but it's just what I need: a recipe for holy water."

SETH AND TIM STEPPED AWAY, allowing Sophia to get a closer look.

Casey wanted to reach out and help her – her hand had a slight tremor. *She so needs to stay away from caffeine,* he thought. To mark the place, before searching for a potion to help him with his memory, Sophia slipped a pamphlet in between the pages to stand out above all the other pieces of paper sticking out from the notebook. She turned the fixed and loose pages, flicking past images and descriptions of beautiful angelic beings, symbols, hideous creatures, spirits and demons. The original pages of the book were old, as if whoever wrote them had used ink and a quill.

She paused and tapped an image of a ghostly woman in a nightdress with two heads. One head was a young, beautiful woman, and the other was an old hag with rotten teeth. It was like two people were the same. The image changed as you moved the page, which is what must have caught Sophia's eye.

"*Planctus Mulierem* – banshee. Means wailing woman. This is the woman we saw at the cemetery." Sophia read out the first paragraph:

"*When she crackles or shrieks, someone is going to die. If attached to you, she will curse your family with bad luck and or death. She can be hateful and angry or a beautiful messenger. Lance her with a golden blade to banish her forever, or you can shackle her with a Celtic blood spell in potions.*"

"What's a Celtic blood spell? No, I've changed my mind. I don't want to know," Tim said. "This is too creepy for me. I should have stayed at the estate."

"Do you think it's attached to my family?" Seth asked. "We heard her wail before Colin died." He held the corner of the page, moving it back and forth to see the image change like a hologram.

"We all saw it when we entered the city," Tim said.

Casey watched Tim's aura reach out to protect Seth's and Seth's aura responded, merging into the edge of Tim's. "I think everyone at the tavern had become one family, and the banshee showed itself to us because Hugh was in the car," Casey said.

"Does this mean we have to banish her too before we can leave?" Seth asked.

Sophia closed the book. "I can't do this, Casey. I want to leave. I want to go back to the estate now. Right now!" She marched towards the shop door, leaving everyone astounded by her outburst.

"Wait here," Casey said to Tim and Seth. He went out after her. "Sophia, what's wrong? Talk to me."

She quickened her pace. He had to jog to catch up to her. "Sophia, it's not safe out here. Talk to me, please."

"I don't care, I've had enough. I can't do this," she said, digging her hands into her pockets.

"You have to," Casey said.

"Why!" She halted in the middle of the laneway. "Why? Show me where it's written that I have to help these people."

"Because you're the only one I know who can face these horrors and save the children."

"I can't do it without Father McDonald," she blurted, and began to cry. "He had all the faith, the strength, and the certainty, not me."

"We have to do this," Casey said. "Metatron will protect us no matter what happens. He carries the energy of the Merkaba and we're guided day by day, moment by moment along the path of light. No matter how dark the world is. Even if we die, he will carry us home. Life has changed, and it will never go back. That's the old world, this is the new world. We have to make the most of it , and do what we can until it's our time to leave."

"All I have ever wanted was to live in the suburbs, in an average house, hang out with the locals, study hard and go to Glasgow University," Sophia said. "I wanted to fall in love and have a family of my own, and I wanted God to take the sounds of other people's thoughts out of my head, and the premonitions from my dreams. All my life I've been preparing for the apocalypse. Well, it's happened, and we failed. I should be free. Of all the things I wanted, God has removed the sounds of other people's thoughts and the premonitions, and I can't bear the silence and not knowing, Casey. This is not me. This is not who I am." Sophia was choking on her tears.

There was nothing Casey could say that could make her feel better, so he simply held her in his arms and shared her pain. He saw no future. Something was happening, or going to happen, but he couldn't sense the outcome and it frightened him.

"I think I'm going to die," Sophia said.

He moved her hair from her face whilst he searched for the right words. "Like with a panic attack?" He didn't want her to tell him any more. It was best if he said nothing.

She stayed wrapped in his arms and said, "I don't see a future. Before, I always knew what the future held. But now it's blank, Casey. I can't see it anymore. It's a blank white screen."

She wiped her tears and, with a deep breath, walked back into the shop. Tim and Seth moved aside, and pretended not to notice her tears.

Without a word, she opened the book at the beginning. The first section seemed to be all about herbs and potions. She sighed as if exasperated, looking at the picture of a *Turritopsis Dohrnii*, a squid. "*Immortalitatis*," Sophia said. "Immortality – why would anyone want immortality?"

"What's a squid got to do with immortality?" Tim said.

Sophia gently pinched the corner of the page and continued looking through the notebook, not bothering to answer him.

"Let's just get what we need and come back later," Casey said, seeing the color in Sophia's aura changing to pale pastels. Her energy was being drained, and he didn't know why. Placing his hand on the small of her back, he allowed his energy to flow into the back of her solar plexus. Vitalizing red hues filled her aura, enriching all of her energy fields. She turned and smiled, but her hand was still shaking.

"Here," Sophia said. *"Memorias Invenire* translates to 'memories find'."

"That sounds like the ticket," Tim said, trying to sound chirpy.

"All the ingredients are here, it shouldn't take too long to make it," Sophia said.

"I don't know if this is a good idea," Casey said.

"But if you think it's important, maybe you should," Sophia said.

They were all anxious as they waited for him to answer. "I don't think now's a good time, guys." Casey ran his fingers through his hair and cleared his throat. "No, now is not a good time." He shoved his hands in his pockets.

"When will it be a good time? Not back at the tavern," Tim said. "There's no better time than the present. When we get back to the estate it might be too late."

"There's a massage table in the back room, Sophia. We can set it up for Casey while you prepare the potion," Seth said.

"Okay, I'll do it. How long will it take?" Casey asked, trying to sound confident, but the idea terrified him. What if the ghosts from his nightmare showed up? He believed a haunting presence lurked in the shadows, waiting for him to be in a vulnerable state in order to pounce and devour him. That's what would happen if he took this potion.

Casey took his sketchbook out of his backpack and opened it to the drawings. He studied the images; he didn't want any of these characters to follow him into this reality. Shoving the sketchbook back into his bag, he went into the room where Sophia was preparing the potion and paced in front of the bookshelves.

"Sophia, I don't think this is a good idea. Something feels very wrong."

"It will be okay," Tim said, playing with some crystals. "These are gorgeous." He looked at Seth.

"They are nice. Whenever I came into the store with my friends, I tried not to look interested, but I like that one you're holding."

"These spheres remind me of our friend Shaun. He has gemstones similar to these."

"This one's my favorite," Seth said, taking it from Tim.

Casey watched Tim and Seth. There was a lot more going on between them than either of them was saying. He could see it in their auras, the colors changing and expanding towards each other until they overlapped. Casey sat on the stool at the side of the counter and waited. He fiddled around with the register, trying to work out how to open it to distract him from what was about to happen. The memories of his dreams might be best forgotten. As he touched the register, he saw an image of a middle-aged woman who he assumed was the owner of the store. He pulled his hand away – he sensed she had cast a spell over the register. Casey got up and browsed through the store noticing a faint underlying energy in the room. A curse for thieves.

"We need to pay," Casey said. "Everything we take or use, we need to pay for it."

Seth and Tim stopped touching the crystals. "What do you mean?" said Tim.

"We don't have any money, and I'm sure a card won't work," Seth said.

"We need to pay for everything we're taking, because there is a spell of misfortune protecting the store from thieves. If we take anything without paying, the spell will activate."

Casey took a pamphlet, found a pen and wrote an IOU on the back for two hundred dollars. "Should I make it pounds?"

"I sure dollars will be fine, Casey," Sophia mumbled as she concentrated on the mixture. He wrote the address of the estate and stuck the note under the register. He watched Sophia. She was heating the mixture over a Bunsen burner in what looked like a tiny cauldron. She sensed him watching and smiled with her eyes. "I'm almost finished, I need one more ingredient." she said.

"What is it? I'll find it," Casey volunteered.

"Okay, sure. I need two frog's legs."

Casey stopped moving. "Are you serious?" he said, stretching his neck out.

Sophia laughed. The sound of her laughter filled him with hope. He sat down again on the stool and waited. "How come you can read Latin?" he asked.

"Father McDonald. Bible studies. He encouraged me to read Latin. He said demons can't understand Latin. It would be useful if I ever needed to cast out demons. I never thought he was serious though." Sophia raised her eyebrows as she continued stirring the potion with a crystal stick that looked like clear plastic. Her hand was a little steadier.

"Well, I hope you remember your lessons," Casey said.

"What about salt?" Seth said, moving towards the counter with Tim.

"What about salt? What do you mean?" Casey said.

"If you make a circle with salt and stand in the middle, nothing can harm you," Seth said. "I passed a page that mentioned a circle of salt. I think it was for a demon trap."

"Maybe we should take the book with us?" Tim said.

"I'll have to increase the IOU if we take the book," Casey replied.

Sophia stopped stirring. "I'm done. It says here the potion loses its potency in thirty minutes. Maybe you should get out your sketchbook in case you have trouble verbalizing what happens and can only draw the images."

"Okay, maybe I should clear a space at the table stacked with books in the back office. Let's forget about the massage table in the healing room, Seth. I prefer to sit up, anyway. I don't want to fall asleep."

17

HUGH: SPIDERS

I nside Hugh's boots, his toes were freezing. He rubbed his legs and stood up. Sitting in the chair, his body had stiffened from the cold while watching over Ernest. The boy's sleep was restless. He looked at his watch and only fifteen minutes had passed. A fly broke the silence and buzzed around the room in the stillness and landed on his watch. Frustrated, Hugh swatted it away. He was glad he was wearing his old digital watch rather than his smart watch. The battery would have died in the first few days after he had arrived at the tavern. He always kept a backup charger in the car, but it still wouldn't have done him any good. The constant alerts, the flashing green lights as it checked his pulse rate, were things he didn't miss.

The chair creaked as he got up to check the thermostat again. It was still on high. He hovered his hands over the radiator bars for warmth, then rubbed them together and shivered. The chill was worse than the meat locker at the local butcher's where he'd worked as a teenager.

It might snow, he thought. Frost covered the windowsill. It melted when he dragged his finger through it. There was a pungent smell in the room that was getting worse. He opened the window a crack. Warm air from outside entered the room. He pushed the window all the way up, welcoming the early evening breeze. There wasn't even a hint in it of the icy chill that pervaded the tavern.

He wrapped his arms around himself. The cold and the smell intensified the closer Hugh got to Ernest. It was coming from Ernest's mouth. Hugh drifted his hand towards Ernest's mouth and nose and checked his breathing. It was slight. Hugh's touch was light as he searched Ernest's wrist for a pulse; it was rapid, as if he was running. Careful not to disturb him, Hugh laid his hand on the boy's forehead. He was burning up. Ernest's head turned towards Hugh, and his eyes flew open. They were yellow. Hugh pulled his hand away and stumbled back from the bed.

"You should've died in the car with us." Hugh knew it wasn't his mother's voice, but it sounded so real.

Confused and unsure, he hesitated, transfixed, waiting to hear her voice again. He snapped out of his trance and rushed from the room, grateful to leave the apartment.

It was time to check on Bo; he had agreed to check on the children at fifteen-minute intervals until Gwen, Eleanor and Patricia came back from the kitchen. Gwen was helping Patricia and Eleanor regain their wits over a fresh pot of tea and sage leaves. He wished Billie and Gary would come back with Kraig. They should watch over Ernest. *What was Kraig thinking to leave and not tell anyone?* It seemed like an eternity since Seth and Tim and Casey and Sophia had left too. "Hurry, guys." Hugh braced himself before entering Bo's room.

Bo was struggling to breathe. Her room was in darkness.

Every time he entered the room, he had to open the curtains and the window.

Something scurried across the room. A child giggled. Bo was in her bed, and the giggling was coming from under her bed. He stepped closer. Muffled giggling and shuffling moved towards the wall, away from him. Hugh lifted the edge of the blanket up off the floor and got down on his knees. The Miss Amelia doll lay on the floor, pushed up against the wall. He stood up. Something scurried across the dark room. He headed towards the window. The doll was back in the chair, looking up at him. He wanted to chuck it out the window. He backed out of the room and shut the door. The devilish giggle of a child became a deep, sinister laugh. Fearing he was losing his mind Hugh ignored the shivers running down his spine. He was about to close the door to the apartment when the laughter stopped, and Bo whimpered.

Rushing back into the bedroom, he held his hand to his mouth as green vomit, thick as mud, trailed down the side of Bo's mouth. Gagging, he wiped her mouth and the edge of the pillow with tissues. She was still in a deep sleep, breathing through her nose. The chair behind him rocked, and the floorboards creaked. The chair was empty. He couldn't get out of the room fast enough. He slammed the door behind him.

"Shit. Shit. Shit! What the hell!" He raced down the hall and down the stairs. He caught himself as he slipped on his way down to the kitchen.

Eleanor was eating broth. Her primary focus was whether they should leave with the children. She didn't understand what was happening but was adamant the best course of action was to leave. To get into her van and just leave.

Gwen noticed Hugh listening at the kitchen door. "How are they?" her voice quivered.

"Resting. No change. Ernest may have a fever." Hugh gave Patricia an apologetic smile.

Patricia didn't respond. She kept her head down and stared into her bowl of broth. With micro movements, she titled her head back until her eyes met his. They were full of shame.

"We'll get this sorted," he said to Patricia. "It'll be alright. I promise."

Hugh poured himself a mug of tea. He welcomed the heat travelling down his throat, almost burning his esophagus, but it was better than the frigid air upstairs.

"We can't just sit here," Eleanor said.

"We have no choice," Hugh replied. "Has Gwen explained what happened when we tried to leave with Bo? Whatever is here with the children won't let the children leave. Besides, we have to wait for the others."

"Why, what are they going to do?" Eleanor slammed her spoon down.

"Well, I suppose an exorcism," said Hugh.

"What? There is no such thing as ghosts and demons. I've lived here for three years. The stories aren't real. It's all a myth. It's all part of the mysteries of London. It brings in the ghost hunters and tourists. The tavern's not haunted, I guarantee it. It's nothing but a bunch of Chinese whispers."

Hugh stepped closer. "Before all this I hadn't experienced any hauntings or ghosts, but now I've seen things I can't explain. Go and look at Bo and Ernest and tell me there isn't something possessing them. Tell me you just see two normal sick children. Is this normal behavior?" he asked, gesturing towards Patricia, who continued to stir her broth, her eyes glazed as if detached from reality.

"Hugh, calm down." Gwen touched his forearm as he leaned on the table.

"Why were you and Gary sleeping, Eleanor? Why were any of you sleeping?" Hugh said, frustrated.

"I don't know about you, Eleanor, but I feel like I'm being watched, that something or someone is waiting for me to fall asleep. I can feel it, and it's freaking me out." Gwen glanced behind her.

Eleanor shifted uncomfortably in her chair.

"I'm afraid to sleep, worried I won't wake up again," Gwen continued. "And each time I sleep I wake up more and more tired."

Patricia stopped stirring. "I sleep with my eyes open. I hear voices, people screaming inside my head. Dogs are barking, growling, snapping at me. Everything is strange, the air tastes different, sounds are muffled. I feel the sensation of people around me, looking at me, you know, like when you're on the subway and you look up from your phone because you sense someone is watching you, and there is. I'm seeing things it would be easier to believe result from an overactive imagination rather than being part of my reality."

"I've felt like I shouldn't be here. It's like when I sold my parents' home after they died. I grew up in that house," Gwen said. "But in an instant it felt like it belonged to someone else. To me it feels like the earth is no longer my home, but I don't know where home is. I know it's foolish. Ever since the whiteout when everyone disappeared, I don't feel I belong here anymore."

Eleanor sat back from the table. "You both sound crazy. This is my home. Things have changed, I'll give you that, but it is still my home. The air might be different because there isn't as much pollution or as many people, and we're just not used to clean air."

"It's more than that," Gwen said to Eleanor. "Did you have the dream?"

"What, the one the crazies claimed was the one conscious-ness, the one-self of all creation? Don't make me laugh. Did you?"

Gwen glanced at Hugh and looked away. "No."

Eleanor pushed her bowl away. "We need to take care of the earth. We've had a humongous wake up call."

There was a faint vibration coming through the floor. "What's that? Can you feel it?" Hugh said.

"Feel what?" Gwen asked.

In an instant, the kitchen erupted into life. Drawers and cupboards slammed open and closed. Cutlery and dishes became dangerous projectiles. Hugh ducked and dodged flying plates. A sharp carving knife hurtled towards him. He squatted down in a hurry and bounced back up. The knife drove through Eleanor's eye socket, forcing her head backward as the knife lodged in her brain. Hugh grabbed Gwen's hand and pulled her off the kitchen chair onto the floor. Hugh flexed forward, away from the pain in his back as he reached around. A knife had wedged into his back. Patricia ran screaming from the kitchen and out of the tavern. Hugh crawled behind Gwen and helped both of them out of the kitchen. Each movement of his arms caused him pain under his shoulder blade. Heat rushed through his body. They entered the main bar, and he grappled for the knife in his back. Gwen stood up and ran after Patricia. Hysteri-cal, Patricia was running across the road. She threw herself back-wards against the wall and scratched at her throat as if she was being strangled. An unseen force lifted Patricia off the ground and dragged her up the side of the wall.

Hugh pulled the knife out of his back and dropped it to the floor. He ran outside and jumped up to grab Patricia's legs. It hurt him to reach up.

"You're bleeding!" Gwen cried out. "Help her, Hugh!"

He jumped into the car and reversed it up to the gutter and climbed on top. He still couldn't reach Patricia. Her hands dropped away from her throat, and she hung in mid-air, then dropped like a rag doll onto the hood of the car.

Hugh lowered her to the ground. Patricia had claw marks and bruises around her throat. Hugh checked for a pulse. "She's gone," he said.

"We can't just leave her here," Gwen said.

"Get her feet," Hugh said. "We'll take her inside and put her and Eleanor in one of the empty apartments."

They left Patricia on one bed, and went back downstairs for Eleanor. Hugh eased the knife from deep inside her brain. He flinched as he felt it hitting the bone. Together they lowered her onto the bed opposite Patricia.

Gwen rummaged through the apartment's medicine cabinet. Shaking, she helped Hugh pull off his jacket and lift his shirt so she could attend to the cut under his shoulder blade.

* * *

ONCE HUGH'S wound was bandaged, Gwen said, "I'll check on the children."

"I'll check on Ernest, you go check on Bo," Hugh said, tucking in his shirt and throwing on his jacket before following Gwen out of the apartment, and locking the door.

Standing in front of Ernest's family's apartment with his hand on the doorknob, Hugh took in a deep breath then went inside. Ernest's bedroom door was wide open and his bed was empty.

Gwen called out to Hugh. He ran down the hall and found Gwen standing at the threshold of Bo's room. Guarded, he walked up behind her, not sure if he wanted to see what was inside. He feared Bo was dead. Light was streaming from the room.

Bo sat in the middle of the floor with Ernest and her dolls. The blinds were open.

"We're having a tea party. Come play with us, Mommy," Bo said.

Hugh and Gwen looked at each other, and he saw her eyes pooling with tears. She held them back and walked into the room. Hugh lagged behind, mesmerized by the doll Miss Amelia. A spider crawled out of its mouth.

"Are you hungry? Ernest, would you like a sandwich?" Bo handed the boy a tiny plastic plate with plastic triangle sandwiches.

"Thank you," Ernest said. "But can I have some soup with bread like my mommy was eating?" Ernest looked at Gwen as if to say he knew what she had been doing.

"You should share, Mommy. Miss Amelia said you're being greedy," Bo said.

Hugh couldn't take his eyes off the spider crawling into the doll's broken eye.

"Wakey, wakey," said Ernest in a deep female voice.

Hugh snapped out of his trance. "Who are you?" he said.

"You know who I am. I'm the reason the children still have their souls."

Bo continued to play as if nothing strange was happening. Her skin was pale gray and could have been mistaken for that of a corpse.

"While I play with the children, why don't you get some broth and bread for them?" Gwen said.

He was staring at the doll again and out of the corner of his eye he thought he saw a spider crawl under the sleeve of his jacket. He slapped at the sleeve and shook his hand.

"Are you alright?" Ernest giggled. It was the same giggle Hugh had heard coming from under Bo's bed.

He ignored Ernest and answered Gwen. "Okay, sure, I won't be long." He didn't like leaving Gwen alone. Bo and Ernest may be two weak children, but the evil spirit controlling them had powers he couldn't even imagine. What they might do if he made it angry scared him.

Out in the hallway, he paused. *What was that noise?* A kind of faint scraping sound. Hugh rubbed his wet palms on his pants and ran his fingers through his hair. He took a deep breath before he continued down the hall and entered the adjoining wing. The door he'd locked only moments ago, securing Eleanor's and Patricia's bodies, was open.

"Hello?" The scraping stopped. He pushed the bedroom door open wide, expecting to see Eleanor and Patricia on the beds. *"Oh, Jesus!"*

They were gone. Hugh straightened the ruffled bedcovers, hoping to reveal the shape of the bodies – they had been there, he knew it, he had put them there. He swiveled round, checking the room. Had he fallen asleep and imagined it all? The scraping sound began again, outside the apartment, and he ran out into the hall. Patricia's awkward movements forced her against the wall, causing her to drag her sagging head against it as if she had a broken neck.

What the hell?

She sniffed the air and focused on where he was standing, then twitched and jerked into action. Her body twisted and bent in unnatural ways as she dropped onto all fours and scurried up the wall like a spider. He rushed to the nearest apartment, and opened the door as she jumped towards him and deflected her into the apartment.

He yanked the door closed. Horrified, panting, Hugh

propped a chair against the door and sat down. Exhausted, he held his head in his hands, his elbows on his knees. *The world has gone to hell.* He lifted his head and stood up, ready for another attack. *Where's Eleanor?*

A presence was creeping up beside him; he could feel it. His eyelids were heavy. He was so tired he couldn't remember when he'd last slept. *Where am I? How long have I been awake?* He couldn't remember. He looked at his watch. It made a loud *tick-tock tick-tock.* It was dinnertime. He was hungry. It was a struggle to remain standing. Hugh moved to the banister and held on, afraid he would topple down the stairs.

Downstairs everything was quiet. No one was around. He called out to the bartender and looked over the menu while he waited at the bar. A woman with severe burns on the right side of her face and an empty eye socket served Hugh his gin and tonic and took his order. He sipped his drink as more people entered the bar and sat next to him. There was the murmur of small talk, otherwise it was empty. Unusual for that time of the evening. Every Friday since he started working in the city, Hugh had visited the bar. He finished his drink just as his food was ready. Famished, his mouth watered as he broke the bread and dipped it in the soup. It was delicious.

"Would you like a serving for your guests, sir?" the bartender asked.

"My guests?" Hugh tried not to stare at the waitress's face, but he couldn't help wondering what had happened to her, or who she was. He had never seen her working behind the bar before.

"Yes sir, in your apartment upstairs. Don't you remember, sir?"

The disfigured woman left and returned with a tray. There were two steaming bowls of soup with fresh slices of bread. He hesitated, then took the tray and walked upstairs, not sure where he was going. He looked down through the steaming bowl of soup and saw an eyeball floating on the surface. Maggots crawled over the moldy bread. The tray dropped to the floor. His elbow slid off his knee and jolted him awake. Hugh jumped out of the seat and looked about for the tray of food – there wasn't one. Patricia was inside the room he had propped the chair against. "Holy crap," he said, digging into his pocket for more caffeine tablets.

Unsteady on his feet, he went downstairs, stumbling to keep his balance. It was like he had taken sleeping tablets instead of caffeine tablets, and he moved as if he was waking from a deep sleep. Disorientated, he gave a nervous laugh at his awkwardness. The kitchen was a mess, with broken crockery everywhere. He stepped through the maze of shattered pieces.

A pot of broth simmered on the stove. He lifted the lid; no eyeballs. Bread, a knife, butter and two empty bowls had been laid out on a serving tray, just like the one he had dreamed about.

He ladled the broth into the bowls and, with a final check over his shoulder before he left the kitchen, he headed back to Gwen.

The ticking of his watch was annoying and hypnotic.

"What took you so long?" Ernest snapped.

"Put the tray over there," Bo instructed. She was in the middle of cutting one doll's stomach open with a plastic knife.

"She's a doctor," Gwen said.

He put the tray down on the bureau and glanced at the doll. He couldn't remember seeing it smile before.

* * *

HUGH KEPT CHECKING over his shoulder, afraid he would see Eleanor standing in the doorway. Spiders crawled out from behind the cross nailed above Bo's bed and raced onto the ceiling. Bo slurped her soup and dipped her moldy bread. He watched, confused. Gwen ate the bread too, as if nothing was wrong. She wouldn't eat moldy bread, and she wouldn't let Bo eat it either.

Hundreds of tiny spiders moved across the ceiling, and one dropped into Bo's soup. He took the spoon and bowl out of her hands and searched for the spider.

"What's wrong?" Gwen said.

Nervous, Hugh gave Bo back her bowl. He forced a smile for Gwen. "I thought I saw something fall from the ceiling into her broth."

Bo put her soup on the ground and focused on undressing another doll. Gwen followed his gaze up to the ceiling. "I see nothing," she said, uncrossing her legs and tucking them underneath her. She yawned.

"Nothing at all?" Hugh asked.

"A light fixture," Gwen said, giving him an odd smile.

Hugh studied the light fixture and could see spiders running around inside the cover. It wasn't a light fixture at all – it was a spider's egg sack, ready to burst with more tiny baby spiders. He shuddered.

Bo picked up a plastic knife and pretended to cut open the next doll's stomach.

"Don't you want to play with your dolly a little more before you cut her open?" Hugh said.

Bo tilted her head. "I suppose she could have supper first, but then I shall proceed with the operation." Her childish voice carried a formal old-fashioned tone.

"That's the spirit," Hugh said, trying not to glance up at the dangling spider sack.

"You can feed her some broth." Bo adjusted the doll into a sitting position and gave Hugh a plastic spoon from her tea set.

Gwen smiled at him as if Bo and Ernest were having a normal play date, and there was nothing odd about their behavior. "You need some broth in that spoon," she said with a genuine smile and a lift of her eyebrows.

Groggy, he steadied his hand and took the tiny plastic spoon.

Bo and Ernest laughed at him, pretending to feed the doll with an empty spoon.

He scooped up some broth from Bo's bowl and held it to the doll's lips, and Gwen made a slurping sound.

She was trying to tell him he needed to make the sound. She nodded at him as he mimicked her and slurped on behalf of the doll.

"You now need to eat the soup yourself," Bo whispered.

Bo and Ernest covered their mouths with their hands, leaned into each other, and giggled.

Their laughter was creepy. Hugh raised the spoon to his mouth. A spider raced to the edge of the spoon and climbed out on to his hand. Shaking his hand, he dropped the spoon.

Gwen handed him Bo's soiled napkin. "Thanks," he said and squashed the spider with the heel of his boot. He tried again, and pretended to eat the soup, pouring it back each time as he ladled another spoonful for the doll.

"That's enough," Bo said.

He glanced up without moving his head. The spiders emerged from the sack and crawled around on the ceiling. Maggots dropped from Ernest's bread, creating tiny splashes as they fell into his broth. The level in the bowl never seemed to decrease. He watched Ernest take a mouthful, and he chewed as if the broth had meat in it.

Bo straightened the doll's legs and walked it around the doll's house to the Miss Amelia doll sitting on the chair with a spider over her wonky eye.

"Tell me about your action figure doll, Ernest," Hugh said. "I don't think I've seen you playing with it before."

"It's you," Ernest said. "This one is Gwen, this one is my mommy. The one Bo has is Eleanor, this is Colin but he's dead now, this one will be Billie, and this one will be ..."

Bo whispered in Ernest's ear. They giggled again, but this time Gwen joined in. Had they all gone mad?

They went on and named a doll for every person at the tavern, even Casey, Tim, and Sophia.

Bo sat the doll on the chair next to Miss Amelia, then walked her around to the front door of the doll's house and pretended to knock.

There was a knock at the bedroom door. Hugh went to push himself off the floor, but Ernest stopped him with a gentle hand pressed against his knee. Ernest opened the door of the doll's house – and the bedroom door opened.

Dead Eleanor stood at the threshold, transfixed. Bo turned the doll to walk towards Hugh and Eleanor entered the room. Bo laid the doll down. Eleanor lay on the bedroom floor. Bo placed the plastic knife on the doll's exposed abdomen and proceeded with another operation.

"What the hell ...? Gwen, did you see that?" Hugh said.

"Shh, the doctor has to concentrate," Gwen said.

Bo pulled a pretend mask over her face and cut the doll open.

"Isn't she cute?" Gwen said.

Hugh checked Eleanor for a pulse. She was cold with a blue

line covering her beautiful caramel skin. She had been a lovely woman. The buttons on her shirt popped off one at a time as Bo dragged the plastic knife along the torso of the doll. Bo took her time pulling back the imaginary skin of the doll, and Eleanor's shirt opened. Bo repeated her actions and pushed harder onto the doll. A cut appeared down the center of Eleanor's abdomen, opening up her stomach.

Hugh lunged for the plastic knife in Bo's hand. "Stop this." He chucked the knife away from her, picked Eleanor up under the arms and dragged her out of the bedroom, back to the empty apartment, and placed her on the bed again, next to Patricia's empty bed, and locked the door before returning to Bo's room.

"Game over!" he said to the children. "It's bedtime for you both."

They both whined. Surprised they were even listening to his orders, he kept up the facade.

"Maybe you would like Ernest to stay for a sleepover?" Hugh said, hoping Gwen would chime in with some ideas. He noticed the doll that represented Eleanor was in bed, and that's when he noticed the action figure doll hanging out the window of the doll's house. The children were nothing but the devil's puppets.

"Yes! Mommy, can Ernest stay for a sleepover, please?"

Gwen squeezed her lips closed. Hugh looked up. The damn spiders were still there. He didn't know what was worse, the spiders, or the maggots in the bread and soup.

"Only if you both go straight to bed. It's late," Gwen said.

"Yeah!" Bo and Ernest cheered. They jumped up and embraced each other. Ernest pulled the action figure away from the dollhouse window and dropped it to the floor. Hugh felt himself falling. He caught himself on the bureau. Then collected the action figure representing him and the doll representing Gwen and put them safely inside the house.

"I want you two to tidy up this room, and put all your dolls to bed," Gwen said, standing up.

Bo stepped over the toys and hugged Hugh. He patted her on the back and gave her a little squeeze. A stale smell of sickness escaped her body. She had soiled bedclothes and dry vomit on her collar. He wondered if he should suggest giving them both a quick shower and clean night shirts while they could. The smell was hideous. He hesitated, afraid to speak.

Bo hugged Gwen. "This is the best day ever. Hugh can have a sleepover too, Mommy. It's okay with me, and Miss Amelia."

Under the watchful eyes of Miss Amelia, Ernest copied everything Bo did. Humming, Bo and Ernest put the dolls to bed in cardboard shoe boxes.

"Okay you two, in the shower, while Mommy and I get a mattress to make up a bed on the floor for Ernest and some clean pajamas for you both," Hugh said, leaving the bedroom for a glass of water from the kitchenette.

"Be quick about it. Listen to Hugh or there'll be no sleepover," Gwen said, leading the way to the bathroom. She turned on the shower while the children stripped out of their dirty night clothes.

"Make sure you wash yourself," she said, handing them each a face cloth.

They went into the Hugh's apartment and took the mattress from the spare bedroom. "How are you holding up?" Hugh asked Gwen.

"I could use some fresh air and a shower too," Gwen said. Tired, she slouched, and her speech was slow. "But we have to stay awake."

"The others will be back soon, and this nightmare will end."

Hugh gave Gwen a hug. "Take the bedcovers and maybe you should grab some pajamas from Ernest's room."

He dragged the mattress into Gwen's apartment. He could hear the kids playing in the shower. They sounded like any children having fun with water. He made room for the mattress. Something fell down the neck of his shirt. He looked up and the spider nest had disappeared. There were just little black dots all over the ceiling. The white sack fell to the floor. He tore off his jacket and shirt, searching for spiders. To be sure there were no spiders, he shook out his clothes and redressed, walking to the kitchenette for bug spray as he did so. He pulled the blankets off both beds and gave them a good shake. Just the thought of the empty sack and the tiny spiders going down his shirt made his skin crawl.

From the bathroom he heard Gwen say, "It's time to get out of the shower."

He helped Gwen dry and dress the children. It took little convincing to get them both to get into bed. They were very excited. Miss Amelia was lying on Bo's pillow. Hugh didn't recall putting the doll there. Hugh was looking forward to getting away from the children. He looked back at the dolls sleeping in the shoe boxes. His body tingled with fear.

"Can you read to us, Hugh?" Bo asked.

"No, it's late," Hugh said, and the bedroom door slammed.

"Come on now, get some sleep," Gwen said.

Hugh was glad she was trying to take control.

"One story, please?" Ernest said as he got out of bed and collected a book off Bo's shelf and handed it to Hugh. Ernest took Hugh by the hand and led him to the chair Miss Amelia had been sitting on. Hugh didn't want to sit where that ugly doll had been. Gwen was sitting on the edge of Bo's bed, so Hugh thought he might as well read the story and get it over and done with.

Ernest turned off the overhead light and jumped back under the blankets. Gwen switched on the lamp, which gave just enough light for Hugh to see the spiders crawling out of the book.

18

CASEY: THE FORGOTTEN NIGHTMARES

C asey sat at the desk in the back room of the emporium with his sketchbook and charcoals in front of him.

He liked the shop; it was fresh and clean – the air was light and the energy inviting. He thought Jade would like this store and all the herbs. She worked in the veggie and herb gardens at the estate, and had a special kinship with plants, though she wasn't aware of it. Casey found it interesting, and enjoyed watching her nurturing the plants just by her mere presence. The plants reached out to her like she was the sun; her aura would expand so she could feel what the plants needed with her energy, as if they were speaking to her.

Casey drew himself back to the present and tried to focus on the task at hand. The memory potion sat next to the sketchbook. He only had to reach out and take it. Tim's and Seth's energy around him was light, playful, kind spirited, and excited – just the energy he needed right now. He wanted something close to normal because he was worried about what was going to happen. He looked up and drawn on the ceiling was the image of a pentagram. Casey had never seen one close up. *It's like in the drawing in the leather notebook,* he thought.

Seth, Tim, and Sophia followed his gaze.

"What the hell, man?" Tim said. "Is that a demon trap? This woman believed the mysticism written in her notebook."

Sophia went back into the shop and collected the book.

They all leaned over the pages.

"It's a demon trap alright, if there is such a thing," Sophia said. "Well, let's hope it works."

"What if we get everyone from the tavern to come here?" Seth said. "If there are any demons possessing Bo and Ernest, the demon trap will do the job."

"You're forgetting the demon or whatever the entity is controlling Bo and Ernest won't let them leave the tavern," Casey said.

"We should take the book back with us to the tavern," Sophia said.

Casey studied the pentagram on the ceiling. He didn't know if he could trust it. He knew nothing about witchcraft or Wicca or any of those sorts of things, but he trusted Sophia. If she thought it was okay to do this, then he would stop acting like a wimp and do it.

He wiped his hands on his thighs and reached for the potion. He put the cup to his lips and drank. It tasted a little like rosemary, and radishes. He felt it clear his nose and sinuses. He breathed in the bitterness of the radish and let it clear his mind.

"How long will it be until it takes effect?" he asked.

The weight of his eyes compelled him to close them. He listened for Sophia's answer. The bitterness and heat from the potion moved throughout his body. His head tingled as if he was getting his hair washed. It was the best part about having fast-growing curly hair: the hairdressers would always massage his head. That was something he missed from the old world. It was the simple things he missed. He wouldn't be able to get a professional haircut, a head massage, a shave, or one of those warm facecloths they use to open your pores after the shave. It hadn't been long since he started shaving, and he would've liked to have felt the warm cloth.

He felt himself lean back in the seat and tilt his head back, imagining soothing warm water being poured over his head. The warmth travelled through his entire body as the thought filtered through his mind. He was still waiting for Sophia to answer his question, or maybe she already had, and he hadn't noticed? What was the question?

Unable to open his eyes, Casey watched his mind's eye transformed into a projection screen flooded with images that moved in quick succession from right to left, as if going backwards in time. A slimy white *Homoharenae* flickered across the screen, twisting with disjointed movements. It wasn't afraid of Casey, and snarled. Flashes of bodies hanging from gallows splashed across his mind as the images on the screen gained momentum and showed death, murder, and destruction, which felt real.

The sound of victims screaming in pain filled his head. There was a man who was supposed to be trustworthy, but he was cruel, and laughed in the face of justice as he violated the public's trust. Dark medieval streets filled Casey's vision: horses and carts, babies in sacks and wheelbarrows. The images were making him dizzy. Miss Amelia and the girl. The young girl crying as her birth mother abandoned her, selling her to Miss Amelia for a silver coin. An image of the girl cooking and cleaning for her keep. She prayed at night that Miss Amelia wouldn't give her to Doc. The scene changed, and an old hat floated down from the sky. A flash of a demon's face frightened him. Babies screamed. The *Homoharenae* leaned over a sleeping body, feeding on the dreamer's nightmares, draining the sleeper of vitality. Casey found himself inside Sophia's bedroom at the estate. He cried out for her to wake up. The pale slimy *Homoharenae* leaned over her but fled when it saw Casey.

Sophia was so still as she slept, he had to concentrate to see her chest rise and fall as she breathed. Her perfect hair rested on her shoulder. She was Sleeping Beauty, unaware of his presence. He smiled and kept his eyes on her as he left her to her dreams, then suddenly he felt himself ripped backwards, out of Sophia's bedroom and flying through the night sky.

He hovered over towns and saw generation after generation of people in pain and suffering. Time moved so fast, he felt dizzy. Casey lost control. He was on a merry-go-round of time, not knowing what was real, or which time he was in, or where he belonged. Pain vibrated in his temples, and his head throbbed. He wanted to stop the images. Sophia floated in the darkness, falling, just like the old hat. There was nothing he could do but watch her fall – forever falling. He tried to open his eyes, and as he did a flash of light blinded him and he was in the middle of London. The prison was burning. Prisoners trapped behind the walls screamed for help.

"I want to wake up," Casey said. "I want to wake up. Enough, enough! I don't want to know anymore."

If these were the memories of his dreams, or his astral travels through time and space, then maybe they were best left undisturbed. History was repeating time and time again. All the horrid ghosts and monsters of the past were now free to roam. It was hell on earth. He didn't want to hear the desperate cries of the babies Miss Amelia tossed into potato sacks like unwanted kittens. She was a monster trapped inside a doll, a doll that controlled Bo.

Casey floated outside the burning prison. Doc wanted Bo for

the Legion. In return, Doc would have sovereignty over London while the devil reigned on earth. The *Homoharenae* masqueraded as the man in the hat, the warden in Casey's dreams, tricking him with his ticking clock. It was nothing more than another hellhound feasting on a banquet of unsuspecting souls. But it had another job, too – to keep Casey away from Sophia.

The merry-go-round stopped and Casey felt his bones had aged and he was a middle-aged man, a poet, or a holy man condemned to death. Casey sympathized with the dead priest, but he didn't want to feel his pain. He struggled to free himself before he experienced the holy man's fate.

Casey's body stiffened. It was too late. Terrible pain filled his mind and body as a horse dragged the holy man by his ankles, on his stomach, to the place where he would be hanged, disemboweled and quartered. The images flashed across the screen of his mind and filled his body with dread as he experienced the last moments of a man from centuries ago. He struggled to untangle himself from his agonies and broke free, rising into the sky, aiming for heaven among the brightest stars. The city below and its pain and suffering disappeared.

He was flying. He was among the stars. His ascent stopped. He could feel the warmth of the sunshine illuminating the moon. A beam of white light shone down from a cluster of stars near Orion's belt. Sophia was in his heart, calling out to him to return. He listened, tumbled forward, and dived down through the stars, back towards the city, following Sophia's voice, and as he did he remembered the shop, the potion, and the chair. Casey searched the unfamiliar streets for the emporium, looking for Sophia's quintessence, her effervescent light. A rainbow of color from Tim and Seth should also guide him back to his own body. Sophia's essence glittered on the horizon like a star as Casey drew closer, and night became twilight. He had been roaming on the edge of darkness. It was good to see the effervescent light as he drifted down and entered the building, passing through the demon trap to nestle safely back in the chair.

For a moment he watched himself drawing at lightning speed, using reams of paper. He was hungry for the empty page. Tim and Seth stood beside him and watched astonished as both his hands moved, drawing different images at the same time. His brow was covered in beads of sweat and exhaustion. The muscles in his forearms bulged and flexed as he tightened his grip on the charcoal.

Casey immersed himself in his body, inhaling his stink of perspiration. Every muscle was sore, as if each of them had expelled a memory they had locked away to keep him safe while the *Homoharenae* had tried to steal him away. He no longer felt the influence of the *Homoharenae*, but Casey knew it waited in the shadows. All it needed was for Casey to fall asleep.

They had to destroy or banish the *Homoharenae*, had to stop it stealing their life force. There was a lot more evil to destroy, more than he cared to admit, and he didn't think Sophia would be strong enough to defeat all of it. The book the owner of the store had left was important. He could use it to find the keys to help Sophia destroy the evil possessing the children so they could head back to their sanctuary at the estate. But it was going to take the hand of God to scrub the devil from the face of the earth. He had to stay vigilant and guard Sophia.

His hand broke the charcoal. His eyes flew open. He cried out, and took a deep breath. His body went stiff, then limp. His muscles spasmed, then relaxed. He felt his chest rise; his breathing increased, and his spiritual heart opened – the energy vibrant. He hadn't realized it had been closed. A fountain of love for Sophia welled inside his open heart, and in his stomach an overwhelming fear.

Tim handed Casey a glass of water. "What the hell man, what happened to you? Do you have any idea how many images you have drawn? We had to search the shop for more paper."

Scattered over the table was every evil atrocity committed in London through the ages. Everything Casey had seen, he had drawn. Embarrassed, he reached out and scooped up the pictures into a messy pile.

"Wait!" Sophia said, touching his hand. "We've already seen everything. You can't hide anything from us now."

All the trauma and pain was in each picture. All the sinister actions of every evil entity he had drawn came from one place only forty minutes away, at the intersection of Old Bailey and Newgate. Casey couldn't recall if Sophia had told him how long it would take for the potion to react, but he didn't care, he would not go back into his memories no matter what; he would glue his eyes open if he had too.

"Try to tell me – what did you see and feel?" Sophia asked.

"I don't have the words to express the madness and horrific pain." Casey glanced over the pictures of evil and its victims. His fingertips bled. He had used his own blood again to create the color red. They were all silent, Sophia in particular as she stared at the picture of herself falling in the darkness.

Sophia cleared her throat. "What do you think was the most important thing that you needed to remember?"

Casey thought about it. The images were a jumbled mess. He didn't know.

"I think the most important thing is to remember that the lost spirits and entities are not all bad, some are victims, lost and suffering, and they need our help. With that notebook, I can help them," Casey said, pushing himself out of the chair, desperate to rinse his face and arms. "We can help them." he said, facing

Sophia and taking her hands. "Together, we have to stand together. We cannot let the evil separate us."

Sophia squeezed Casey's hands and pecked him on the cheek. "I'll pack up the things we need so we can get going. Tim, can you help Casey? And Seth, can you come with me?"

Sophia touched Casey on the shoulder before going back into the front of the shop.

"There's a book somewhere on the table I want to take. Can you put it in my bag?" Casey asked Tim.

"The big one that looks like it's made of deer hide, about Sumerian teachings?"

"Yeah, that's the one." Casey splashed water on his face.

"But it's empty," said Tim. "The pages are blank."

19

SOPHIA: ROMAN RITUAL

O n a rack in an alcove along the side wall, Sophia found clothes made of cotton and hemp. Rifling through them, she wondered about Isabella Sumer, whose name was above the door of the shop. What magic did she know? Where had she gone?

Sophia selected a long-sleeved shirt of white lace with a high neck, and a pair of white hemp pants. She used the only dressing room near the counter to prepare for the ceremony ahead, and the energies she'd channel to help her save the children. Wearing white allowed the energies from the light to filter through her unencumbered. Her old clothes she folded into a nice, neat bundle, and placed on the stool in the corner. Then she rushed to put her coat back on; it was cold without it. As she added another hundred pounds to their IOU for the clothes, a book fell off the shelf. She picked it up. It was a hardback titled *Roman Ritual*. Sophia turned and studied the energy in the store, wondering who had knocked the book off the shelf. Who wanted her to find it? In her heart, she sensed a strong but gentle energy, and wondered if it was Isabella. She couldn't quite tell if the energy was male or female. It could even be an angel or Father McDonald keeping his distance.

She placed *Roman Ritual* on the bench beside Isabella's leather notebook. The leather was strong and comforting under her hand. The notebook looked worn and loved. She held her amulet between her fingers, tracing the lines of Penelope's web and the flower of life with her fingers. *Please God; guide me with your loving light. I seek your wisdom and protection, show me mercy. There are things I know I must do, but I don't know how to do them. I pray for your guidance.* She placed her hand on the leather notebook and moved it across the cover to the lock, and unlatched the metal hook. With lightning speed, the pages turned, stopping on a page headed 'Holy Water Ritual'. She skimmed through the Latin text for the ingredients and hoped her level of Latin was sufficient to understand what they were, and that her connection to the light of God was strong enough to honor what she had to do.

"I would appreciate guidance, I am grateful for any help the universe sends me." In this moment she felt very alone.

Inside her head she heard her own voice ask, *What do you want?* Sophia remembered how, months ago before she left the church, she had promised herself she would think from the perspective of what she wanted, rather than what she didn't want. As soon as she made the shift, the fear in her stomach disappeared and a sense of peace, security, vitality and calm washed over her. She felt herself moving closer to the place of God, rather than running from the negative place of fear and anguish. *I want, with the blessings of the light, to save the children from the evil that haunts their souls. Help me and Casey to use the unfamiliar tools to slay the beasts that haunt this city, so we may escape to a place of harmony. Amen.*

Sophia heaved the bag of crushed pink rock salt off the ground and placed it on the table next to the smaller plastic bag filled with rock salt flakes. She rolled down the stiff paper of the enormous bag exposing the pink salt, then opened the smaller bag of flakes and poured a quantity from each of them into a copper bowl next to a vessel of water. She hadn't done this before and she hoped it would work; she had to believe God had confidence in her and that this wasn't only a test of her faith, but an opportunity to strengthen her will.

Sophia took off her necklace and separated the two parts of the locket. Leaving the side of the flower of life on the chain, she placed it in the copper bowl of salt. With a delicate touch she lay the other side of the locket with the symbol of protection, Penelope's web with the twelve seals of Solomon, on the bottom of the vessel filled with water.

Casey walked into the shopfront with Seth and Tim. They stayed just within her peripheral vision and waited for her to finish.

"It's okay if you come in, but don't make any sudden loud noises. Treat this place with respect, as if you just walked into the house of God. Oh, and if you hear me say *Amen*, I want you all to repeat it, please."

"Sure, no worries," said Casey, moving forward to the counter. "Your aura is translucent with purified white light."

"Yeah, no problem," Tim said. "Why are you dressed in white? Do we need to change?"

"White is a symbol of purity," Sophia explained. "And no, you don't have to change unless you want to."

"Whatever you say is fine with me," said Seth.

She cleared her throat and raised her arms, looked up to the ceiling and closed her eyes. She imagined herself standing before the altar of God and began the ritual.

"Salt and water, creations of God, with the light the Almighty has invested in me I excise from you all impurities in the name of the Father, the Son and the Holy Ghost, so you may become a means of salvation to those in need of good health in mind, body and spirit. May you, salt and water, intercede wherever you are sprinkled and chase away every evil aspiration, every rapscallion and Mephistophelian hypocrisy and every unclean spirit. For the time is coming when He will come to judge the living and the dead, and will cleanse the world by fire. Until such time, salt and water, it's your time to cleanse, heal and protect. Amen."

"*Amen.*" Their combined voices harmonized as Casey, Seth, and Tim joined in.

Sophia picked up the flower of life she had put in the bowl of salt and withdrew the other part of her locket from the vessel of water and clicked them together again. She dried the wet locket on a corner of her white lace top.

Pouring the bowl of salt into the vessel of water she said the blessing: "Join the power of these two elements, God, I beg thee." Sophia ran her finger along the inside of the bowl, pushing the remaining salt into the water, watching it dissolve as the two elements combined.

"In the name of God the Father, the Son, and the Holy Spirit, Lord hear our prayers and pour down the power of thy blessings into these two elements and make them ready to purify, as combined agents of thy grace, to dispel sickness, to cleanse and free from every harm so no disease remains, through the power of the Holy Spirit, forever and ever. Amen."

"*Amen,*" said Casey, Seth, and Tim.

Sophia poured the holy water, made with the combined purified salt and purified water, into two bottles and topped up the flask handed down to her by Father McDonald that she kept inside her coat pocket. She took up her necklace and put it on. With a sense of love and gentleness, she rolled up the opening of the enormous bag of salt and held it out to Seth. "If you don't mind."

Seth was looking at her, spellbound. "Not at all."

"What's wrong?" she asked him.

"I feel a sense of grace radiating from you. I feel like I should call you ma'am or something." Seth blushed.

"It's okay," Tim said. "I felt the same way, the first time I met her."

Sophia checked off the items she had prepared while Tim packed them into bags. "Sage sticks combined with frankincense, rosemary, and sage leaves. Myrrh cakes, the bag of mixed herbs, matches and crystal and mineral shavings." Everything she might need was ready. She drew in a deep breath. A clatter broke her train of thought.

Casey bent down to pick up a metal dagger with a carved wooden handle.

"Casey, are you alright? Casey!" Concerned, Sophia froze, waiting for him to speak. She dared not imagine the visions or physical pain that could penetrate his mind and body from holding a dagger. His eyes glazed, his breathing deepened, as if in a trance. His head tilted back. He was far away. "Casey, Casey!" She pulled the dagger out of his clenched hand.

He took in a long breath through his nose.

Sophia picked up the dagger's holster from the shelf and returned the dagger to it. Casey reached out for it. He paused and let out a puff of air like releasing the valve on a tire. "Wow, that was hectic. It's okay. I want to keep it. Add another fifty pounds to the IOU, Tim." Casey tucked the dagger into his backpack.

"What happened?" Tim said, shouldering the bag of supplies.

"Holy power. The dagger is timeless. The flashes of history were painless. It was like travelling through a wormhole of time, back to before the erection of the pyramids, and beyond and into the universe."

"We 'd best be going," Seth said, hefting the bag of salt. "It's getting late."

Sophia looked around the emporium one last time to make sure there wasn't anything she had forgotten.

Seth held the door open for them and was about to pull the door closed when he called out for them to stop. He passed the bag of rock salt to Casey and ran back into the rear of the shop and came out with a set of car keys. He aimed the remote control into the street and a set of lights flashed a few car-lengths down the road. "Why walk when we can drive?" Seth said.

Sophia held on to the book and climbed into the back of what turned out to be a campervan with Casey.

"This is neat," Tim said, looking back between the front seats at Casey and Sophia sitting either side of a table by a large window.

"I've always wanted to get one of these motorhomes and travel around Europe," Seth said.

"You still can," Tim said.

* * *

THE UNFAMILIAR CRIES of creatures that did not belong in any city filled the twilight. Tim closed his window. While she was not scared or concerned for herself, Sophia wondered how Casey was dealing with the memories he had regained from his dreams. She would not give in to temptation and peek into his mind; she wanted him to talk to her when he was ready. The pictures he'd drawn were clear, but their meaning eluded her. It was disconcerting to be in the dark. The sketch of her falling in the night was unsettling.

Leaning over the table, Sophia lowered her voice and said, "Casey, can I see your sketches?"

"I left them behind."

"Why?"

"They may have been from my dreams, but they weren't my memories. They were the memories of the dead. They're not mine. I have to let them go, otherwise they'll continue to haunt me. What I want to know is why I had those dreams."

"It's the *Homoharenae's* influence. It's got to be," Seth said, looking through the rear-view mirror.

"Could be." Sophia thought about the pamphlet Casey had written their IOU on, and wondered about the common dreams people had experienced. Had someone transported them to another world? Or back to God? *Maybe they were the chosen ones, taken by God. If so, does that mean we're the forsaken, left with the menacing spirits, ghosts, and demons from hell? Have we been abandoned to live a continual nightmare as the horrors of hell's reign gain strength?* She held the leather notebook in her lap.

Casey avoided looking out the windows. "Can I hold it?"

Sophia placed it on the table in front of him. "You have the dagger. I think the book, and the dagger and the medallion, belong together. Keep the book with you."

"What medallion?"

"It's at the back of the book," Sophia said.

He unlatched the book and turned to the back. "There's nothing here."

"It's under the leather edge." Sophia ran her fingernail under the leather and popped out a round silver medallion of St Benedict's cross. "Take care not to lose them; I think Isabella kept them separate for a reason. You might need them one day."

"Did you have a premonition?" Casey asked, putting the medallion back.

"No. But if anything happens to me, promise me you'll take care of the others."

"What are you talking about? Nothing is going to happen to you. Forget about that stupid drawing, that could've been anyone from the past."

"Just promise me," Sophia said. She could feel Seth watching her through the rear-vision mirror.

"I promise," Casey said, taking her hand.

Sophia smiled. "Turn to the last few pages, it tells you how to use the medallion to protect yourself, and how to use the dagger."

He went to the back of the book, turned the pages backwards, and as he did, he passed a drawing of Sophia's necklace.

"What does it say?" Seth asked.

"Pretty much what Jade told us when she first saw it."

"Who's Jade again?" Seth said.

Tim adjusted himself in the front seat. "She's one of our friends. Jade and Kevin are trying to find her dad back in the United States."

"I thought you said they went to Israel?" Seth said.

"No, that's Shaun and Rachel."

"It's a ten-spoke wheel with stars at the end of each spoke, and each star has twenty outward points, which is what signifies the aspect of protection. We also know the stars as the Seal of Solomon, which amplifies the locket's message of protection. The lines of the wheel and the stars are interlaced by two lines that join at the center; it represents unity – to preserve all of humanity. But the other side of my locket has this image," she pointed to the opposite page, even though Seth couldn't see it. "It's multiple connecting spheres, which is the flower of life, and it holds the secrets of the universe. It's a symbol created from one sphere, the first seed of life spiraling out until it contains all the sacred patterns and secrets of the universe. We can see the flower of life throughout history."

Casey could feel her energy spike a little as she connected to her necklace. She went on, "I remember how excited Jade was when she told you it's in the atom, the building blocks of life, and it's found within everything: a piece of fruit, an icicle, a person, an animal. It's a part of everything."

"That's what this says," Casey said, taking the book from Sophia and moving his finger across the translated text. "The Penelope's web is for protection, it has the strength of the stars of Solomon and the universal connection to the tree of life. It mentions the seven sisters, but it refers to them as a star cluster in the heavens, near Orion's belt."

Casey looked over at the double-sided medallion that sat over Sophia's heart. "It must be ancient. You're one of seven sisters."

"It's thousands of years old," Sophia said. "I want you to wear it." She said putting it over his neck.

He knew there was no arguing. He tucked the necklace under his shirt. Casey returned to the book. He was aware of its possible age and turned the pages with mindfulness. He reached the image of the dagger on one page, opposite it was a page dedicated to the binding of the medallion and the dagger.

"The book is not seven thousand years old," Sophia said, as if reading his mind. "Most of the writing is Latin, which only makes it two thousand seven hundred years old."

"Are you channeling Jade now?" Casey asked with a chuckle.

Sophia just smiled and waited for Casey to finish studying the image of the dagger. She took the book back and translated the Latin, reading out the basic information, leaving out its history, which he most likely already knew from having held it, and told him what she thought was important. "To kill a demon with the dagger you will need to drive it straight into the heart of the host, and in doing so you will free the soul and kill the demon, but in its authentic form you need to cut off its head while reciting this passage." She pointed to the inscription under the drawing.

"*Cum postestate omnipotentis, aut spiritum daemonii immundi, et terebrare in te judicia, et non erit ultra ferrum: et hoc non factum est, in nomine spiritus sancti: Amen.*"

"Translate, will you?"

"I can only give you a rough interpretation. I think it says, *With the power of the Almighty, unclean demon or spirit, I pierce you with the blade of judgment and you shall be no more, and it is done, in the name of the Holy Spirit: Amen.*"

"That's serious stuff," he said. Taking the dagger out of its holster, he examined the carvings on the blade and the handle. He sheathed it and sat it on the table next to the book. He unstrapped the bowie knife Kevin had given him as a Christmas present. Sophia watched Casey strap on the holster like a gun belt and fasten it to his waist. He secured the dagger. There was a circle in the leather near the buckle. "What do you think goes in there?" He asked.

"I don't know, maybe a gemstone or emblem. The drawing only shows the dagger, not the belt and holster," Sophia said.

"What about the silver medallion of St Benedict's cross?" Casey said, pushing it into place. "It fits!"

He stood up and leaned on the back of Tim's seat to talk to Seth. "I want you to look after this for me," he said.

Seth took his eyes off the road and looked down. Casey was handing his bowie knife to him. "Sure thing," Seth said.

Seth drove through the streets of Whitechapel back to the tavern. Sophia could see Casey shy away from the window. They were moving through streets filled with horrors from the past that only he could see. *Though I walk through the valley of the shadow of death, I will fear no evil, for thou art with me; thy rod and thy staff they comfort me …*

* * *

Sophia braced herself as the van pulled up outside the tavern. She closed her eyes and prayed for guidance under her breath. She heard nothing but silence.

"Why is Hugh's car up over the gutter and on the sidewalk?" Seth said as they scrambled out of the van.

The tavern was in darkness. The front door wide open.

Seth raced ahead. "Billie, Dad …"

Sophia heard the beast approaching before they heard its growl or saw the red eyes glowing like hot coals in the night. She pulled Tim out of the way by his jacket and cast a blinding white light. The jackal held its ground, growling and snapping at her as the church bell began to ring. She magnified the intensity of the light and the jackal disintegrated. Seth turned on the tavern lights.

"Dad! Billie! Hugh! Anyone here?" Seth hurried from the bar and dining area out into the kitchen. Sophia was the first to spot the blood on the floor.

"I think you should start cleansing, Sophia," Casey said.

"You might be right, but we need to save the holy water. We should find the others first and set up a safe area to recharge in during the exorcisms. We should break up into pairs, and clear a passageway to exit the tavern when the time comes." Sophia said.

"I'm sticking with you. I will not let you do this on your own," Casey said.

Sophia reached into her coat and took out a smudge stick and lit the end. Smoke billowed around them. She sprinkled the crystal dust over the top of the sage and moved away from the kitchen. The trailing smoke was black. *That's not good.* She felt foolish hoping the smoke would be white. The black smoke meant there were menacing spirits that need cleansing from the earthly realm. She chanted her way up the stairs, "God Almighty, guide us through the lurking evil, let no breath of disease harm us, your servants, as we make passage. Amen."

At the top of the landing, Sophia drew in a sharp breath. A giant spider with the face of Patricia sat on the floor, blocking their way.

"Mom!" Seth screamed.

"It's not your mom, Seth," Sophia warned. The lights flicked off and on. "Everyone, don't take your eyes off it."

The spider was now on the ceiling and moving in time with the flickering of the lights, readying itself to jump down on them. The lights went off and Seth screamed. The lights flashed on again, and the spider was spinning Seth into a ball. Sophia illuminated her own light. The spider climbed down the wall, dragging Seth behind it. Seth struggled against the silk binding him. Casey dropped his bag to the floor and pulled out the dagger. He chased after the spider, threw himself onto Seth, and sliced the silk tether away from the spider. He slit the silk web down the center. Tim was helping Casey free Seth from the bindings when the spider turned on Casey, pinning him down with its hairy legs. Casey lunged up, stabbing it in the heart with the dagger. "With the power of the Almighty, unclean demon or spirit, I pierce you with the blade of judgment and you shall be no more, and it is done, in the name of the Holy Spirit: Amen." The spider collapsed on top of Casey. Seth turned his head so as not to look at his mother's face as he pulled Casey from under the creature.

"Drag it in here," Sophia said, opening up the door marked three.

"That's 1533, are you sure?" Casey said. "During the memory recall potion I saw each room haunted by a horrendous past."

"Maybe for you, but not for the rest of us or that thing," Sophia said. "Seth, Tim, drag it inside."

She held the smudge stick up high as if it was a torch while Casey wiped the black blood off the knife. "Hold the dagger up." She took out her bottle of holy water and blessed the knife. Casey collected his bag and threw it over one shoulder. Seth locked the door from the inside and slammed it closed. He took the chair lying on the floor and propped it against the handle.

"Pick a room so I can clean it out to create a safe zone, Casey," Sophia said.

"Are you kidding? Ghosts haunt every room in this place. Pick a number and that's the era you must cleanse."

"Seth, what was the best era for London?"

"How about room six?" Tim said, opening the door. "It seems peaceful."

Casey wiped his tired eyes. He was sick of always having to explain everything. Frustrated, he said, "How would you know? That's 1941. I hear sirens."

"That's incredible – 1941 was during the Blitz when London was being bombed. Not a good time period," Seth said.

"How is room number six 1941?" Tim asked.

"Okay. I'll explain once. We don't have time for this, but one plus nine plus four plus one equals fifteen, break fifteen down to its simple form one plus five equals six."

"I don't get it," Tim said.

"Maybe 2012 was an okay year," Seth said.

"Okay, that would be room number five. Let's hope it was a good enough year and dominates everything else in history that wasn't so good. The predominant experiences will govern," Casey said, and headed across to room number five.

Sophia followed him with the smudge stick. She could smell the frankincense mixed with the sage and watched Casey hesitate before placing his hand on the door. With very little patience, she waited in the corridor, pulling her hair back. The smoke was a pale gray. It was an excellent sign. She tried to relax.

"Come on, man, is it good or what?" Tim said.

Casey, reluctant, forced himself to open the door for Sophia. "I'll be back in a minute," Sophia said and walked into the room, closing the door behind her.

The trailing vapors of spirits rushed in a whirlwind around her. The smoke intensified, and the embers flickered. The dark gray smoke trailed back into her face and eyes. Sophia closed her eyes and prayed out loud. "God bless this space, keep all that enter free from harm. Make sure that all evil cannot step forward into this place of holy sanctuary." Sophia stepped on a piece of gravel that must have come inside on the bottom of someone's shoe, and moved around the room from left to right, cleansing every corner of the room. After adding more minerals to her smudge stick and spraying holy water, the smoke turned white. She opened the window and encouraged the ghostly vapors of the spirits who had refused to leave via the blessings, to exit. Once she was certain she had cleansed the apartment, she opened the door for the guys.

"Grab the other end," Tim said to Seth. They lifted the dining table into the middle of the room and Sophia unpacked. Casey opened up the book to a page she couldn't quite see and laid the dagger down on it. She had to focus on what she had to do next.

Casey helped her unpack the rocks and minerals, smudge sticks, the bag of mixed herbs, mixing bowl and thurible and placed them on the table. He lined up the bottles of holy water on the kitchen bench.

"What can we do?" Seth asked.

"Take the gigantic bag of purified salt and sprinkle it in a wide circle around us, then do the same around to the edge of the room. Make sure you get plenty under the doors and windows. Make sure you do along the window ledges too. But don't use all of it. If anything disturbs the salt, replenish it."

Sophia opened Father McDonald's Bible. Now she was ready to exorcise the demons from Bo and Ernest. Taking the holy water, she dabbed her forehead and chest in the sign of the holy Trinity. She took a handful of herbs and dropped them into the bowls. She opened the packet of crushed minerals and took a few pinches, dropping them along with a few drops of frankincense oil into the mixture. Gently she placed a brown cake of myrrh on top of the mix and set it alight. Her heart was thudding. It was difficult to speak and she was out of breath. She had to calm herself down, reduce her heart rate, or she would hyperventilate. No more caffeine pills for her.

Sophia refocused on the task at hand. *An exorcism. How did I get here?* She marked the sections she would read from the Bible with pink sticky notes. She snapped the book closed and tucked it into the inside pocket of her coat, and exhaled.

Casey was studying the Latin in Isabella's notebook. He was still on the page about the dagger. He became aware Sophia was watching him and picked up the dagger and tucked it into its holster around his waist before she could protest.

"I don't know if it can be used against ghosts and evil spirits. I don't think it can help free Ernest and Bo, they wouldn't survive," Casey said.

Sophia walked out into the hall. As Tim was about to shut the door, she said, "No, leave it open."

Her head exploded with sound; her gift had returned, but she wasn't hearing the living, she could only hear the dead. In the distance she heard murmurs and chatter, up close were cries and pleas. The voices were male, female and androgynous, but all were in agony, screaming in stereo. Her eardrums felt they would burst. It was as if she had been thrown into the middle of an insane vengeful crowd, full of hatred and pain. She tried to keep her attention focused on the cleansing prayer, watching the smoke turn from black to gray to white, cleansing the hallway as they passed through the evil. She continued to recite prayers, but could no longer hear her own voice. Sophia redirected her focus inward on her heart and concentrated on feeling the passion her words created as the smoke turned white clearing the hallway.

They stopped at Gwen's apartment. The door was wide open.

"I'll go check on Ernest," Seth said.

"No, we stay together," Tim said. "That's when people die in the movies."

"Are you serious, Tim?" Casey said.

Sophia gave him a half-smile. "We should stay together. As soon as we make sure Hugh, Gwen, and Bo are safe, we will check Ernest."

"What are you planning?" Casey asked.

"I want to get everyone back into the protected room."

"That sounds easy enough," Tim said, looking confident.

Sophia concentrated on dampening the sounds of the ghosts in the hallway, then moved into Gwen's apartment and stood outside Bo's bedroom.

"Bo and Gwen are in there, and they are not alone," she said.

The bedroom door was closed. The door handle was icy cold as she pushed inward. Standing at the threshold, holding the door open, she looked at the row of shoe boxes with dolls lying down as though sleeping. At the end of the row, on the floor, Hugh and Gwen were curled up in a ball, sleeping too. Bo slept on the bed, her breathing shallow and uneven.

The chair rocked. Seth and Tim rushed into the room and tried to wake Hugh and Gwen. "Get them out of here," Sophia said.

Seth and Tim first picked up Hugh.

"Take him to room five and lay him in the protected circle," Sophia said. "Help me with Gwen, Casey." Sophia put her bowl down at the threshold of the room and together they carried Gwen back to room five.

Sophia ran back for her bowl of burning herbs. As she crouched down to pick it up, the smoke was an intense black. The bedroom door slammed in her face, knocking her onto her backside.

Sophia picked herself up and went to check on Hugh and Gwen. They were in a peaceful sleep. She reached for the canister of holy water in her pocket and sprinkled a little over each of their faces.

"Are they going to be alright?" Seth asked.

"I don't know." *There's a lot I don't know these days,* she thought.

20

HUGH: PLAYTIME OVER

Bo and Ernst laughed as hundreds of baby spiders poured from between the pages of the book in Hugh's lap and climbed up the sleeves of his jacket. One by one the spiders dropped from the ceiling onto Hugh's face. He slapped at his face as they crawled down the collar of his shirt. The book fell to the floor, Hugh stomped on the book and slapped at his chest and forearms, squashing the spiders and flicking them away from his body. In a mad panic, he yanked his shirt off.

"What are you doing, Hugh?" Gwen asked.

In fits of laughter, Bo and Ernest tried to control themselves to sing a song together:

"Oranges and lemons,

"Say the bells of St Clement's …

"When will you pay me,

"Say the bells of Old Bailey …"

"The spiders are everywhere!" Hugh said. His feet were becoming entangled in a web. "Gwen, they're in your hair!"

She reached her hand to her head and screamed. He tried to

reach out to her, and a spider crawled into the side of his mouth. He tried to blow it away.

Sophia flashed into his mind. "You're safe," she whispered.

Hugh choked on the spider as it crawled down the back of his throat. He gagged.

"It's just a dreadful dream, Hugh. It's time to wake up, trust me. Listen, your alarm is ringing. Wake up now!" Sophia clapped her hands in front of his face.

Hugh could hear his alarm. His eyes flew open. Sophia stood above him, studying his face. His face was wet. Sophia flicked water off her fingers at him, getting it in his eyes. Hugh jumped up and spat on the ground, trying to spit out the spiders. He coughed and cleared his throat. With rigor he slapped and slapped at his body until he slowed to search his arms for spiders. Gwen was sitting up on the floor, her legs out-stretched, waking up. Hugh saw the pink rock salt at the edge of the room; he was not in Bo's bedroom. Disorientated, he twisted around.

"It's blessed salt. It will keep us safe for now," Seth said.

"Where's Bo?" Gwen said, getting to her feet. She combed her fingers through her hair as if making sure nothing crawled in it.

She must have felt the spiders too, Hugh thought. He shook out his jacket and pulled at his collar.

Gwen made for the door.

"Wait!" Casey said.

Hugh, dumbfounded, followed Gwen out of the room and back to her apartment. He staggered.

Gwen was the first into Bo's bedroom. It smelled of sulfur and was shrouded in darkness. Bo, restless in bed, still wore the dirty nightgown. The air was icy cold. There was no mattress on the floor, there was no evidence of soup or bread. *There was no Ernest. Was it all a nightmare?* Hugh tried to recall how the last couple hours had played out. The images of himself sitting on a chair in the hallway barricading something in one apartment were vivid. The loud ticking of his watch sounded unusual.

"Where's Ernest?" Hugh said, running to check on him. Seth was behind him.

Ernest's room was icy cold and stank of rotten eggs. Ernest was in bed, just as he had been over an hour ago. Hugh looked at his watch and it had stopped. "Seth, what's going on? Is your dad back, is Billie here? Did you see the kitchen?"

"One question at a time, but we need to have this conversation in room five, it's safe in there." Seth bent down to lift Ernest off the bed when an invisible force repelled him away from the bed and slammed him up against the far wall, knocking the wind from him.

Hugh rushed to Seth and helped him up. "Let's just get out of here. We'll come back for Ernest." As they left the bedroom, the door slammed shut behind them.

"Why can't I get into Bo's room?" Gwen said in the corridor.

Hugh went and comforted Gwen. "We can't get Ernest out either."

"We need to return to the safe room. I think Sophia needs to perform the exorcisms before we'll be able to take them anywhere. If you all can wait in there, I'll help Sophia," Casey said.

Hugh thought Casey and Sophia had wisdom beyond their years, but he doubted if he should follow them willy-nilly. Should he listen to them at all? "What are you, seventeen, eighteen?" Hugh looked at Casey. "And you're what, fifteen, sixteen?" He turned to Sophia.

He'd made a colossal mistake getting them involved. All the strange things had started when they'd arrived. Bo and Ernest were fighting a strange virus, that's all. Casey and Sophia were causing this paranormal activity. Casey had stopped and started his car when he showed up at their estate. Perhaps they thought this was funny. It's got to be those two, maybe they're evil, maybe they're the devil's puppets. Uncomfortable, he moved from one leg to the other.

"Age has nothing to do with it," Casey said.

"What is it, Hugh?" Gwen said, stepping closer to him.

"Why are we listening to a bunch of teenagers? Everything is just crazy," Hugh said.

"What, you don't know?" Tim said. "We teenagers know everything. Haven't you seen the bumper stickers?"

"Tim, not now," Casey said.

"If you know about hauntings, emotional loops, and hey, let's not forget demonic possessions, and don't need our help, just say the word, and we'll leave you to it. If you haven't noticed, we *can* come and go as we please. It's only Bo and Ernest who can't," Casey said, frustrated. "I'm sure Sophia would be happy to jump into the camper van with me and get the hell out of the city."

"We shouldn't argue," Sophia said. "Let's go into the safe room. Hugh, Gwen, go back to your apartment and try to remove Bo. See if you can bring her back. But if you can't, then you listen to us, and do as I say. Then maybe, just maybe, we will all get out of this alive."

"Hugh, they weren't here when the kitchen became a war zone …" Gwen said.

Seth stepped forward. "What happened in the kitchen?"

Hugh looked at them all. They were all young adults; he shouldn't be thinking of them as a bunch of teenagers. If God needed instruments, these two would be pure of heart. It was the boy Alex who had guided him to them, and deep down he knew they had a special connection with a life force he wasn't privy to.

"Okay, it might be futile, but I've got to try to get Bo out of that room. If I can't … I'll do whatever you tell me to," Hugh said.

They all went into the safe room.

"The negative energy in the hallway was causing friction between us," Sophia said once they were inside. "Go, Hugh. Do what you have to do, but hurry."

"I'm going with you," Gwen said. "She's my daughter."

"Stay here, please," Hugh said. "I'll be right back."

Hugh didn't wait for Gwen to answer, or check to see if she was following him. Determined, he stormed into Bo's room. The sound of his watch echoed in his mind, distracting him. He forgot what he was there for. The bedroom door squeaked closed. Bo sat up in bed, watching his every move.

"It's so nice you came back for us. It's time to put the dolls to sleep again and complete the surgical explorations." Hugh inspected the room. Gwen must have opened the curtains and the window. A warm breeze entered the room, reminding him it was spring. The curtain flapped and moved in time with the ticking of his watch.

Drowsy, Hugh said, "Bo, honey, there's no time to play doctors, we need to go because …" He couldn't remember why, but he sensed it had been urgent. It was a beautiful day outside. "Why don't we go outside?"

"No, not outside. The light will hurt your eyes and there is work to be done. Help me, Hugh, then we'll go outside."

* * *

As soon as he'd seen the dolls lying flat in the shoeboxes, he'd had a sense of déjà vu and searched his memory for a similar image. He felt he has seen these dolls before, and the rocking chair. The old porcelain doll with the wonky eye and frizzled hair was staring at him with her one beady eye. She had a name, but for the life of him he couldn't remember what it was. Even the warm breeze drifting through the window seemed familiar. Déjà vu had never felt so real to Hugh before. Bo climbed out of bed and stood next to him whilst he was daydreaming. He hadn't noticed her get up. She tugged his hand, and guided him down onto the floor in front of the dollhouse. He crossed his legs, still mesmerized by the warm breeze and the filthy doll on the rocker.

"Where's your mother, Bo?" Hugh asked, staring at the doll.

"Downstairs with Eleanor and Patricia having dinner – bread and soup."

He looked deep into her eyes and said, "What soup and bread?" There was something gnawing at him, a thought or a memory he was struggling to grasp.

"Come on, Hugh, stop daydreaming and help me," Bo said.

Hugh looked at her again as if she had said something profound about daydreaming and helping her. A warm breeze touched his face again. He looked back at Bo, then glanced at the ceiling – the spiders. "Oh, no," he said, getting up off the floor. "This is just a dream. I'm trapped inside another nightmare."

I have to wake up; I have to wake myself up.

"Maybe if you jump from the window you'll wake up," Bo said.

"That's possible. Like when you're exhausted, and you feel yourself falling, just before you drift into sleep, then you jolt awake in fright."

Bo encouraged him to move. "Yeah, just like that. Let's do it!

Can you feel the lovely breeze coming from the window? Maybe we could go downstairs and play outside for a while first. It's so beautiful out there. It was such an icy winter. But now the sun is shining. Wouldn't it be nice to be in the sunshine again?" Bo smiled at the doll.

Hugh shivered and rubbed his arms, trying to stay warm.

"You can go into the sunshine to warm up, you just need to step outside."

He shivered at the front door of the tavern and couldn't remember walking down the stairs. He was so cold, but the breeze on his face felt warm. Bo reached up and took his forearm, forcing him to stop hugging himself for warmth and take her hand instead.

She walked him to the door. "Before you go out, why don't we put a rope around your waist and if you get scared, you could find your way back just like when you went into the whiteout and the jackals attacked the other men, but not you."

Hugh recalled the sound of the dogs tearing apart the other men who had entered the whiteout with him that day they first woke up. "Okay," he said. Bo smiled at him, and he knew the rope was already around his body. "I'm not sure if I want to go outside anymore. What if the jackals are outside?"

"They won't be, silly, it's just a dream, remember, you said so."

He massaged the back of his neck. Everything was wrong. He wasn't sure if he was dreaming or if it was real. Maybe there was no apocalypse after all and he had gone insane, locked up in a mental institution. Hugh thought the latter was the best outcome he could get. "It's got to be a dream, and I have to wake the hell up!"

"Hell is already awake, Hugh," the sound of Bo's voice was like a melody.

Hugh stood in the open doorway of the tavern and felt the warmth of the sun. "Bo, are you coming, maybe we can wake up together?"

"Later. I have to finish my important work. It's very important I understand what's inside everyone's body, and what's inside the brain."

"Why, Bo?"

"Because I'm a man of science. I'm a doctor."

"What?"

The tavern changed into a morgue and Bo transformed into a young professional gentleman wearing an apron over his waistcoat, his shirtsleeves rolled up to his elbows. The man focused on dissecting a cadaver. Blood covered his apron and hands – he wasn't wearing gloves. Blood was draining from the body into a trough. Nothing was hygienic.

"Hand me the clamp so I can open up your brain," Bo said to Hugh as he stood at the side of the operating table.

The doctor stared at him. "What are you waiting for, man? Get a move on," said Bo's voice.

Hugh avoided eye contact, not sure where to look. It was weird seeing the man but hearing Bo's voice.

"If you want to understand medicine, you need to focus."

It was very primitive, unhygienic; it was incredible that they called it medicine. There was a knock at the door. The man took off his apron and pulled down his waistcoat, but left his sleeves rolled up to his biceps, as he wiped his hands on a piece of linen from under the body on the table before he checked the time on his fob watch. "I dare say it will be the delivery from Miss Amelia. I'll make haste."

It was Hugh's chance to escape. He rattled the door handle. The door stuck. The doctor had locked him in. He looked down at the body. The head was bald; the face was gray and the torso flabby; it didn't resemble him at all.

The doctor was quick to return. He carried a potato sack and placed it on a table. The contents spilled out, and he arranged the dead babies in a row.

"That woman, Miss Amelia, is getting too big for her britches. I think it's time we alerted the authorities after her next delivery. We'll still have the grave robbers."

I'm having a nightmare within a nightmare.

"Where's the tavern, where's the tavern?" Hugh said.

The doctor picked up a handkerchief and a brown medicine bottle. "You won't be going anywhere."

"What ..." In an instant Hugh was lying naked and flat on the table. He was the body on the table. The doctor covered him with a linen sheet. Hugh shivered. He tried to move, but Doc strapped his head and hands to the table.

The doctor clamped the handkerchief over Hugh's mouth and nose. "Don't fight it. The chloroform will put you to sleep, you shouldn't feel any pain, when you wake up you will remember nothing," The doctor said.

The chloroform didn't knock him out straight away; he had a chance, but the doctor pressed the handkerchief harder against Hugh's nose and mouth. The doctor punched him with his free hand in the stomach, forcing him to take in a deep breath, filling his lungs with the sweet-smelling chloroform, then before he could blink he was standing at the threshold of the tavern feeling the warm breeze on his neck.

Bo stood beside him in her filthy nightgown and reached out her hand to him. "Come play with me, Hugh."

He could still smell the sweet drug travelling to his brain. "Okay, it will be good for me to get some fresh air. I need to clear my head."

"Okay, you don't want to miss the sun before it goes down."
Bo tugged on the rope. "I've got you," she said.

As soon as Hugh stepped out into the warm air, he felt the
rope around his neck. It was too late to stop the momentum of
the fall; he had stepped off Bo's window ledge on the second
floor. His stomach fluttered and weightlessness filled his chest.
He wasn't waking up. Pain shot through his body as he jolted to
a stop a few feet from the ground. The rope had drawn tight
around his neck. *Wake up!*

21

CASEY: LEAP OF FAITH

"He's taking too long," Casey said. "I'll go and check."

"I'll come with you," Gwen said.

"Me too," Tim said.

"Everyone just stay put. Okay?" Casey said, stepping over the line of salt.

He walked down the center of the hallway, staying focused on Gwen's apartment. He could feel things were about to go from bad to worse, fast.

Casey knocked on Bo's bedroom door. He twisted the knob and pushed the door. "Hugh, are you in there?" He couldn't open the door. Casey threw himself against it, driving his shoulder into the door, but it wasn't any good, it wouldn't open. Dark energy drifted under the door. Something terrible was happening on the other side of that door.

"Hugh, Bo! Open this door!" This time he feared Hugh wouldn't be curled up in a ball, sleeping like a kitten in front of the doll's house. Danger and urgency fired all of Casey's senses as he heard the bedroom window open, and a clatter as if someone had climbed on to the ledge. He went to the window in the living room. His heart was racing at the thought of sticking his head out of the second-story window. His head spun, and he crumbled to the floor. He clenched his ear as the panic attack filled his ears with the sound of chiming bells.

The bedroom door bust open. Bo was laughing and pointing at him from within her room as she watched him squirm in pain. With lightning speed Bo moved to the top of the bedroom doorway and hung from the ceiling on all fours, peering down at him. "Scared of heights, are we?" She laughed and laughed.

Casey forced himself to reach for the window frame and drag himself up. He squeezed his eyes tight shut, stuck his head out, then opened his eyes wide. Hugh was hanging inches off the ground and grappling with the rope above his head, trying to free the tension around his neck. Within a second Casey channeled his energy towards Hugh and levitated him up, releasing the tension on the rope. He floated Hugh towards him. Casey leaned further out the window. Hugh was an arm's length away. He was alive, but the rope was still tight around his neck.

"Duck," Casey said as he went to step back from the window to guide Hugh's body through it, but he didn't have time to step back. Hands wrapped around his thighs from behind and tilted him out the window.

The night wind pushed against his face and through his hair. He directed his energy to the ground, repelling himself from crashing down. He hovered inches above the road.

Casey raised his hands with open palms as he embraced Hugh in waves of energy, preventing the rope from going taunt and snapping his neck. He rose to meet Hugh. Hugh's face was a deep purple. Casey pulled the dagger from its holster and cut away the rope before lowering him to the ground. Hugh pulled the rope off his neck and sat in the middle of the road, holding onto Casey's shoulder, coughing. Casey scrutinized the second-story window. Eleanor watched him with one eye open, the other socket was hollow just like the doll Miss Amelia.

"We have to get back inside. Eleanor just tried to kill me!" Casey touched the dagger at his thigh. He wasn't sure if he had the stomach to stab Eleanor, but he had to do something before she hurt anyone else. If he wanted to destroy the demon that was using her body like a puppet, he would have to use the dagger. The book had said: *You must drive the dagger through the heart of the possessed to free the soul and banish the demon.*

"We have to free her soul," Casey said, and reached under Hugh's arm to help him to his feet. He was still coughing and holding the back of his neck. Hugh's neck was red and looked painful. The rope had cut into his skin.

"You alright?" Casey asked.

Hugh tried to speak. He was having difficulties.

"Can you talk?"

In a hoarse voice Hugh said, "What – the – hell? I don't know – how much more – I can take. These – aren't – my problems." He rubbed his neck and stomped on the rope as if it was a serpent.

"There's no going back now, Hugh," Casey said.

Dark, smoky black spots appeared in the air along the street. Casey watched them expand until ghosts from the past littered the modern streets. They multiplied and were from different eras. Casey didn't know what century he was witnessing. It was all happening at once. He wished he knew more about London and its past. There was no space between time periods. He saw apparitions of cars driving through apparitions of ghosts riding horses and carts. Men rode tall penny-farthing bicycles with giant front wheels through trams. One second it was daytime, and the next it was night. The seasons rotated in a blink from spring, to summer, to fall, to winter. He was getting nauseous from the constant changes as history collapsed into one time frame; it felt like he was spiraling in a whirlpool of history.

He looked down to focus his eyes, trying to get some perspective. He needed to make sure he and Hugh stayed inconspicuous. Most of what he witnessed was emotional energy, memories, but some pockets were deep black, and a tingle raced up his spine as evil took form. Everything turned gray – he shouldn't have focused in on the negativity. Color melted away from the streets. Men harassed and bullied women of the night. Casey hoped to stay under their radar. He wanted the whirlpool of time to stop. It was night again. A priest was walking down the street towards him, ringing a bell. Again, the prison door opened, and shackled together the prisoners marched towards the gallows. The warden was behind them, his hat tilted forward, casting deep shadows over his face. He wasn't alone, he walked with a woman, it was the heavy-chested woman with the babies, Miss Amelia. *I've got to move before they see me.*

"We got to get you back inside," he said to Hugh. Swirling black energies moved along the street like vultures of death behind the priest, who guided them to their next host.

Hugh pulled his collar up over his neck. "I have had so many caffeine tablets, my heart is racing. I don't understand why I keep falling asleep." His voice was hoarse.

"It's the *Homoharenae*," Casey said. "Sometimes I don't know if I'm awake when I see the apparitions or if I'm asleep having a nightmare ..."

"What's that?" Hugh asked as they stepped up onto the sidewalk.

"The Sandman."

"Isn't the Sandman supposed to sprinkle magical dust in

your eyes so you sleep well and have wonderful dreams?" Hugh said.

"Not this kind of Sandman. That one's a myth. The *Homoharenae* is real."

* * *

Hugh held onto the banister and walked up the stairs first. Casey shuddered, thinking about being touched by the forces beyond this world. Hugh pushed open the door to the safe room, and they both rushed over the boundary of salt into Sophia's sanctuary. Casey felt his head clear, and his body felt lighter. Even though Sophia's anxiety filled his solar plexus, he saw celestial lights shine from within her. It was beautiful, but it made him nervous, too.

Gwen dropped to her knees, seeing Hugh empty-handed.

"Sorry," Hugh bent down and embraced her. "I'm so sorry." He lifted her off the floor.

In a soft voice Sophia asked, "What happened?"

Casey hesitated. "Bo hung him out the window."

Gasping, Gwen held Hugh's face and with a soft touch brushed the marks on his neck.

Hugh wiped her tears away. "We will get Bo back, we'll do it their way." He coughed, pulled back from her and rubbed his neck as he tried to regain some sense of control over his emotions. "So, who do we exorcise first?"

"Here," Sophia said, handing him a glass with two fingers of holy water she had poured from the bottle on the table.

"What is it?" Hugh looked at the glass and smelled it as if it was alcohol.

"Holy water," Casey said, watching Seth move around him with the smoking thurible. He watched the white smoke drift around him and raised his arms. The gesture reminded him of being measured for a suit for his mother's funeral. It was too sad to think of his mother's funeral, so he associated the moment with being hosed down by some hazmat unit.

Seth smiled. "Sophia has shown us how to combine the elements required for the cleansing of the tavern." He held the thurible up and passed it over Casey's head before proceeding to Hugh. The smoke was grey and then turned white. There was a quick gust of wind that exited the room via the open window.

Tim was grinding two rocks together over dry batches of herbs he had arranged on the table for them all. "Sophia, do I add the blessed salt now or after I light the herbs?"

"Before, but you can do it before and after."

"It will be difficult to add it later," he said, looking at the thurible.

"Not if you're using one of the two clay bowls we got from the emporium. Put some salt in your pockets. Give some to Hugh and Gwen too," Sophia said, staring at Casey.

"I'm okay. What's your plan?" Casey asked as Sophia put salt and herbs in his pocket.

Sophia pulled away, but he could tell she wanted to stay close in his aura. He felt crazy, because he wanted to kiss her. He wanted to hold her tight and tell her how he felt.

Sophia inspected the batches of herbs on the table. "This is what we are going to do." She handed him a clay bowl already prepared. "While I do the exorcisms, you guys will cleanse this place together, and make a pathway for us to leave as soon as the children are free of the evil spirits possessing them. Okay," she said, drawing in a big breath. "Gwen, you'll be with me while I perform the exorcism."

"No! I'll do it," Casey said, handing the bowl to Gwen.

"No, Casey. It has to be this way," Sophia said. "I want you guys to break into two teams and tackle the cleansing of the tavern. You have the book and dagger, Casey, I want you to take Tim. Hugh, you'll be with Seth."

Casey saw the way Seth and Tim glanced sideways at each other. "Why don't I go with Hugh?"

"You guys don't know how to mix the elements," Sophia said.

"Why can't Hugh be with us?" Gwen said.

"Who will watch over Ernest?" Seth said.

"I'll exercise the demon from Ernest first, Seth. I think it might be easiest." Sophia gave a nervous chuckle.

"I'll show them," Seth said.

"And I have the dagger," Casey said.

Casey could see Sophia would not argue, she was trying to conserve her energy for the battle. "Are you sure you don't want me with you?"

"You're the one who can see what is haunting the tavern. You'll know when it's safe to leave. The others will rely on you to confirm when it's good to go."

Sophia didn't wait for him to answer. She avoided his eyes, and he could feel her heart pounding as if it was his very own. She began the blessing.

"Luke 10 verse 19, *Behold, I give unto you power to tread on serpents and scorpions, and over all the power of the enemy: and nothing shall by any means hurt you.* Ephesians 6 verses 10 to 13, *Finally, my brethren, be strong in the Lord, and in the power of his might. Put on the whole armor of God, that ye may be able to stand against the wiles of the devil. For we wrestle not against flesh and blood, but against principalities, against powers, against the rulers of the darkness of this world, against spiritual wickedness in high places. Wherefore take unto you the whole armor of God, that ye may be able to withstand in the evil day, and having done all, to stand.* Amen." She picked up the thurible and packets of herbs. Gwen followed with one of the bottles of holy water.

As Gwen and Sophia went to step over the final salt boundary that lay in front of the apartment door, Casey called out to her.

"Wait, watch out for Eleanor. It's not her. She's dead, but possessed. She pushed me out the window while I was trying to save Hugh."

"We'll be careful." Sophia smiled at him.

Instead of watching her leave, he took out his dagger and rubbed it with blessed salt for good measure.

THE PACKET of herbs in one pocket and the salt in the other weighed down Casey's jacket, and made it feel uneven. He didn't want to put his hand in his pocket in case the heat from his palms liquidized the blessed salt. Hugh carried the bowl and recited the chants Tim had taught them – they had both written them on their forearms. So far, so good. In the bar and restaurant, within seconds the smoke had changed from gray to white. A faint clang of metal against metal came from the downstairs. Casey brushed his face against his rolled-up sleeve at the elbow. He unzipped his jacket with one hand as they descended the creaky stairs into the basement.

The glow of the burning herbs turned Hugh's shadow into a giant. Casey felt the pressure of the dead all around him like a crowded, steamy room. He coughed and turned his head. Gray smoke drifted over Hugh's shoulder into his face. The sweet smell of herbs turned sour and stung his nostrils – it was thick at the back of his throat. Casey turned on his torch to drive away the haunting shadows. Miss Amelia stormed past, Casey pressed his body against the wall, and sucked in his stomach as she raced up the stairs – she smelled of burning old tires. He wondered if she was running from them, or to Bo. Had Sophia already started the exorcism?

Entering the depths of the basement, the herbs in the bowl sparked and popped as they passed the crowded cells. Casey watched Hugh sprinkle salt into the bowl and the embers glowed brightly. The energy in the basement was getting lighter, the smoke turning from black to gray. Casey relaxed a little. He had his bottle of holy water ready. Most of the ghosts and entities left in a burst of light that turned to falling luminescent dust. He side-stepped to avoid getting any of the dust on him. It surprised Casey how easily the herbs, minerals, and prayers moved the ghosts from this realm to wherever they belonged.

Out of the corner of his eye, he could see a mass moving across the ceiling. He put his hand on Hugh's shoulder for him to stop. Casey gingerly raised his torch beam up to the ceiling. Something big shied away from the light, and scurried down the corridor and around a bend.

"What was that?" Hugh said.

"Let's keep going and finish up," Casey said.

As soon as the words were out of Casey's mouth, he could hear the thudding pounding of four legs, or more, racing along the ceiling. It wasn't a ghost; it was solid. A great mass was heading straight for them. Casey felt the essences of the herbs, prayers, and holy water might not be enough to hold it back. He stepped in front of Hugh and aimed the torch like a gun to penetrate the darkness and reveal the demon. It was Eleanor on all fours. The demon controlling her had bent her legs and arms out of shape and her head was upside down, her chin at the top and her eyes at the bottom.

"It's Eleanor!" Hugh yelled, peering around Casey. "How the ...?" He stepped back, away from the creature.

"It's not her, she's the demon's puppet," Casey said. Eleanor twisted her head the right way up and was poised to jump. Casey raised his hand and pushed her back with his mind. The demon floated in mid-air under his control. He thrust his head and hand downward, pinning the creature to the ground. It squealed and squirmed as if in pain. The body snapped in and out of shape. Bile bubbled from her contorted mouth. The bones in her face distorted. The sound of her bones breaking echoed through the basement.

"Far out, this can't be happening!" Hugh said, spraying the holy water over the creature.

It wriggled to be free. "Add more herbs and salt to the bowl, and add another myrrh cake," Casey instructed.

The bowl in Hugh's hand sparked and burst into flames.

"Don't drop it," Casey said.

Eleanor's face was completely distorted in anger and pain. Her body was no longer identifiable as human.

The mind power pouring out of Casey through his third eye became visible waves of electromagnetic energy. His head hurt. He had to do something, or his head was going to explode. Casey removed the dagger from the pouch. Eleanor didn't look like a spider or some other unrecognizable creature, but he couldn't help thinking she was still in there. This was real, he wasn't sleeping, he was wide awake, and he would have to stab her in the heart. The sound of her racing heart filled his head.

"What are you waiting for? She's already dead. That thing is not Eleanor," Hugh said.

Casey stepped closer. She reached out for him. He raised the dagger above his head and drove it through her back and into her heart. "With the power of Almighty, I pierce you demon with the blade of judgment, and you shall be no more, and this woman Eleanor's soul will be free, and it is done, in the name of the Father, the Son and the Holy Spirit, Amen."

He twisted the ancient dagger into her chest. The creature howled and wailed. He pushed down, keeping the pressure on the dagger until Eleanor went limp. Casey knew the beast was in pain, he knew it felt agony, but for the first time in a long time, Casey couldn't feel the pain or the agony as it died. The dagger and the medallion of Saint Benedict protected him. The demon exited her body and turned to ash. Casey and Hugh kneeled by Eleanor's body. Casey took the bottle of holy water from Hugh, tipped some holy water onto his finger and made the sign of the cross on Eleanor's forehead, and said a prayer.

"Blessed are you O Lord, grant Eleanor eternal rest, let everlasting light shine upon her, and may her soul and all the souls of the departed, here in this space, through the mercy of God, may they rest in peace. In the name of the Father, the Son, and the Holy Spirit, Amen."

Together they moved the broken body into a cell and covered it with an old tarp.

Casey was feeling the weight of his emotions pressing down on him until his whole body ached. He wondered if he should just blast everything away. Taking in a few deep breaths, he called on his life power to repel every entity, poltergeist, ghost, and demon for miles around with the force of his energy – then stopped. It was no use. He would only push them aside. It might not be so crazy to think one day, somehow, they would have to deal with the whole of haunted London, just as they had done in the country. Maybe if they didn't, they would be the next victims.

"Come on," Hugh said. "Let's get back upstairs to the people we care about."

"I'm with you," Casey said, and took the lead, calling out the ritual as he walked to the end of the basement. "In the name of God the Father, the Son, and the Holy Spirit, Lord hear our prayers and shine down the power of thy blessings into this place and purify, with thy grace and mercy, to dispel sickness, so the unclean may be clean, turn darkness into light, and bring freedom from every harm, as so no evil spirit or lost soul or disease may remain. Forever and ever, Amen."

He saw the ghost of every criminal from the past, including weeping widows and abandoned children. They all disappeared into multiple sparks of light, or whispers of smoke and ash, until the basement was clean and empty of dark and lost entities. Casey knew what it was like to feel the absence of someone's soul, and remembered the sorrow and emptiness he had felt when his mother's soul had left the world. Today that same feeling was comforting.

"Let's go. We're done here." The weight of the books in his backpack from the Hallow Curative Emporium was digging into his shoulders. Next, they needed to find out how to draw out the *Homoharenae* and destroy it. Casey's body was becoming heavy, he wanted to lie down and rest. He searched his pocket for caffeine pills, but he was out. He pinched his nose and rubbed his eyes.

"When we get back to the safe room, I want us to spend some time figuring out how to destroy the *Homoharenae* and execute it," Casey said, dropping his voice to a whisper.

22

_____

SOPHIA: EXORCISM OF ERNEST

S ophia whipped around to Gwen. "Oh, no, I forgot to do something. Help me, quick, find a glass bowl and a white towel."

"I have a glass bowl in my apartment, so Patricia should have one too. Check the kitchen cupboards under the breakfast bar," Gwen said, moving towards the linen closet near the front door.

How could I forget to cleanse my hands? I've watched Joe do it a hundred times. Sophia searched the lower cupboards for a glass bowl and found one on the bottom shelf. She filled it with tap water, and placing it on the bench facing what she hoped was east, added seven drops of holy water. Gwen placed the folded hand towel next to the bowl. Sophia lit the herbs in the bowl and placed it in the thurible. Three times she poured water over each side of her hands with the water from the glass bowl, and then dried them with a white hand towel. The smoke trailed from the thurible and she waved the smoke into her face and breathed deep. With her head tilted back, she felt discomfort in her neck.

She raised her hands up high and closed her eyes. "Dear God, take this as a symbol of my desire to cleanse myself of all impurities, so I may be worthy of your guidance. The Lord redeemeth the soul of his servants: and none of them that trust in Him shall be desolate. Amen."

A bell tolled. It echoed inside her head. Sophia covered her ears. *Not a good sign,* she thought. *The wailing woman and the bell both foretell death. I hope I can save both Ernest and Bo.* Cringing from the sound and trying to stay focused, Sophia imagined white light surrounding her and the childlike energy of her sisters dancing in the golden fields back home. The chimes faded.

"Ready?" she said to Gwen.

"No. But I don't think I ever will be." Anxious, Gwen twirled her hair and kept looking over her shoulder.

Sophia fixed her eyes on Ernest's closed bedroom door. Gwen's movements distracted her, and she wondered if Gwen was the right choice. When Casey finished cleansing the tavern, he would come to her. He would help her with Bo's exorcism. The thought comforted her. Casey was her angel, her reason for living.

Butterflies filled her stomach, and her heart was pounding. Sophia dropped her shoulders and pulled them back; it felt like wings emerging from her spine. The doorknob was cold.

Darkness filled the room. The air was frigid, thick and stale. Sophia radiated light into the room. The bedsheets had fallen off Ernest onto the floor, and his shirt was wide open, exposing bony ribs. His little lungs expelled frosty, rancid air. Gwen shivered, her hands shaking as she created a space on top of Ernest's chest of drawers for Sophia to lay out her tools. Sophia got the feeling Gwen didn't want to look at Ernest. He was frail with pus-filled blisters on his face, brow and the back of his hands.

"Thank you," Sophia said. She hugged her coat to her body gratefully. She searched for her necklace, to pull it out and lay it outside her clothes with Penelope's web of protection facing outward when she remembered she had given it to Casey for his protection. Sophia slipped her hand inside her coat and drew out her flask of holy water. In one hand the metal flask was freezing, and in her other hand the Bible channeled warmth and comfort. She kissed her Bible, swallowed, drew in a deep breath, and proceeded to Ernest's bedside reciting the Lord's Prayer.

Sophia looked into Ernest's gray face. He panted faster as she drew closer. The bed vibrated and the glass in the window frame rattled.

"Sorry if this hurts, but you'll feel well in no time," Sophia said to Ernest, hoping he could hear her.

She showered him with holy water. Steam rose off his body. Cuts and welts appeared over his arms, face, and neck. "Blessed are you, oh Lord, cleanse the body before me of all forms of evil and return the soul of Ernest," Sophia returned the flask to her inside pocket and took the thurible from the dresser. She waved it above his body. "Return his youthful spirit renewed by the power of the Holy Trinity, Amen." Sophia made the sign of the cross over Ernest's body.

Gwen tried to suppress a cough as she took the thurible from Sophia. Her hands were shaking, from the cold or fear, Sophia didn't know which. Ashes spilled over the floor as Gwen removed the bowl from inside the thurible. She scooped up the waiting fresh batch of herbs and minerals and placed them in the bowl. Sophia held Gwen's hand until it steadied, then sprinkled the salt over the top before replacing it back inside the thurible. The rattling of the windows intensified as if a gale-force wind was blowing.

"We can do this," Sophia said.

She spoke loudly over the noise, reciting the ritual of exorcism. Against an unseen force, she dragged the thurible from the top of Ernest's body down to his feet and across his chest before giving it to Gwen. "Take the thurible and cover every inch of this room until the smoke turns white. Don't miss an inch."

Ernest's body rose from the bed. Sophia had experienced the phenomena of levitating, but it wasn't because evil dwelled inside her. She dwelled in the light, and the smell of sweet-perfumed incense had filled her senses. Darkness bound Ernest. He was possessed by unclean spirits or demons. She wished Casey was with her to describe the entities in the room. She splashed the holy water over Ernest again, but he kept rising. His body flopped. The holy water slashed the exposed parts of his legs and arms. His back arched and she worried his spine would snap.

She splashed the water over Ernest again and shouted out, "In the name of God, the Father, the Son, and the Holy Spirit, Lord hear our prayers, drive the evil from this child, and shine down the power of thy blessings into this place and purify, with thy grace and mercy, to dispel sickness, so the unclean may be clean, turn darkness into light, and bring freedom from every harm, so no evil spirit or lost soul or disease may remain. Forever and ever, Amen."

Ernest's body floated down onto the soiled bed. A whirlwind of sadness and evil reached out and touched Sophia's heart. She tensed in pain.

Sophia witnessed a dark mass, casting itself in the shape of a human, brace against the wall, pulling back from the billowing smoke as Gwen held the thurible above her head. Sophia raced to the corner and splashed the evil entity with holy water. "God, our Father in heaven, have mercy on us."

Sophia turned her attention to Ernest.

Gwen fumbled, trying to scoop out the bowl in the thurible to add fresh herbs and minerals. "They're burning too fast!"

"Holy Mother of God, holy virgin of virgins, St. Michael, St. Gabriel, St. Raphael, all holy angels, and archangels, all holy orders of blessed spirits ..." The screams of children laughing and giggling filled Sophia's head. They screamed with fear and joy. The sound of rope slapping on the dirt filled her ears. An image of two girls turning a skipping rope around and around filled her mind. The rope arched upwards, and a girl ran into the middle, jumping over the rope as it hit the ground while her friends turned the rope in rhythm with their song:

Oranges and lemons,
Say the bells of St. Clement's.
You owe me five farthings,
Say the bells of St. Martin's.
When will you pay me?
Say the bells of Old Bailey ...

Hypnotized by the turning rope slapping on the ground, Sophia stopped reading from the Bible and rocked back and forth. The temperature of her body fell as she studied the three girls. They wore identical clothing: black polished sandals, white knee-high socks, and white party dresses with a red sash around the waist. Like a camera lens Sophia zoomed in on the skipping girl's face. It was Bo. The dresses she and her friends wore were the same as the ones Patricia had made. Sophia's vision zoomed out. She thought she could hear the ticking of a clock.

Sophia had to drive the images and the bewitching nursery rhyme away. She shouted to hear her own voice. "All holy patriarchs and prophets, holy disciples of the Lord, all holy martyrs, be merciful, spare us, Lord. Hear us, Lord. From all evil, deliver us, Lord ..." Her heart quickened, her body twitched as if she had fallen between sleeping and waking. She jolted into alertness.

The smoke had died out. Gwen was on the floor. The rhythm of the skipping was hypnotizing her. She dragged her focus her back to Ernest.

Gentle as a warm summer breeze, Father McDonald filled her being. Her body tingled with the loving essences of his spirt. He recited to her Peter 5 verse 8, *"Be sober, be vigilant; because your adversary the devil, as a roaring lion, walketh about, seeking whom he may devour."* Sophia picked up her Bible from the floor.

Father McDonald continued to read, and she read from Luke chapter 10 along with his familiar voice: *"Behold, I give unto you, power to tread on serpents and scorpions, and over all the power of the enemy: and nothing shall by any means hurt you, standing in this rejoice not, that the spirit is subject unto you, but rather rejoice, because your names are written in heaven.* Amen."

The chest of drawers toppled over, and the herbs and minerals fell to the bedroom floor. Exhausted, Sophia wiped the sweat off her brow and took a sip of holy water. She returned to the foot of Ernest's bed and continued to clean the unclean spirits from Ernest, reading from Mark chapter 16:

"He that believes and is baptized shall be saved; but he that believes not, shall be damned. And these signs shall follow them that believe; in my name shall they cast out devils; they shall speak with new tongues; they shall take up serpents; and if they drink any deadly thing, it shall not hurt them; they shall lay hands on the sick, and they shall soon recover. Amen."

Sophia placed her hands on Ernest's body and said, "By the power of God I cast you out, demon!"

Ernest exhaled and a thick black mist spiraled out from his mouth. In a whirlpool of energy, it fled through the ceiling. The visible welts and gashes on Ernest's face, neck, and arms vanished. His cheeks turned rosy red. Sophia remained on guard; she had expected more of a fight.

"Are you alright?" She turned to Gwen, who was still on the floor, looking shocked and horrified. Sophia leaned down to help her up. The window had stopped rattling. The black energy had vanished, the turmoil in the air subsided and the curtains stopped fluttering.

"I'm okay," Gwen said. "Is that what is inside my baby girl?"

"Let's hope not," Sophia said, and rubbed her eyes.

Ernest's breathing was easing, relaxing. In a split second, he sat bolt upright, crying.

Gwen rushed went to him and held him tight.

Sophia held back her tears. She needed to stay strong for Bo. She was so very grateful Father McDonald had come to her aid. *Thank you, father.* The darkness in the room lifted, and the air smelled of the burning herbs. She felt bathed in the light of God. She dropped to her knees, closed her eyes, and gave thanks.

Seth and Tim ran into the room, jolting Sophia. Seth went to Ernest.

"Are you alright?" Tim crouched beside her.

When she didn't answer, he held her in his arms. "Come on, Sophia, you've got this."

She opened her eyes and smiled at him.

"Billie found her father. He's a mess, he looks like the jackals got to him, but he's still alive. They're in the back seat of Hugh's car, ready to go whenever you are."

"Will Ernest be okay?" Seth asked Sophia, taking over from Gwen.

"He should be fine now. If we're lucky, he might not remember what happened, but he could still have nightmares for a while. Take him and leave now," Sophia said. Her mouth was so dry and her stomach rumbled. She took out her flask and had a few sips of holy water.

Gwen stepped away from Ernest. "No, they can't leave without us!"

"Have you cleared a pathway?" Sophia said.

"Yes, I think so," Tim said

"Then go. Don't wait for us. It's important you don't stop for anything. Get him out of here," Sophia said.

Seth picked up his brother. Ernest couldn't stop crying. He wrapped his legs around Seth's waist and his arms around his neck and buried his head in the nape of his neck.

"Tim, I want you to go with them," said Sophia.

"No, my place is with you. I have to help you. When you leave, I leave," Tim said.

"No, you're going. Get them as far as possible from the city. Take the rest of this bottle of holy water. Let Ernest sip it until it's finished," Sophia said, shivering.

Tim took his jacket off and removed his sweater. He handed it to Sophia and put his jacket back on. "You need it more than me."

He held her coat while she put his sweater on over the white top from the emporium. "If you get back to the estate, and by some slim chance Kevin's back, ask him to take Ernest through the portal membrane and heal Ernest's emotional pain. Then get him to open a portal and come back for us if we're not back, but Casey, Gwen, Bo, Hugh and I will be only an hour behind."

"Why don't we just wait for you outside the city?" Tim said.

Sophia moved Tim out the door and into the hallway behind Seth. "Don't wait, please leave. Take turns driving with Seth. Don't stop for anything." She led them down the stairs.

"Why the urgency?" Tim said.

"I might need to level this place."

Tim hugged her and kissed her on the cheek. "I'll see you soon."

Seth opened the back door of Hugh's car and handed Ernest to Billie. He ran back and hugged Sophia. "Thank you. I won't forget what you've done for my brother. I owe you one."

Sophia was feeling light-headed.

"You need to eat something before the next exorcism," Seth said.

"I can't eat. I need to keep my vessel empty so the universe can fill me with the light of God. I'll eat when all this is over. Now go."

23

CASEY: HOMOHARENAE

Impatient, Casey followed Hugh out of the basement. Even though he had cleansed the ghosts and energy in the basement, he still refused to touch the walls going up the stairs. There would be memories still lodged inside them that he did not care to feel.

"Hurry, Hugh. Why are you moving so slowly?" Casey felt his legs sinking into each step. "What's taking you so long? We have to get back to Sophia and Gwen, they need our help."

No sooner had he spoken, he found himself on the stairs heading up to the apartments. Seth, carrying Ernest, rushed past. Ernest's emotional pain filled Casey as their arms touched.

"Where are you going?" Casey cried out after Seth.

Sophia and Tim were at the top, heading down the stairs.

"What happened? Is he okay?" Casey said to Sophia.

They ran straight past him.

Casey lost his balance and tilted over the edge of the banister. "What the hell?"

Hugh reached out and caught him. "What's going on?" Hugh said, amazed.

Ernest looked over Seth's shoulder at Casey and Hugh before Seth carried him out the tavern door. He was free to leave. *She did it,* Casey thought.

Hugh looked back at Casey. "Sophia must've completed the exorcism. But why are they ignoring us?"

"I don't know," Casey said, concerned.

Out in the street, Hugh's car started. Casey tried to turn around and go after Sophia, but he couldn't move his legs. He grabbed onto his pants at the knees and pulled at his legs. It was no use, his legs were sinking into the step.

"What the hell? What is this?" Hugh said, struggling. The lower portion of his legs had disappeared.

"Quicksand!" It was up to Casey's knees. Hugh grabbed hold of the banister, trying to pull himself up and over the rail, but he only sank deeper.

"Stop struggling!" Casey said, watching Hugh submerge to the hips.

The patterns on the carpet swirled up like colored sand in an hourglass, defying gravity. It whirled around them, up to their necks, crushing their bodies. The overhead light changed to a dull yellow glow, and shadows crept in from all sides.

His nose and mouth went under the step, but before his head submerged Casey heard the crack of a whip. As he fell through the floor he reached out and grabbed hold of Hugh. He linked his arm with Hugh's and stopped their descent into nothingness. Darkness blinded them as they hovered. Casey, in control, continued the descent. He felt his chest rising and falling – at least he was breathing – but he longed to feel the ground under his feet. Casey's aura expanded, trying to sense what was around them, but felt only nothingness. He swallowed his rising hysteria; he didn't know where they would end up.

Like at the peak of a roller coaster, his stomach dropped when he saw the silhouette of buildings. Their speed increased and the walls of the buildings rushed past them. They smacked down into the middle of a street. Casey felt a punch from inside his chest and his heart palpitated as he coughed and coughed.

"Where are we?" Hugh said. "Why aren't we dead?" He looked up into the starless night.

"I don't know." Casey stopped coughing and cleared his throat.

"By the design of the buildings, it could be the late seventeen- or eighteen-hundreds? Have we gone back in time?" Hugh got up and dusted dirt and mud off his clothes.

It smelled like manure to Casey.

A horse pulling a cart headed down Old Bailey behind Hugh. Casey shoved Hugh out of the way just as the cart toppled over onto two wheels, missing them.

"What the hell? Where did that come from?" Hugh said.

"You saw it?" Casey said, helping him up.

"Yeah, this is crazy." Hugh stepped sideways as a man with a cane rushed past, followed by a boy on a skateboard.

Casey gazed about him. The dull gas lamps spaced out along the street provided minimal relief from the evil lurking in the darkness. At the top of the street a beam of light cast a shadow over the figure of a tall man in a hat. Though he was far away, his haunting laughter echoed down the street. With a sudden burst of speed, he moved, heading for Casey.

"We're asleep, we need to wake up and get back inside the tavern before it disappears."

"Don't move," Hugh said. "Can you hear that? It's dogs or jackals."

Casey listened; he could hear them. "We still have to move. We have to get inside the tavern and back into our bodies."

They ran from the intersection into the building where the tavern should be. It had transformed into a gin palace. Their bodies lay on the stairs.

"Quick, Hugh. Get back into your body." Casey slipped back into his body and tried to wake up, but he was very drowsy, and his body was heavy as if someone had sucked the life out of him. It would be great if he could lie down and sleep for a month. Casey raised his heavy hand, slapped his face and rubbed his head, trying to clear the fogginess. Hugh slept on beside him. Casey pushed himself up. "Hugh, wake up." Casey nudged Hugh. "Hugh, wake up!"

Hugh moaned.

"Open your eyes, dammit!" Casey said.

"What's happening to us?" Hugh said.

"Come on, safe room now," Casey said, dragging himself up the stairs.

* * *

SOPHIA RADIATED light as she sat in the middle of the sacred circle of salt facing east. She was in a deep trance.

"Sophia!" Hugh said.

"Don't startle her. She's meditating. Regenerating," Casey said. "Where else can we go?"

"My apartment, this way," Hugh said.

The apartment appeared to be the same as the safe room. Casey pulled his backpack off and dropped it onto the breakfast bar. He dug into his pockets and grabbed a handful of blessed salt. The pink salt made no sound as it fell upon the carpet.

They sat down in the middle of the protective circle with

Isabella Sumer's notebook. The book seemed heavy as he dropped it in his lap. Casey unlatched the lock and flicked through the potion section.

"What are you looking for?" Hugh asked.

Casey didn't stop flicking through the pages as he spoke. "When we found this book at the emporium, we noticed there was a section on mythical creatures, and Seth pointed out a creature that looked like an image I saw in a dream. It's called the *Homoharenae*, the Sandman, and I'm hoping I can find a way to kill it. The *Homoharenae* makes you fall asleep and when you do, he draws the life force from you until you die."

"Shit. That's crazy. Is that what's been happening to us?"

"I believe it is." Casey flicked past images of creatures he never would've believed existed. He dreaded to think that if the *Homoharenae* was real, what other mythical creatures might be too. He turned the pages, and Hugh reached out his hand for him to stop.

"That's the woman we saw by the cemetery when we entered the city. The banshee," he said, reading the English translation. "Whose book is this?"

"It belongs to Isabella Sumer, the woman who owned the shop where we got the herbs and crystals; she made the flyers about the shared dream, and the portal at Stonehenge." Casey riffled through the book until he found the page about the *Homoharenae*. He studied it, trying to read the Latin before shifting to the English written at the bottom of the picture.

"There were two ways to kill it. One: *Whilst in its sand-like form, blast it with fire until it turns to glass, then shatter it into a million pieces.* Or, two: *Freeze it whilst it is in any form then shatter it to pieces.*"

"How the hell are we going to do that? If there's an icebox or freezer, we could push him in. There is a cool room at the back of the kitchen," Hugh said.

"Good idea."

"But how do we get it out of our dreams and into reality to lure it into the freezer?"

"I've got an idea. You go to sleep, and I'll meditate, so the *Homoharenae* thinks I'm sleeping, otherwise it won't show itself and approach you, but when it does, I'll be able to see him, and I'll be ready to …" Casey said.

"How will you see it?" Hugh said, scared.

"I see spirits, entities, memories, ghosts – you know that, right? I can see the energy that surrounds you. I see it change when you are near Gwen, or when you are afraid like now, and I hope I'll be able to see the *Homoharenae* too."

"What do you mean, my energy?"

"Some people call it an energy field, some call it an aura. When you're with Gwen it changes to blues, reds, and a soft pink. We don't have time for this right now."

"That's just creepy. Are you sure your parents weren't part of some government experiment, and you're not the result of some drug test?"

"Not that I am aware of, but listen, we can do this." Casey looked up at the door as if it just opened.

"I don't like your idea, it's too risky. Look what just happened. He had us both before we even left the basement," Hugh said.

"We just had a lucid dream, we had a shared dream, and I think I pulled you into my dream, and I can do it again. We have to flush him out now, or we will not get back to Sophia and Gwen. I feel like it is trying to keep us separated. I'm so scared that there's a reason it has been keeping me from Sophia."

"Okay, but what … what are we going to do again? How can

we freeze the *Homoharenae,* and how can we flush him out to freeze him?" Hugh said, rubbing the back of his neck.

"Maybe I could create a snowstorm in my dream and hope it freezes. We need to trick it."

"Okay, why not? If you can take me into your dreams, then you are in control, right?"

"Well, sort of, I seem to mesh with local history a lot. It's as if time collapses." Casey felt uncomfortable and stood and paced the circumference of the circle, searching his mind for ideas. His stomach was doing backflips. He felt he was on the verge of knowing something important, but he could not grasp what it was.

"But can you control what we do?" Hugh asked.

"Yes, I can control us, but not the environment. So, a snowstorm is out of the question."

"But you're going to govern my consciousness and unconsciousness. That's asking a lot," Hugh said.

"What we need is an enormous bottle of wart remover." Casey sat down again.

"Liquid nitrogen?"

"Yes. We need a hardware store or a pharmacy," Casey said. "Can you guide us to one while we are in the dream state?"

"Wait! I can do better than that," Hugh said, looking excited. "Eleanor was a brilliant cook and makes some spectacular deserts with liquid nitrogen. There is a cylinder in the kitchen under the chef's bench."

"All we have to do is lure the *Homoharenae* into the kitchen and blast it with the nitrogen," Casey said. "Okay, let's go over this one more time. You'll go into a sleep state, under my control, while I'm in a meditative state. Then I will guide you into the kitchen and you pretend to be asleep within the dream, which should appeal to the *Homoharenae's* desire for your life force enough for it to materialize. I will watch over you. When it shows itself and it's out in the open, I will blast it with the liquid nitrogen."

"Okay, but will you be awake or asleep when you do that?"

"Awake, I'll be awake. Meditating so my brainwaves change to theta waves – dream state, which I hope will fool the *Homoharenae* and give me enough control over the dreamscape," Casey said.

"Well, as long as you know what you are doing, I'm in," Hugh said.

Stuffing the notebook in his backpack, Casey tried to stand, but he had pins and needles all down his legs, and moving up into his torso. He couldn't feel the bottom half of his body. He tried to step forward and collapsed. Hugh reached down to pick him up. Casey could see Hugh touching his arm, but felt nothing. Pins and needles were advancing up his chest and head. Stars filled his eyes, then darkness – he was nothing but consciousness. They were already in a dream state.

Casey had dreamed of the safe room; their bodies were still in the basement, lost in a void. He rummaged through his mind for a way back into the basement and his body. Casey called out in his mind to Sophia and Hugh, anyone he thought might hear him. He sorted through his mind, trying to create a sense of order around him, but he still could not see the way. Panic was rising inside him, accompanied by the fear of being lost in this nothingness. It was madness.

Calm down, calm down.Okay, so I'm asleep within a sleep. I'm two levels down. As soon as he thought this, a steep spiral staircase appeared in the nothingness. Casey floated towards it and stood on the bottom step, wondering where it went. He had to rise into consciousness. A different staircase came into view with steps made of ice. Casey shivered from the cold, and each step he took felt a little colder. He crouched down to hug himself, but there was no body for him to touch – he was trying to get back to his body in the basement, and he needed ice. Standing on the cold icy steps, he continued up the stairs before pausing again. If he was dreaming he could make up whatever he needed.

An image of the kitchen flashed into his consciousness, and he was standing as an ethereal body of light in the kitchen. Hugh lay on the ground next to the workbench. He almost raced over to him, to see what was wrong when he recalled their plan. Among the kitchen mess was a cylinder of nitrogen and he had to find it. The bench. Hugh had said it was under the kitchen bench, and there it was.

Making slow deliberate movements, Casey headed for the nitrogen until he saw a white figure that looked like a wet human-like salamander moving across the ground towards Hugh. Casey froze and watched the *Homoharenae*. It sniffed the air, as if it sensed Casey, but it didn't see him or know where he was. Casey floated inches above the floor. He moved to the canister and turned it on. He found the nozzle and had it pointed in the direction of the *Homoharenae* when the creature stood up, leaned over Hugh's body and sucked out his life force. The *Homoharenae* was a little too close to Hugh for Casey to spray the nitrogen. He had to get it away from Hugh. Hugh's back arched and his body looked like it was being dried out. Hugh slapped himself and wriggled around as if something was crawling over him. He was going to die if Casey didn't do something quickly.

Forcing all his energy into his ethereal body, Casey willed the hose to move. He tapped the nozzle against the canister, surprising the *Homoharenae*. It stopped sucking Hugh's life force and looked up and saw Casey shimmering. It jumped over Hugh's body and lunged towards him, but before it could reach

Casey, he aimed the hose and sprayed the *Homoharenae* with the nitrogen. It turned to glass in mid-air and crashed to the floor, smashing into a thousand pieces.

Casey ran down to the basement and saw himself and Hugh collapsed midway up the stairs. He lay down into his own body and merged back inside. Wriggling his toes and fingers, he woke up sluggish, his body heavy as if still trapped inside his nightmare – Hugh beside him, moaning. Casey shook him awake and Hugh's eyes flew open as if he had been struggling to move. He panted and slapped his body.

"Spiders, so many damn spiders," Hugh shivered. "Thank God, I thought you would never come back for me. It paralyzed me. The damn thing paralyzed me. Did you get it?" Hugh stood, swaying on his feet.

"Yeah. We got it, Hugh. Give yourself a minute," Casey said.

"We don't have a minute," Hugh said. "They were leaving, remember, when we were heading to the safe room in your dream?"

They both stumbled up the stairs for the third time, and for the first time they entered the main foyer of the bar. Casey could feel the cool air on his face coming in from outside. He stuck his head into the kitchen and saw ice and broken dishes all over the floor.

24

SOPHIA: EXORCISM OF BO

S ophia needed a minute to herself before she could start working on Bo. She entered the safe room, took off her coat and placed it on a stool at the breakfast bar. It was like taking off her heavy armor. She felt lighter, but meager, vulnerable and ungrounded. She wondered when she had become so dependent on the coat. In the past she had had no tools but the light within her, but that was when Father McDonald had cared for her.

She pulled her ankles up onto her knees and sat lotus-style in the middle of the circle of salt. "Blessed are you, Lord, Almighty God, thank you for your strength, thank you for the blessings to restore Ernest's mind, body, and spirit. I give thanks to you for my eyes that see the divine beauty in everything. I am grateful for the gift of hearing and the expressions of your voice in the sounds of nature, which sing a song to my heart, I thank you. Blessed are you Lord for the sweet fragrance of the red rose and white roses and the essence of all colors, which reflects your brilliant light that fills the world. I am nothing without you; I feel your light within me. Amen.

"The Lord is my shepherd; I shall not want. He maketh me to lie down in green pastures: he leadeth me beside the still waters. He restoreth my soul: he leadeth me in the paths of righteousness for his name's sake. Yea, though I walk through the valley of the shadow of death, I will fear no evil: for thou art with me; thy rod and thy staff, they comfort me. Thou preparest a table before me in the presence of mine enemies: thou anointest my head with oil; my cup runneth over. Surely goodness and mercy shall follow me all the days of my life; and I will dwell in the house of the Lord forever."

Opening her eyes and unfolding her legs, she stood, feeling the carpet under her soft feet. She faced east and stretched her arms, neck and legs, preparing herself for the battle ahead. The flutter of nerves calmed, and her head cleared. Now her heart once again was armored with love. She was ready.

The glass bottle, half full of holy water, reflected a beam of light from the iridescent ceiling light. Sophia hummed a hymn, replenishing her flask with holy water. She put on her coat. It pulled on her shoulders as she weighed it down with supplies. Placing sage between her gum and cheeks, she patted the top pocket confirming Father McDonald's Bible was by her heart. She pushed away from the table, her spirit rising up, strong. She found a glass bowl and washed her hands three times, one after the other, and dried them slowly on the hand towel.

Gwen entered the room and took batches of herbs and minerals for the thurible. "Are you ready? Sorry if I'm rushing you. It's, I just want to get this over with and get my daughter back. I can't imagine the trauma she is experiencing."

Sophia folded the hand towel, then focused on her body, took a deep breath and exhaled. "Let's do this." *Please God, let the exorcism of Bo be easier than Ernest.* "We're very close to going home. How is she?"

"Terrible. Very restless. Her breathing is labored. She's unconscious. Sophia, help my little girl."

"Maybe unconscious is a good sign. It could mean whatever demon has claimed her is busy elsewhere. Where's the doll?" Sophia said.

Gwen's hand flew to her mouth. "I don't know. I didn't see it."

Sophia cleansed Gwen's aura again, trying to calm her down. "Let the smoke of the sage fill your being, breathe it in and center yourself. Bo needs you to be strong."

"Where are Hugh and Casey?" Gwen asked, sounding calmer.

"A few times I've felt Casey close, but I can't open myself up to him right now, because whatever demons are in the tavern can possess me too. I'm not immune. We need to be vigilant if we want to save Bo. This is going to be tough, Gwen, I will not pretend otherwise. Any time, if it's too much for you to bear, I want you to leave the room and come back when you're centered, if you can. Don't listen to anything that comes out of Bo's mouth, it's not her. The demon will try to confuse us. When you are unsure, recite the Lord's Prayer. Can you do that?"

"Yes." Gwen blew her nose.

"Good," Sophia said.

* * *

THE BEDROOM WAS LIKE A REFRIGERATOR, the sulfur smell was strong. The lights wouldn't turn on. Sophia pushed energy into her aura, her own source of light, and illuminated the room.

"Wait," Gwen said and ran from the room. She returned with a flashlight and scented candles. Gwen placed the herbs, holy water, rock salt, myrrh cakes and matches in a row along her daughter's chest of drawers as she'd done in Ernest's room. Her hands trembled. She was like a frightened nurse laying out a surgeon's tools.

Sophia scanned the room for the doll and began sprinkling holy water from her flask while reciting the cleansing prayers. She wanted to find the doll and splash it first to get rid of the entity inside it. There was more than one entity in the room trying to claim Bo, and Sophia would have to deal with them one at a time. She could feel them creeping around her, trying to smother her light. As they brushed up against her, the hair on her arms rose, and the hair on her shoulders moved. Foul breath puffed back her fringe. Sophia blinked several times, trying to focus on a translucent figure floating in and out of her field of vision. Her senses heightened, blessed with the vision beyond the veil that was so thin it wouldn't be long until they all saw the beasts from hell and the trapped spirits of the dead. She ignored the roaming evil.

"Gwen! Ignite the thurible and cleanse the room just like you did in Ernest's room. Don't miss a single inch."

Gwen recited the cleansing prayer, and the door slammed closed.

A silence washed over Sophia, and she listened into the quietness; the crackling burning of the herbs in the thurible amplified like the sound of a bonfire.

Black smoke trailed Gwen. She screamed in pain, kicking out. Sophia shone her light at Gwen's leg. The doll had a hold, biting Gwen on the shin. Blood dripped down Gwen's leg. Before Sophia could help, Gwen dropped the thurible and grabbed the doll, ripping it from her leg. She flung it across the room, and it hit the wall with a loud thud.

Sophia went after the doll. It giggled, darting behind furniture. Sophia splashed holy water at it. It was quiet. It had stopped moving. She picked up the fallen thurible and handed it back to Gwen. The herbs were still crackling and burning within it as if it was a roaring fire.

In her mind, Sophia saw images of roaring flames. Her house, where she was born, was burning. From her cot, the screams of her sisters awoke her as they cried out from their bedrooms across the hallway. The nursery door opened and allowed thick black smoke to fill her room. Sophia stood up in the cot she was getting too big for and held onto the wooden side. The smoke was hurting her eyes; she cried and coughed, her face was streaming with tears and snot.

Bo's eyes were open. She was watching Sophia. Her mouth opened and she released a scream that came from many souls and demons. It filled the room. The windows rattled, then blew out, and Sophia was back in the image of her mind when the nursery window had blown out in the heat of the fire. She watched the fire enter the nursery through the open door. It raced along the ceiling. Within a split second, light surrounded her, and she was outside of herself. Sophia reached out her tiny hand towards the wing of an angel that sheltered her from the fire as it consumed the room. Her sisters' screams faded into silence. She had been too small to remember the day her family had died, but she had stored it in her subconscious and now it surged forward into her consciousness. *It's just a memory.*

"Now I know your weakness," Bo said in a harsh voice.

Calmness washed over Sophia. *"Fight the taunts. Remember, those in the astral plane can read you like a book, from the cradle to the grave. Don't let them get the better of you,"* Father McDonald whispered into her mind. *"Focus on the child. The demon is just trying to rattle you, stick to the Scriptures."*

Sophia stood at the foot of Bo's bed and splashed her with holy water.

The doll sprang out from under the bed and lunged up at Sophia, grabbing hold of her throat. Gwen rubbed salt on her hands and reached out for the doll. It was crazy that a doll with porcelain hands was trying to choke her. As soon as Gwen with her salted hands touched the doll, it wailed in agony. Gwen pulled the doll away from Sophia and held it at arm's length as it wriggled to free itself. Sophia made the sign of the cross with the holy water. Gwen dropped the doll as if it was burning hot and went to stomp down on its squirming body, but it combusted into flames before she could. They both jumped back. The flames died down as quickly as they came.

"Mommy?"

"That's not your daughter," Sophia said.

Bo was sitting up.

Sophia splashed the water over her.

Bo screeched. "It burns, Mommy, it burns."

"Gwen, refill yourthurible. Don't listen to her," Sophia said.

Sophia turned her attention to Bo. "Come out of her, unclean spirit, by the power of God I command thee to leave this child that belongs to the kingdom of God."

"You don't deserve to be my mommy. I hate you, I hate you, I hate you!" Bo spat at Gwen.

Gwen started crying.

"Leave the room," Sophia said.

"Yes, leave the room, Mommy." Bo giggled, and then the laughter turned into the roar of a beast.

Bo aged a hundred years. She was as gray as a corpse. "Help me."

"What's happening to her? Help her!" Gwen cried.

Sophia struggled to find the right passages in her mind. She flicked through her Bible and all the post-it notes flew out. The demon laughed. Sophia's hands were shaking. She accidently dropped the book and rushed to retrieve it.

"Mommy help me, it burns. Make her stop."

Sophia splashed holy water over Bo again. Bo's upper body fell back onto the bed, pushing into the mattress to get away from the blessed water. She squirmed and wriggled, releasing harrowing screams of pain as her skin bubbled with steam. Her body convulsed.

"Stop it!" Gwen said and put down the thurible.

"I compel you demon to leave this child and return to whatever dark hell you have spewed forth from. What is your name? Who dares to defy a servant of God?"

"No, Sophia." Father McDonald's kind voice filled her mind. *"Don't engage in conversation, for it is many, and has many names. It's not important. Drive it out! You can do this. If it tells you, do not repeat it out loud or even say it in your head, Sophia, or the demon will get inside you. Repeat after me ..."*

Gwen advanced towards Bo as if she was going to hold her daughter's shaking body as it lifted up off the bed.

"Don't touch her," Sophia said.

Sophia ignored Gwen's pleas to stop the exorcism and blocked out the demon inside Bo that reached out from the darkness.

"Focus on my voice," Father McDonald said, *"and repeat after me ..."*

Sophia listened and spoke " *... forthwith Jesus gave them leave and the unclean spirits went out, and entered into the swine and the herd ran violently down a steep place into the sea and were choked in the sea.* Amen."

Sophia splashed the holy water over Bo's suspended body and made the sign of the cross. "In the name of the Father, and of the Son, and of the Holy Spirit," she said. Bo's body returned to the bed.

Sophia felt as though she was in a trance. The sound of her sisters' screaming coming from Bo's mouth had stopped, but it left Sophia with incomprehensible pain and suffering.

"You are weak!" The insidious laugh of the demon echoed from inside Bo. "Ha, ha, ha, ha …" Bo sat with her legs crossed and her hands on her knees, rocking back and forth with a smile on her face, enjoying herself.

The voice sounded like a legion, and it terrified her. It laughed and laughed. She wanted to clap her hands over her ears and stop the sound of the laughter.

"You're so weak. It's pathetic. You are not a chosen one. You're fallen like the rest of us."

She had wondered a few times that day if she was one of the forgotten. Maybe Father McDonald was just a deluded old man, and she wasn't the prophet he had led her to believe.

"Look at what has become of humanity. What is there to save?" the demon counselled.

While she been collecting the herbs and minerals in the emporium, she had wondered why God had not called to her the way Isabella described in the flyer. Why had nobody at the estate had the collective dream?

"That's right, he left you behind. He abandoned you."

That's how she'd been feeling, abandoned by her sight – she could no longer see the future. She had been deserted.

Bo studied her, bemused. "Ahh."

"Sophia," Father McDonald whispered.

The book in her hand flicked opened to Luke 9 verse 42, and she read as if in a trance: " *… as he was yet a coming, the devil* *threw him down and tare him and Jesus rebuked the unclean spirit, and healed the child and delivered him again to his father.* Amen."

Sophia pulled herself out of the depths of darkness and raised her hands up high. "I am a child of God and he walks with me! Blessed are you, oh Lord, who for the salvation of humankind has built the greatest mysteries, hear our prayers and shine your blessed light through me, into this world, and into this child before me. Purify her mind, body, and soul. I pray I may be your divine agent placed in service for this very moment. Strengthen me to drive away these evil spirits and dispel the sickness within this child we call Bo. Cleanse everything in this place, let no evil or infection fall upon the living souls. Amen. Depart this world, evil demon, return from whence you came. Be gone. In the name and unity of the Holy Spirit of God – be gone. And so be it, forever and ever, Amen."

"Amen," Gwen whispered through tears.

Sophia waited. The overhead lights flickered on. Bo collapsed. Sophia had to be sure. She entered Bo's mind. It was quiet, nothing was lurking there. There did not appear to be any doors open to other realms within her. She exited Bo's mind and searched her outer energy bodies and could find no psychic holes in her aura.

"It's her."

Gwen ran to her. Sophia felt the energy changing in the room and everyday sounds returned. Casey called out to her from the other side of the door. She wondered how long he had been there.

Casey burst into the room with Hugh.

He stopped and stared at her. "What's wrong with you? You look exhausted, you're so pale. You're weak."

"Help them take Bo out of here. Let's not waste any time. I'll just be a minute," said Sophia.

"Thank you," Gwen said, clutching Bo to her chest and leaving the room.

Bo looked at Sophia over Gwen's shoulder. "Thank you."

She needed to be alone. Sophia walked back to the safe room with Casey.

25

SOPHIA: DEVIL'S TRAP

Sophia's muscles felt like Jell-O, and her arms and legs were heavy. Throbbing pain filled her head. Sharp stabbing pains radiated through her stomach – she was much too young to have an ulcer, but Mother Catherine had warned her that if she didn't stop worrying and have a little fun, she would sure as eggs end up with one. Sophia chuckled.

"Are you alright?" Casey asked.

"Yeah. Just hunger pains." She thought she would feel elated after channeling so much of God's light, which was incredible, but she felt the opposite. Heaviness, like the onset of a cold or flu, weighed her down. She collected her belongings. "I'll meet you downstairs," she said to Casey.

"Hugh and Gwen are heading to the campervan, let's go now," Casey said.

He was standing inches away, and she wanted to fall into his arms, but if she did and let go, the last of her strength would drain from her. He was so handsome; she adored his curls. Tears pooled in her eyes. The exorcisms had exhausted her.

"That's splendid news." Sophia leaned against the breakfast bar. She wanted him to leave. She didn't feel right, she needed to centre herself. It felt very important not to let him fuss over her. He needed to leave.

"Are you sure you're okay? Your energy is so low; I'll get some gummy bears from the kitchen. Maybe a sugar hit is what you need, or I can give you a zap of my energy."

"No, not this time. I have to go to the bathroom." Sophia said, removing her coat. It was so heavy and hot. She placed it on a stool at the breakfast bar. She was burning up.

"I'll wait," Casey said. He looked very concerned and agitated.

"I'll be fine, women's problems. I'll be down in a few minutes."

He pursed his lips as if trying not to speak, reluctant to go. "If you're not downstairs in three minutes, I'll come back."

Casey left the apartment door open. Something had disturbed the circle of blessed salt across the threshold and broken the protective seal. She grabbed her stomach and tried to walk to the bathroom. Her knees buckled. She caught herself falling. Braced against the wall, Sophia slid down to catch her breath. She felt the need to purge. She gagged, her throat tightened, and she broke out in a sweat. Her stomach rippled. "Dear God, what is happening to me?" She coughed into her elbow and blood splattered over her white sleeve. She pushed herself up. The walls were cold under her steaming hands. Her breathing was labored as she shuffled towards the bathroom. She stopped, feeling faint. Her feet were burning, she had to keep moving. It was like walking on hot coals. A coughing fit brought her to her knees. "I pray Almighty God, Lord of the universe, bless me with haste. Archangel Raphael, healer of the sick, I need thy help ..."

"He can't hear you."

Sophia jolted, disturbed by the frightening voice. She tried to focus on her breathing and relax, but she couldn't catch her breath.

"Casey!"

Victorious laughter filled her head. She vomited blood over her arm. She called out again. "Casey!" but it was only a whisper.

"Feel the fear, your true weakness, the ugliness inside you. Feel how the absences of your beloved God and His brethren leave you hollow, with only your true essences. They have forsaken you, and you are mine. Your God cannot hear you while I am in thee, no more than he can hear me. Now you're mine to do as I will. You will continue to feel pain as long as I desire."

It laughed with joy again and again.

"How precious you were. I see what they meant you to be – no mere mortal, you were one of God's chosen, but no more, you are mine. You shall not transform and walk with God, for you did not please him. You missed your return …"

Sophia coughed, wiped the blood on her sleeve. "You know so much about God and his angels, do I detect jealousy, demon?" As she expelled the words, her stomach twisted in pain. She shuffled along the wall, trying to get back to her coat on the stool. She could see the shine of the metal flask of holy water poking out her pocket.

"You will never return to the heavens. This is my world now and I will take your physical body, and your ethereal light, and do as I please."

The heat in her feet radiated up her legs to her knees. She stumbled. She no longer felt she was in complete control of her body.

"I'll destroy you before I let you leave. You are another menacing child of God, just like all your ancestors."

Sophia fell to the floor inches away from the blessed salt in her coat pocket. She wouldn't give up her power to the demon.

"Do you think I cannot hear your every thought? I am not a demon, I am a god! I sent the *Homoharenae* to occupy your soulmate; I orchestrated all that you see. Your God lost the battle in Heaven. This world is my sovereign realm, and I shall rule it and destroy all your God's remaining children."

Her coat combusted into flames. She lay on the floor on the edge of the circle.

"I am one with God and all things of God; when my friends cry, I feel their tears upon my face as they will feel mine and come for me." The laughter was consuming. As her body ate itself from the inside, Sophia coughed up small amounts of blood. She was dying, she could feel death all around her. She had been full of ego believing she had banished the demon from Bo. She had cleansed Bo and given the demon access to her own being. Pressing her fingers upon the granules of salt she collected them and brought them to her mouth. The fire in her legs radiated up into the rest of her body. "If you want me, you'll have to kill me." With all her strength she pushed herself up onto all fours, but as if her bones were brittle, her wrist snapped, she fell back to the floor and lay at the edge of the broken circle.

The curtain flapped in the night breeze, a slow cloud drifted across the full moon. With all her strength, Sophia pushed herself up. Excruciating pain radiated into her arms as she crawled. With her good hand, she rubbed her body with the salt and thought she could feel the pain ease. "That won't help you now," the demon said, amused.

Sophia kept scrubbing her face and neck until she had navigated her way around her entire body. "God, creator of the universe and all things, I know you have not forsaken me. I am coming home. Shine your guiding light so I may see the way. With this blessed salt I shall hold the demon in steadfast and forbid it to leave. If I must perish to annihilate this evil within me, so be it …"

"What are you doing? You cannot destroy yourself, it is against your beliefs. Your God will never allow you into his kingdom, foolish child."

"You don't know what my beliefs are, you only can see my fears, for you are blind to the love of my God. You cannot hear the trumpets that I hear, you cannot smell the fragrance of God, you cannot breathe in his light – without me, you are nothing."

Dragging her leg up to her chin, she rose with outstretched arms and sprinted to the window. Inside, light illuminated her entire being.

26

CASEY: THE WINGS OF AN ANGEL

"What's taking her so long?" Hugh said.

"I don't know," Casey said, looking out the side window of the campervan, willing Sophia to walk out the tavern door. It didn't feel right, he had a terrible feeling he shouldn't have left her alone. "I'll be right back."

Casey squeezed between the two front seats, entering the back of the van where he had sat with Sophia only hours before, going over Isabella's book and the dagger. Bo was sitting at the table being cuddled by Gwen. Bo looked well. She had no recollection of what had happened. She was excited about the van and wanted to know what was in every cupboard, but Gwen moved her next to her and buckled her in.

"Sorry, I'll be right back," Casey said.

"Hurry," Gwen said. She looked tired and drawn.

Casey opened the door and jumped from the van, letting the door swung on its hinges as he ran into the street. He stopped and shouted, "If I'm not back in five minutes, go without us."

"No," Hugh said, standing on the first step out of the van holding the door open. "We'll wait."

"No, I want you to go. I can fly Sophia and me out of here."

Casey listened. A slight wind was blowing; a solitary object tumbled down the street. His heart skipped a beat as he looked around in case he was dreaming, but the landscape hadn't changed. It was dark and hard to see. A hat tumbled towards him. "No, please no." He ran towards it. It was a piece of rubbish, the flap from a cardboard box. A cloud drifted across the moon as he kicked the rubbish out of the road. Shattering glass broke the silence. Sophia was falling, just as he had seen in his dream. He raced forward. The light surrounding Sophia was mixed with a black mass. Casey sprang into the air to catch her.

She went limp in his arms. Blood covered her clothes and mouth. He lowered her lifeless body to the ground and felt for a pulse. He started compressions.

Hugh ran from the van. "What happened to her?"

Casey watched her spirit detach from her body and float a few feet away. A thin thread of light tethered it to her body. He had seen this before when people were dying – spared pain and suffering, they hovered above their bodies. "No!" he yelled at the sky.

Dark energy wrapped around her spiritual body. Casey knew she would want him to move away from her physical body, but he couldn't bring himself to just let her die while she battled the dark energy.

"Come and take me!" Casey yelled at the mass. "Take me!"

Hugh pulled at Casey. "You can't help her now. We have to go."

Sophia's spirit glowed like an angel. Wings expanded behind her. A great light split open the night sky and the archangels fell from the heavens to join Sophia in battle.

Casey left her body, and flew into the sky. He drew his dagger. By the light of the full moon, he witnessed hundreds and thousands of dark energies from across the city fly towards them. He would not stand down from this battle. With his dagger, he cut away the evil entity holding Sophia's spirit hostage.

"I pierce you demon with the blade of judgment, and you shall be no more ..."

Hugh worked on Sophia's body the moment Casey took flight. With his mind, Casey pushed Hugh out of the way. "Leave now," he yelled, "before we all die."

The angels and demons battling in the night sky must have prompted Hugh to flee, to get Gwen and Bo out of the city, because he started walking backwards to the van while looking up at the sky.

Casey knew what he was doing. "I will be fine. Go!" Casey yelled down to Hugh.

Casey watched Hugh drive through the streams of entities entering the intersection of Newgate and Old Bailey as he sped out of the city.

Casey catapulted himself into the mist of evil and joined the battle, fighting beside Sophia and the angels.

Sophia entered his mind and touched his heart.

"Leave," she said. "The angels have this under control."

Casey looked around and saw the entities evaporating in bursts of light. One shot up from the ground and he pierced it with his dagger.

"Casey, it's my time to go," she said.

"No, I won't leave you," Casey said.

"You must!"

She had sparkling etheric wings. Sophia floated like an angel. "There is no foreseeable future, now I understand why the visions stopped. It was because I was going to die, this is the end of my earthly existence."

"I love you. There is nothing here for me if you go. Take me with you."

A blinding light surrounded Sophia, and Casey found it hard to keep his eyes open. It was Metatron.

And Metatron spoke. "This is not your battle. This is not your time. Your time will come soon enough. You have a job to do. Her job is over. She must return to God."

"Sophia, no, please don't make me go."

"My body has already perished," Sophia said.

"She sacrificed herself," Metatron said, "and she pleases God. But there are many things that do not please God. You must cleanse as much as you can to right human wrongs, and take back from hell what was once God's, because a great fire and flood is coming. Nature will return and grow, just as in the days of Noah. You're never alone, Casey, for I am with you, and I am with you by the order of God. You must lead the last living souls to the portals for ascension before the devil claims them as his. Go, Casey. If you do not leave, I shall remove you."

"But if she dies, who will protect us?" Casey said.

"You will find a way."

"I can't. I can't leave her. I won't leave her. Return her to her body now!" Casey rushed at Metatron. "You returned me to my body twice, once when I drowned and once in the barn when I became infected. If you breathe life into her, will she not live?" Casey said through tears.

"No, she will not live. Her body has gone to heaven."

Sophia inhabited every cell of his body. Her light was pure love. She embraced him from the inside. "Stay with me," he pleaded.

He felt the emptiness as she left. He looked down and knew

that what Metatron had said was true – her body was no more. The sky was bright with light as if it was midday, all the evil and darkness gone. A rainbow hugged the city. Casey's heart was breaking as Sophia entered a stream of magical light rising into heaven, with the archangels by her side.

"This isn't okay! This isn't how it's meant to be!" He screamed at Metatron. "She is to be my life partner, I want to love her, to make her laugh and smile. I'm supposed to protect her forever. I am broken without her."

Metatron spread his wings. "Come into my embrace."

"There's nothing important to me in this world anymore."

"She has pleased God and she will walk with him in heaven. You must help the others. There's many more that need saving before humanity may rise again from the ashes."

Goodness, strength and love channeled into him from Metatron. Casey tried to fight it.

"Show me where she will be." In his mind, Casey saw twinkling stars inside his being. Every drop of dew on every leaf or blade of grass sparkled with the light of God. Casey saw the fires ravage the earth, the ice melt and the waters rise. Stars rotated in the sky and combined into the sign of infinity.

"Look towards the heavens, Casey. One day you will be with her again. Time is of the essence. You need to gather as many people as you can, so that one day they may rise again. They will have a choice whether to go with you when the portals to heaven are open."

Metatron wrapped his arms and wings around Casey and squeezed the breath from him.

* * *

A DOG BARKED. Casey heard it panting as it neared. It licked his face, and an unpleasant odor filled his nose. Casey felt the warmth of the sun shining brightly behind his eyes. He opened his eyes, sat up, and held his dog Lucy at arm's length. It was still night. A single star twinkled in the sky, growing smaller until it disappeared amongst millions of other stars. The grass was heavy with dew; he was no longer in London; he was back at the estate lying on the front lawn. Casey wiped the tears and saliva from his face. In his fist was Sophia's necklace. Joe stood under the porchlight, watching him. Casey could see Joe knew something was wrong. Casey stood up, and they walked towards each other.

Joe sniffed back the tears, and drew in a jagged breath before putting his arm around Casey's shoulders. "We'll see her again."

EPILOGUE

Isabella Sumer's leather-bound notebook remained on the front seat of the van beside Hugh, where Casey had left it; his backpack lay discarded on the floor. A green flyer stuck out of the top of the notebook. Hugh reached over and tugged it out from between the pages. It was all about the meeting at Stonehenge. The dream was real, and he should have listened to it. He should have at least gone to see what happened to the others. Maybe once Gwen and Bo were feeling refreshed, instead of going to the farmhouse he had prepared, it might be best to head off to the sacred ground.

He couldn't imagine the pain Casey felt losing Sophia, but Hugh had lost his parents as a young boy, so he had some idea of the grief Casey might be experiencing. Hugh had thought about it a lot over the past six hours as he drove back to the estate. Even though he had hardly known Sophia, her death deeply saddened him. She had put her life on the line for them.

Hugh adjusted the rear-view mirror to check on Gwen and Bo in the back of the campervan. They were flopped over in their seats, their heads resting on the table. Behind him in the black SUV were Tim, Seth, Kraig, Billie and Ernest. Seth had waited outside of London for Hugh's van when he saw the evil spirits rise from the earth, as the angels descended from heaven for Sophia. Hugh still couldn't believe what he had witnessed.

When they met up, Hugh told Seth and the others that Casey would meet them at the estate, and that Sophia had died. Without hesitation, Tim bolted down the highway, back towards London, running to get Sophia. Seth ran after him. Felled by the weight of his grief, Tim dropped to his knees and wept. Seth touched Tim on his shoulder and waited until he was ready to leave.

The dawn light was no comparison to the light of the angel that had come for Sophia. As he approached Casey's estate, there was no sign of the protective dome. Smoke rose from the chimney as they pulled up to the gate. Tim walked up from behind and opened it for them to enter. The ground shook. They all froze. The vehicles wobbled as if a giant had woken and was stumbling across the moors.

THE END.

REFERENCES

All biblical citations have come from the King James version of the Bible which can be found at: https://www.kingjames-Bibleonline.org/

Amelia Dyer (1837–1896), known as the "Reading baby farmer", a serial killer, was hanged on 10 June 1896: https://en.wikipedia.org/wiki/Amelia_Dyer

John Rogers, St Sepulchre's vicar, was burned as a heretic in 1555: https://en.wikipedia.org/wiki/John_Rogers_(Bible_editor_and_martyr)

Thomas Neill Cream, the doctor and blackmailer known as the "Lambeth Poisoner", was hanged in 1892 for poisoning several of his patients: https://en.wikipedia.org/wiki/Thomas_Neill_Cream

John Frith, Protestant priest and martyr, was held in Newgate before being burnt at the stake in 1533: https://en.wikipedia.org/wiki/John_Frith

Robert Southwell, Jesuit priest, and poet, was held at Newgate for treason before being hanged, drawn and quartered at Tyburn in 1595: https://en.wikipedia.org/wiki/Robert_Southwell_(Jesuit)

Oranges and Lemons – the history of the nursery rhyme: https://en.wikipedia.org/wiki/Oranges_and_Lemons#Earlier_version

Information about the Newgate Bell and the bellman's verse can be found at Crimscribe.com:

https://crimescribe.com/2018/08/08/newgate-prison-ask-not-for-whom-the-bell-tolls/

GLOSSARY OF LATIN WORDS AND PHRASES

Biblia Vulgata: the Latin translation of the Bible known as the 'common version'

Glycyrrhiza Glabra Ferula: licorice

Harenae (Latin): sand

Homo (Latin): man

Homoharenae: my combining of the Latin words for 'sand' and 'man' to create the idea of the Sandman

Immortalitatis: immortality

Memorias Invenire: find memories

Passiflora Incarnata: known as purple passionflower

Planctus Mulierem: mourning woman

Salix Alba: the white willow plant

Turritopsis Dohrnii: immortal jellyfish

Cum postestate omnipotentis, aut spiritum daemonii immundi, et terebrare in te judicia, et non erit ultra ferrum: et hoc non factum est, in nomine spiritus sancti, Amen.

With the power of the Almighty, unclean demon or spirit, I

pierce you with the blade of judgment and you shall be no more, and it is done, in the name of the Holy Spirit, Amen.

AUTHOR'S NOTE

Enjoy this book? You can make a big difference.

Reviews are the most powerful tools in my arsenal when it comes to getting attention for my books. Much as I'd like to, I don't have the financial muscle of a New York publisher. I can't take out full-page ads in the newspaper or put posters on the subway. (Not yet, anyway.)

But I do have something much more powerful and effective than that, and it's something that those publishers would kill to get their hands on: a committed and loyal bunch of readers.

Honest reviews of my books help bring them to the attention of other readers.

If you've enjoyed this book I would be very grateful if you could spend just five minutes leaving a review (it can be as short as you like) on your favorite online bookstore, or on Goodreads, which you can access through my website as well as books one, two and three in the series. https://jmhartwriter.com/buy-now/

Thank you very much.

ACKNOWLEDGMENTS

I would like to thank my supportive family and friends for their encouragements. Thank you to invaluable editors Stephanie Smith and Linda Funnell, proofreader Ellie Stevenson, and Creativindi Cover designers, as well as JMH World Publishing's ARC team who have been a tremendous support throughout the process. No book is complete without the vital service of editors, proofreaders, and great book cover designers.

ABOUT JM HART

Now semi-retired, JM (Jeanette) moved to a peaceful county town south of Sydney, to focus on her grandchildren and writing.

JM Hart is the author of *The Chronicles of the Supernatural Series*. She makes her online home at http://jmhartwriter.com

You can also connect with Jeanette on social media. Click the links below.

If the mood strikes you, you can send her an email author@jmhartwriter.com

GET FREE COPY OF BOOK ONE THE EMERALD TABLET

Building a relationship with my readers is the very best thing about writing. I occasionally send newsletters with details of new releases, special offers and other bits of news relating to the Chronicles of the Supernatural series.

If you sign up to the mailing list I'll send you monthly free or discounted eBooks and updates of my series the Chronicles of The Supernatural. You can sign up here and get a free copy of the first book in the series, The Emerald Tablet, if you don't have it already: https://dl.bookfunnel.com/uab5dvpv6w

www.ingramcontent.com/pod-product-compliance
Lightning Source LLC
Chambersburg PA
CBHW020347120726
47904CB00002B/491